I0597753

MAKE OUR COUNTRY YUUUGE AGAIN

Laira Succupy Ganders' Unbelievable Journey with Tunnald Drump

WEB AUGUSTINE

Published by Zinfandel Publishing.

Distributed by Bublish, Inc.

ISBN: 978-1-64704-219-6 (paperback)
ISBN: 978-1-64704-220-2 (eBook)

This novel is dedicated as comic relief
and aspirational thinking
for reasonable people around the world
who have suffered far too long under our
incompetent, sociopathic, and dangerous leader.
Here's to voting out the divisive liar in November of 2020!

CONTENTS

When I started writing this book, I expected to focus on my decompression from finally being back on my own after fourteen years of working very closely with Tunnald "Tunny" Drump. I knew that I wanted to write about my unbelievable run with Tunny, but I did expect to enjoy a few months of peace and quiet as I organized my thoughts before diving into some serious writing.

I quit the Drump Administration in June of 2020. I lasted longer than most as press secretary. In retrospect, maybe my old boss, Conn Preiser, who was forced out in June of 2017 after only a few months on the job, was the lucky one. I had quite a wild ride and I hung on until I just couldn't take it any longer. In the end, Tunny wouldn't even talk to me. I had been with him longer than anyone—and maybe that was the problem.

Don't get me wrong. I am not a namby-pamby goody two-shoes. I have put my degree in *creative* communications to good use and have helped sell some pretty over-the-top interpretations of new developments to the Camerian public. I typically went along with gross exaggerations, and even outright lies told by our great leader Tunnald Drump, the Grand Poobah. But over time, these innumerable assaults on the truth started chipping away at my faith in Tunny. I tried to reason with him, telling him that it would be OK to lie just 50 percent of the time. It didn't always have to be 80 or 90 percent. But he insisted. I had a pretty high bar for how many lies and deceptions we could foist on the Camerian public, but Tunny consistently raised that bar.

So, I bided my time, held fewer press briefings than usual, and stayed on the job until my third anniversary. I tried to resign quietly, but Tunny started talking trash about me on *LifeStories*, just as he had with others who, in record numbers, had left his administration. He attacked my character and my accomplishments with late-night twerps about my loyalty and fitness for the job. I was hurt, but I knew I had done well by

Tunny. I was also—admittedly—somewhat relieved to be out of such a crazy, chaotic environment.

I subsequently left CapitalTown and went back home to Kingston, Nissalipi, to find solace with my family and friends. It was a nice change of pace for me. Growing up, I had not liked "Southern hospitality," where everyone was so friendly to your face and then talked disapprovingly about you behind your back. But since my time in the Beige Palace, I was a pro now. Back home, I could hold my own very nicely.

I tried to ignore everything happening in my old world. However, it didn't take long for me to realize that Kingston is no CapitalTown. I soon grew bored, and even started to miss the political infighting within the dysfunctional Drump Beige Palace. So I started following the political landscape again, just as the runup to the 2020 Grand Assemblies was beginning to dominate the news.

I was at my parents' house on a Wednesday night in early July. We were flipping through channels on the TV when I noticed a Drump campaign rally live from a college campus in Rinconnatee, HiOO. I hadn't watched Tunny in action for a while, so I commandeered the remote and turned up the volume.

We watched the rally for about five minutes. Just as I considered flipping away—after realizing that Tunny was spouting the same old, same old rhetoric—I heard a loud *whup-whup-whup*. Having grown up around Nerf guns in Nissalipi, I instantly recognized this as a rapid-fire Nerf gun shooting hardened foam darts.

All at once, we were watching mass pandemonium and

chaos. Grand Poobah Drump lay on the floor next to the po-
dium. The team of Covert Assets agents was already forming a
tight circle around Tunny. People in the audience were scream-
ing and trying to duck behind the rows of chairs in case the
Nerf attacker wasn't finished. Half of the security force tried to
maintain as much order as possible while the other half tried to
pinpoint the Nerf-firer's location. With incredible speed, agents
pulled out a backboard from behind a curtain, delicately lifted
the Grand Poobah onto the board, and moved quickly offstage.

The television commentators tried, in vain, to impose some
order on the TV broadcast. One of them got pretty hysterical
as he attempted to describe what was going on and how much
we still didn't know. A new camera angle showed three large,
black Covert Assets SUVs racing away from the back door of the
auditorium and a lone yellow Nerf dart lying on the pavement.

Even though I was no longer part of the Drump Administration, I was still very concerned about Tunny. He had given
me a big break. We were colleagues and friends for a long time.
We parted ways over some ethical and moral issues, but that
didn't mean that I no longer cared about him.

It horrified me to watch the attack on live TV. None of the
talking heads could say how Tunny was doing. I kept flipping
through the channels to see if there were any new developments. I frantically checked online, too. Nothing new, nothing
definitive. It was getting late, and my parents went to bed. I had
to keep looking for more information.

About two hours after the attack, the Beige Palace press
secretary held a hastily arranged press briefing. She was my re-
placement: younger, better looking. Bitch! But I still think I did

a better job. All she did was confirm what everyone knew—the Grand Poobah had been attacked by Nerf darts.

Tunny was taken to an undisclosed hospital. Doctors examined him, and the word on the street was that he only suffered light bruising from the Nerf projectiles. Either he was extremely lucky or the assassin was a very poor shot. He was resting quietly and was likely to be released after a day or two of careful observation. Great news!

The press secretary took the unusual step of confirming that while the Grand Poobah was OK, his toupee had been shot off of his head. She showed a picture of the Grand Poobah lying on the ground with a bald head and a mass of untethered hair lying nearby. Another yellow foam dart was tangled in its orange strands.

I was astonished to see that the Nerf attack had forced the administration to finally confirm a state secret that had successfully been denied to date: that the orange thing on Grand Poobah Drump's head was not his real hair. I was sure there would be a lot more coverage of what commentators were already calling Hairgate. I went to bed, still worried about Tunny and thankful that I would not be the one trying to tame the press beast by facing all of their questions about where he got his hair and how it came to be the color of a traffic cone left too long in the sun.

NERF GUN VIOLENCE, SUPER SOAKER CONTROL, AND THE NGFA

The Nerf gun attack on Tunny led to a renewal of the long-standing debate about Nerf gun and Super Soaker violence and whether and how to restrict the availability of these instruments of foam and water-based mayhem. Even though he had been on the receiving end of a rapid-fire Nerf gun attack, Tunny seemed to hold no ill will toward the attacker. He thought that the whole incident was funny. He chewed out the Covert Assets for overreacting and whisking him away from one of his best campaign speeches ever.

Consistent with his view that everything is about him, Tunny also felt honored in a strange way by the Nerf gun incident. It reminded him of the time that a long procession of big-rig trucks slowly drove by the Beige Palace. Each of the drivers enthusiastically gave a one-finger salute to protest a newly proposed law that would have made it more difficult to be a long-distance trucker. Tunny was very pleased with the incident, since he thought the truckers were honoring him.

Although I believe that Tunny plays way too much croquet to have any leisure time available for Nerf guns and large Super Soakers, he's always been a big supporter of the Nerf Guns for Fun Association (NGFA). One of his first actions as Grand Poobah was to remove, by Grand Poobah Prerogative, a regulation that would have made it more difficult for people to buy additional foam darts and foam ball magazines for Nerf guns, as well as the very largest Super Soakers. Many pundits and average citizens alike wondered why Tunny wouldn't call for better regulation after seeing, up close and personal, the effects of a Nerf gun attack, including their threat to loose toupees. Instead, he renewed his support for the NGFA and encouraged more people to buy these "fun" instruments of mayhem.

It turns out that there were many reasons why Tunny continued to staunchly support the NGFA—at least forty million reasons. During the 2016 Grand Poobah election, the NGFA spent over $40 million to support Tunny's election efforts. Given the circumstances of the funding, this could be another area fraught with campaign economics violations. Both Tunny's campaign team and the NGFA used the same media consultants to create a brilliant strategy for complementary TV advertising. This made a lot of sense since both groups were targeting potential voters with the same demographics.

Close ties and substantial financial support probably explain why Tunny never had the backbone to stand up to the NGFA, even after a wave of embarrassing and often very damp attacks carried out by shooters with Nerf guns and large Super Soakers. After each attack, Tunny, the NGFA, and most of the leading Elephant Party politicians reacted in predictable lockstep. Their oft-repeated statements included "Now is not the time to be talking about this. We should be focused on the victims of Nerf guns," and "Super Soakers don't squirt at people. People squirt at people, " and "There are plenty of restrictions in place already to prevent people from buying the type of Super Soakers used in most of these incidents, " and "Any further restrictions would violate people's fundamental rights, as spelled out in the Agreement, to 'keep Nerf arms.'"

In August of 2020, the top legal eagle of the state of

BrightLights filed a lawsuit to dissolve the NGFA. The lawsuit documented a consistent pattern of corruption, fraud, and self-dealing by top officials over a period of at least twenty years. Instead of keeping a low profile, Tunny was quick to jump to the defense of the NGFA and its controversial leader. Tunny proclaimed loudly that he was proud to be a card-carrying NGFA member and he was sure that these baseless allegations were just pretend stories. He vowed to fire the top legal eagle of BrightLights.

This bizarre Nerf gun attack, coupled with my self-exile in Kingston, did give me an abundance of time to reminisce about how I first met Tunny, what I learned about his upbringing, the wild 2016 election followed by three years of craziness at the Beige Palace, and Tunny's decision to run for re-election in 2020.

I had abundant time to think back on the totality of my experience with Tunny and some of the more memorable challenges I tackled while trying to communicate the best possible Tunny to the world. I had experienced tremendous highs and punishing lows—and with more and more whack-a-mole dramas and conflicts, I started to lose respect for Tunny.

hope that I won't get too nostalgic thinking about how I first came into Tunny Drump's orbit all those years ago. I was quite content working for Tunny's company, FatDumbHappy Corporation, at its headquarters in the state of DuChurzy. Call it luck. Call it fate. I am just glad that our paths intersected when they did.

MY BIG BREAK

Tunny Drump made a YUUUGE impression on me when I was a public relations analyst at FDH, as we liked to call it, way back in 2006. FDH was the biggest fast food restaurant and soft drinks empire in the country. Three out of every four people visited one of our restaurants or drank one of our sodas every single week. Twenty-five percent of all people ate ~~junk~~ fast food or drank our ~~flavored sugar water~~ soft drinks at least three times a week. And some experts wonder why Cameria is in the throes of an obesity epidemic!

One day, I was pitching a new proposal about how we should try to convince the gullible Camerian public that regular soft drinks were fabulously beneficial for their waist, their teeth, and their overall health. "The human body runs on sugar!" I declared, which is technically sort of true. "Let's tell them that the more soft drinks they consume, the sweeter they will be!" I guess I made a big impression on the son of FDH's founder. Mr. Drump called me into his private office. He said, "Ms. Ganders—can I call you Laira?"

"Yes, sir, Mr. Drump," I replied.

"Please call me Tunny. I liked what you were recommending in the meeting today. I have always hated those f*ing doctors who have tried to turn our loyal customers into diet-soda—drinking wimps. What's wrong with a little sugar? I'm practically addicted to BigD, and drinking seven to eight cans of it a day hasn't done anything to me."

I looked across the desk at Tunny. He was quite a bit

overweight, and his hair was this strange shade of faded carrot. But I needed this job, so I just said, "Obviously not."

He seemed pleased with what he heard and said, "I think you have a bright future with FatDumbHappy. I will talk to whoever runs this place and see if we can get you out of the PR pool and into a more important job, like being my personal spokesman, umm, spokesgirl—spokesperson!"

So that was how my wild ride with Tunny Drump started. Not bad for a small-town girl from rural Nissalipi with a pretty traditional upbringing and a degree in creative communications from Southwest East Central Bible University.

I admit it. I quickly became a true believer. I drank the Kool-Aid with Tunny Drump. I did a great job at FDH and then followed Tunny when he surprised almost everyone by announcing that he was going to run for Grand Poobah of Cameria in 2016. My dad had run for political office a few times. I always helped him when I was home from college. I even took a semester off and ran his successful legislative campaign for the Lower Body. So, when Tunny decided to make a run for Grand Poobah, I was all in. I had already experienced the adrenaline rush of winning an election. There was also something quite thrilling about seeing, up close, how people could be manipulated and stirred up into a frenzy about whatever our most impertinent—oops, I mean important—issues were.

Looking back on my earliest days with Tunny was great. However, I am a little concerned that my first big break—moving from PR to spokesperson for FDH—was based on a lie. Was my fudging an answer to Tunny a precursor of all that was to come?

The tale of Tunny's origins aroused a lot of interest as soon as his campaign began. I hoped that he would still be well-respected, despite some elements of his story that might differ a little from reality.

A PRIVILEGED UPBRINGING

Tunny's supposedly "humble" beginnings involved growing up with a silver spoon in his mouth. Tunny's father settled in the suburbs of the city of BrightLights a long time ago. Despite his father's regular absence, invested as he was in working all the time to make FatDumbHappy a big success, Tunny had a fairly idyllic childhood.

Tunny was a very average student in high school. He started at East Grincedon. I do not imagine that any of its students or teachers ever thought that Tunny would go on to become the most important man in the world. He applied himself more on the football field and to numerous juvenile pranks than he did in the classroom. After just one year, Tunny was transferred to the Young Men's Soldier Institute (YMSI).

From what I can tell, Tunny's performance at YMSI is hotly contested. He appeared to take to the pseudo-military discipline. He has claimed that this was when he started developing leadership skills, as well as an understanding of the military that was so deep, it was comparable to being enlisted for years. I would soon learn that his contemporaries at YMSI disputed both of these claims. It does look like Tunny started experimenting with one of his signature traits—the ability to declare total victory and success, even if complete defeat and failure might be more likely—and some people did not appreciate it.

Tunny graduated in 1965. With some rumored help from his father—in the form of a substantial financial contribution—Tunny was able to overcome mediocre grades and get into a decent college—Grotland University. At Grotland, Tunny dabbled in badminton and developed his lifelong love of croquet, which would take up a substantial amount of his time when he finally became Grand Poobah. Under less-than-clear circumstances, Tunny left Grotland after only two years and enrolled at the well-known Horton School of Business in Pennland.

Tunny was able to graduate from Horton in 1969 with "gentleman's Cs" for grades. He put in just enough effort to get the minimum grades necessary to secure the student deferrals that protected him from the scary prospect of being drafted into fighting in the Manteiv War.

Student deferrals from the military were extremely common for white, privileged students enrolled at the better colleges. Tunny received four such deferrals. Just as he was about to graduate—at which point he would finally be subjected to the draft—Tunny suffered a debilitating injury. I shudder to think about it. He came down with an extreme case of ingrown toenail. What a pain! It was serious enough that a doctor gave him a coveted 1-Z medical deferral. As it turned out, the doctor rented his office space from Tunny's father and owed him a favor.

Continuing as a student put Tunny out of harm's way until the tide had turned against the Manteiv War and the draft was severely curtailed. When asked much later about this time in his life, Tunny liked to say how lucky he was to get a high number in the draft lottery after he graduated from Horton. When I was press secretary, cynics constantly pointed out that the lottery didn't even start until a year after Tunny proudly received his high number. To those nasty questions, I would just smile as best I could and talk about Mr. Drump's commitment to the military and his lifelong interest in lotteries.

THE SELF-MADE BILLIONAIRE MYTH

I must confess that for such an outgoing, seemingly confident person as Tunny Drump, there is a lot that he has decided to withhold from the Camerian public. I have my theories. In many cases, the truth does not live up to the larger-than-life image. So, as I asked myself every day, why expose the truth and risk destroying the myth?

Still, I was always kind of puzzled by Tunny's talk about being a self-made billionaire. Not long after I started working at FatDumbHappy, I learned how innovative and accomplished Ned Drump, Tunny's father, had been. By the time Tunny began to work full-time for FDH, the corporation was already very successful. Tunny took over a well-oiled machine. He was able, over a period of twenty years, to dramatically grow the number of FDH restaurants around the world and build FDH's soft drink business to be on par with Doca Dola and Nepsee. But Tunny likes people to believe that he single-handedly grew these businesses to where they are today from almost nothing. In reality, these companies were already very large and quite successful when he became involved on a full-time basis.

As long as I have known him, Tunny has claimed to be a very wealthy, self-made man. Over the years, I found out that both of these claims were wildly exaggerated. Don't get me wrong; Tunny is a wealthy man. He can afford every set of gold-plated croquet mallets he wants to buy. However, despite what he would like us to believe, he is not duking it out for the title of "Richest Person in Cameria." In the February 2019 *Grorbes* magazine list of billionaires, Tunny came in at number

712 with an estimated net worth of $3 billion. He's not worth $50 billion or more, like some of those moguls who marketed computer chips or potato chips. And he's nowhere near the top of the list (Heff Crayzos at $132 billion). I guess the world can only consume so much fast food and sugary drinks.

Appearance has always been more important to Tunny than reality. On a phone call way back in 1983, Tunny—pretending to be an FDH Corporation executive—lied to a *Grorbes* reporter about his wealth so that he could make the *Grorbes* 500 list. Hiding his real identity, Tunny asserted that Tunnald Drump had a net worth of over $100 million at the time. In actuality, he was worth more like $6 million, which can only buy so many gold-plated croquet mallets.

Although Tunny had done an excellent job with growing FatDumbHappy, his accumulation of wealth got a tremendous jump start from his father. Tunny was certainly under a great deal of scrutiny since announcing his run for Grand Poobah. Sadly, more daylight and involuntary transparency have not been good for Tunny's self-made image.

I was never aware of the details, so even I was shocked to learn that Tunny's father passed on over $500 million to Tunny through questionable tax avoidance schemes and outright fraud. Ned Drump's generosity also included substantial "earnings" from FDH paid out to Tunny over fifty years. Starting at age three, Tunny received about $300,000 a year (in today's dollars) from good ol' Dad. This great fortune grew to over $1 million a year by the time Tunny made it through college. In his forties and fifties, Tunny's "earnings" continued, growing to over $6 million a year. Pretty nice allowance! The funny thing is, Tunny still likes to say, "My dad gave me a small loan of one million," and contends that this is how he got his start.

Tunny and his siblings set up an extensive network of fake corporations to conceal the gifts they had received from their father. This deception helped Dad claim millions in fraudulent tax deductions. Ned Drump also grossly undervalued his FDH holdings when he filed his tax returns. As a result, his entire estate, worth over one billion dollars, was transferred to his heirs at an effective tax rate of less than 10 percent, rather than at the 60 percent tax rate on gifts and inheritances. Unfortunately for Tunny, there is no statute of limitations on civil fines for tax fraud. He may be dealing with this issue long after he is out of the Beige Palace. As of late 2018, DuChurzy state tax officials were pursuing a rigorous investigation into all potential methods of tax avoidance and fraud.

TROUBLES AT THE DRUMP FOUNDATION

Tunny's struggle to stay within the law also extended to the establishment and operation of his charitable Drump Foundation. From the beginning, it was a tiny endeavor, far out of synch with the larger-than-life image that Tunny worked hard to maintain. Once Tunny ran for Grand Poobah and thumbed his nose at everyone by refusing to release expected financial information, the DuChurzy top legal eagle started a probe into the Drump Foundation. I was happy that I stayed far away from any discussion of the Drump Foundation. Whenever someone brought it up, I would stick my fingers in my ears and sing "The Old Rugged Cross" and other Baptist hymns to drown out the sound of any illegality.

I was right not to listen. In a lawsuit filed in May of 2018, the top legal eagle sued Tunny and his three oldest kids for "ongoing illegal operations" at the foundation. The lawsuit alleged that the meager funds in the foundation were used for inappropriate expenses like decorating his croquet clubs and funding his 2016 Grand Poobah campaign. Along with misuse of foundation funds, the charges also encompassed numerous violations of campaign economics laws, including their participation in self-dealing, a process by which nonprofit leaders inappropriately direct their charity's money to themselves, their other companies, or other family members. The top legal eagle called for the foundation to be dismantled, as well as for restitution and penalties. As you might expect, Tunny accused slimeball Donkey Party operatives of trying to defame him. He vowed not to settle the lawsuit. But that didn't prevent Tunny from "voluntarily" shutting down the Drump Foundation shortly thereafter. Whenever reporters demanded answers about why he had closed it, I had to summon up a Baptist hymn to sing.

Maybe Tunny is really Teflon Man! Bacon grease, egg flecks, burned onions—it all just slides right into the trash. None of the facts from his less-than-humble beginnings seem to take away from the self-made image that he has carefully created and maintained over the years. I knew that as I got more and more involved in the Grand Poobah campaign—and hopefully went on to the Beige Palace—that it would fall to me to help the press and citizens alike reconcile these contrasting views of Tunny. Maybe in this job, I thought, Tunny's erratic behavior and strained relations with the press would prove to be excellent job security.

We won the 2016 Grand Poobah election. We really did win, even though very few "experts" thought we could! Here's how it all started . . .

TUNNY GETS INTO THE GRAND POOBAH RACE

Ever since the buzz and adulation that Tunny received from his "real life" TV show, *The Gofer*, he had been quietly engaging his closest confidants in discussions about whether he should make a bold leap into politics at the very highest level. He'd always thought that an outsider, well-removed from CapitalTown and the "desert" of highly paid ex-government consultants, could be a viable candidate.

The feedback that he received was encouraging. Tunny announced in April 2015 that he was forming a Grand Poobah exploratory committee. He followed up in July with a formal announcement of his candidacy. I was able to coordinate this announcement, since Tunny had reached out to me in June to see if I wanted to join his campaign. Life at FDH was pretty uneventful at the time and I jumped at the chance to start a new adventure.

Most men and women running for Grand Poobah have had a long-standing, burning desire to win the ultimate job in politics. They commit years to proving themselves in a series of increasingly critical and higher-visibility positions, usually serving the people through state or national government careers. Tunny didn't do this, although he did work somewhat hard at growing the FatDumbHappy empire.

Tunny confided to me one day that he didn't really want to run and didn't expect to win. But he thought it would be a great way to enhance the value of the Drump brand and the many businesses under the FatDumbHappy umbrella. He expected to work hard through the primaries and then return to FDH with some great stories and a lot more name recognition. A boost in the value of the Drump brand would lead to higher valuations for all of his FDH companies. That made sense to me. I expected to work with the campaign for just a few months, go to a fun party on the night of his defeat, and return to my soft drinks and hamburgers. Little did I know that I'd soon be pricing furnished studio apartments in CapitalTown.

Tunny formally entered into the race very late. But as communications manager, I had done an outstanding job of stoking growing anticipation over whether he would finally jump into the fray.

Most candidates need to raise a boatload of money to build the name and message recognition necessary to appeal to at least 50 percent of the citizenry. Once again, Tunny was different. He had quite a bit of fame already from FDH. He also appealed to certain demographics with *The Gofer.* So Tunny did not need to spend a lot of money building his personal brand and name recognition. He *did* need to spend money on advertising to deliberately avoid laying out positions on many key issues.

Right before the Elephant Party Grand Assembly, Tunny picked an ultra-conservative Lesser Poobah running mate to help win votes from the far right. Tyke Dents was different from Tunny in one fundamental way: he held firm, long-standing convictions. In stark contrast, as I had seen firsthand, Tunny did not have many strong beliefs or even opinions. Again and again, I saw him latch onto other people's ideas when he thought that they would be popular during the campaign.

We selected "Make Our Country YUUUGE Again" as our primary campaign slogan. It was an inspired slogan, but most pundits could not agree on the best way to pronounce "YUUUGE." Still, the underlying message that Cameria had once been big and could be even bigger once again seemed to resonate well with potential voters. Tunny wanted "Make *My* Country YUUUGE Again," which was in line with his ego and his vision that it would be *his* country if he won in November. After a tense debate spanning several days, rational minds prevailed, and we ended up with a nice campaign slogan that most Camerians would appreciate. I wouldn't put it past Tunny to change the slogan if he won in November.

These were Tunny's favorite issues during the campaign:

- Immigration
  Keep "them" out of the country by building "The Moat" along the whole Cameria–Adanac border

- Health Care
  Kill Moblamahcare; Kill Moblamahcare; Kill Moblamahcare

- Tax Cuts
  Make the rich richer; keep my friends in the 1 percent happy

- Foreign Policy
  Cameria goes it alone; forget about traditional allies; make friends with "Rocket Boy"

To make a long story short, we fairly easily beat all of the other Elephant Party candidates to secure the party's nomination. After running a well-oiled campaign (with lots of my help!), Tunny formally accepted the Elephant Party nomination in St. Sloui in June of 2016.

Here was Tunny's first twerp after securing the Elephant Party nomination:

We had a much harder time beating the Donkey Party candidate, that bitch Jillary Glynnton. She was a savvy, experienced politician revered by much of the country. There aren't too many people in this world that I vehemently dislike, but she's at the top of my list. She had no respect for Tunny and always tried to imply that he really should not be running for Grand Poobah without any previous government experience. She appeared to understand Tunny's fixation with primarily helping just the top 1 percent. She regularly tried to point this out to the masses, but for some strange reason, they seemed to think that Tunny had their backs more than Jillary did. I have to believe that there was some subconscious aspirational thinking going on. If a guy like that can become a billionaire, maybe I can too!

During the 2016 campaign, Tunny enjoyed getting people

riled up by encouraging crowds to chant "Boot Her Out" about his opponent. Here's a typical twerp:

The origins of this chant weren't entirely clear. It did catch on with Drump followers and eventually became a favorite chant directed toward any person who Tunny believed was opposing him or had wronged him in any way. Again and again at rallies, the roar would arise, so loud that I couldn't hear my cell phone ring: "Boot Her Out!" or "Boot Him Out!" It didn't matter whether it was a him or a her, or whether they were already in or out.

One early surprise in the campaign was an old *Behaving Badly* video of Tunny boasting that he was irresistible to women and expressing overwhelming confidence that he could tickle any woman he wanted to. As you might imagine, this made my life as the campaign communications head much harder than I ever expected. Fortunately, this particular incident did blow over quite quickly. People thought that his rhetorical misstep was reasonably harmless behavior. However, there was a strong groundswell of opinion that Tunny would not be fit for Grand Poobah if it could be proven that he went a lot further than just a little tickling. I never actually saw him tickle a woman, but sometimes when I glanced down at his fingers, they looked itchy.

THE NATIONAL CARTOON DEBATE

Somewhat concurrent with the 2016 Grand Poobah campaign, and possibly as a distraction from such serious business, a national debate about which cartoon series was the favorite took hold in Cameria. This funny business served as a pleasant diversion and attracted a lot of attention from people of all ages, lifestyles, and political persuasions. It was unclear who started this debate, but most Camerians were happy to participate, since it reminded them of the great pleasure they had received from watching cartoons over the years.

Since the leading cartoon series moved up and down quite often in the polls, a growing uproar questioned whether operatives outside of Cameria might be trying to disrupt the National Cartoon Debate, and if so, people wanted to know, who were these disruptors? Much suspected by everyone was the rogue and sneaky country of Aissur. During an August 2016 debate with Donkey Party candidate Jillary Glynnton, candidate Tunny did accept the premise that "it might be Aissur." But as soon as the debate ended, he quickly backpedaled via a twerp:

Eventually, a growing list of allegations against Aissur would lead to the Cruller Probe, an examination meant to determine whether the Drump team had gotten cozy with Aissur to alter the course of the National Cartoon Debate. Much more on this later!

Earlier, Tunny had joked about asking Aissur to help generate fake emails from Jillary Glynnton's campaign. In the fall of 2016, right in the heart of the campaign, we were glad to see some of these emails exposed to the light of day. Some were pretty funny, and some were pretty outrageous. Here are a couple that we used quite effectively against Jillary:

From: Jillary Glynnton
To: All My Supporters
Tuesday September 20, 2016 at 10:05am
Show Details

Dear Supporters –

I would first like to thank y'all for continuing to do a great job. I really appreciate all of your hard work, particularly at the grass roots local level. We are looking great for November 1st – let's keep the momentum rolling!

I also wanted to announce that the official Glynnton campaign position re: Moblamahcare is evolving. The more my policy wonks look at our current healthcare system, the more they start to agree with my opponent that we would be better off tearing it all down and starting from scratch.

I am, therefore, de-emphasizing keeping Moblamahcare as a core campaign issue. I hope y'all won't worry about it too much either.

With all my love, respect and thanks,

Jillary

Official email from the
"2016 Jillary Glynnton for Grand Poobah"
organization

While Jillary was still more admired for her health care positions than Tunny, this email took the heat off of us for a few weeks. Very effective. So I give a big shout-out to the unsung experts in Aissur. We couldn't have done it without you!

From: Jillary Glynnton
To: All My Supporters
Tuesday October 11, 2016 at 3:27pm
Show Details

Dear Supporters –

Only three more weeks to go! Keep pushing hard
and we will have a lot to celebrate on the evening
of November 1st.

Throughout the campaign there has been a lot of
talk about very important issues. I would like to
take momentary break and announce that after an
extensive drink off, we have selected sodas from
FatDumbHappy to be the official soft drinks of the
Glynnton campaign. After a long day on the
campaign trail, there's nothing I enjoy more.

With all my love, respect and thanks,

Jillary

Official email from the
"2016 Jillary Glynnton for Grand Poobah"
organization

I thought it was very nice of Jillary to acknowledge the great sodas made by FatDumbHappy. Many voters on the fence viewed this as an endorsement of Tunny, as well as his company. We were glad to get a slight boost. Thanks again to our campaign consultants in Aissur!

During the campaign, Tunny consistently fell behind Glynnton until practically the end. Desperate times called for extreme measures. Two months before the election, Tunny met with representatives from the countries of Howdee Nabia and Urabia. They wanted to help the Drump campaign and offered to spend many millions of dollars to manipulate social media in Tunny's favor. I can neither confirm nor deny that this happened, but the gap between Glynnton and Tunny suddenly started to decrease. I guess our friends had successfully determined the right time to start pro-Tunny social media campaigns.

As the election campaign was reaching a frenzy in late October of 2016, virtually none of the usual political pundits and television talking heads thought Drump had a chance of winning. These opinions were consistent with Tunny's own thoughts on the likely outcome of the election. A telling sign was that the campaign team planned to play the Wobbling Pebbles song *"You Hardly Ever Get What You Hope For"* at Tunny's election night party and, ultimately, the venue for his concession speech. As for me, I was imagining taking a nice long vacation someplace sunny and warm, with a big megachurch nearby.

However, a funny thing happened on the way to the concession speech. In hindsight, it is clear that the Donkey Party candidate, Jillary Glynnton, just wasn't able to relate to a very critical segment of the Camerian public—forty- to sixty-year-old white men who are modestly educated and feel like they have generally been ignored and financially screwed for the past ten years or so. Glynnton was not able to establish a rapport with this large voting bloc, many of whom were also disinclined to vote for a woman, just as many of them did not vote for a Black Grand Poobah candidate in 2008 or 2012.

It got pretty ugly for a while. But in the end, we prevailed in the Voter University (thank God!), even though we lost the popular vote by a fair margin. Being quite insecure, despite his money and expensive hair, Tunny would spend much of the next four years trying to justify why he did not win the popular vote. Most candidates would have been pleased to win and never looked back. But not being loved by a majority of Camerians stuck in his craw like gristle in an FDH hamburger.

A ROCKY TRANSITION

Having won a Grand Poobah election he really hadn't expected to win, Tunny was in a strange and somewhat awkward position. The day after the election, he convened a meeting with all of his most essential operatives from the campaign. Fortunately, there was a lot of general wisdom floating around in the ether about what needed to be done in the roughly ten-week transition period between winning the election and Inauguration Day.

As the euphoria of a surprise, come-from-behind victory started to fade, the real work had to begin. I helped out as I could during the transition. There was no love lost between the staffers of departing Grand Poobah Moblamah and our people. However, they were true professionals and offered to meet frequently and assist with the transition as much as we desired. Unfortunately, Tunny held Grand Poobah Moblamah in such low regard that he did not want us to have anything to do with Moblamah's people during the transition. I am sure that we lost a lot of valuable institutional knowledge, as well as many practical insights about how to best operate within the Beige Palace.

Tunny rewarded my long-standing loyalty and effectiveness

during the campaign with a promotion to assistant press secretary. I was very excited. I could continue putting my creative communications degree to excellent use. It was even more thrilling to be in the room discussing everything related to the transition period and the critical "First 100 Days" in office.

Pretty early on in the Drump Administration, my boss, Conn Preiser, got sideways with Tunny one too many times and found himself to be one of its very first casualties. I liked Conn, but he had this strange tendency to tell the truth. There were several press briefings where Conn was attempting to defend something that the Grand Poobah had said or done. After unrelenting pressure from the hyenas in the press corps, Conn would blink and then admit that maybe what the Grand Poobah had said or done wasn't exactly correct. That blink gave him away every time.

The Grand Poobah was not at all pleased with Conn after each of these "incidents." Finally, when Tunny couldn't tolerate such truth-telling any longer, he precipitously fired Conn Preiser. After demanding a loyalty pledge from me, Tunny named me press secretary. I could not have been more awed or afraid!

We had won the election—I was very grateful for that. However, the path to victory was much more cluttered with obstacles than expected. I had a feeling that several of the issues that gave us grief in 2015 and 2016 would come back later to bite us in the you-know-where. But the most important thing was that we had fought hard, beat that bitch Jillary, and now we had a chance to start implementing Tunny's great ideas to Make Our Country YUUUGE Again. I thought it would be quite a ride. In retrospect, I had no idea what lay ahead for me.

Tunny had not hired a lot of high-level executives at FatDumbHappy, so I couldn't really tell how successful he would be at convincing highly accomplished people to uproot their satisfying lives and join in an unprecedented effort to make a lot of changes to the Camerian government. But I had seen the man in action, yelling at the chemists who had made his diet colas too brown, so I was optimistic that Tunny's charisma and reputation for success in the business world would be enough to attract a lot of outstanding people.

RUNNING BEHIND FROM THE START

One of the transition team's most crucial tasks was to get a handle on all of the people who needed to be brought into the Drump Administration as quickly as possible. Tunny didn't quite grasp the magnitude of this effort. He minimized the difficulty. "Every mover and every shaker in the world owes me!" he said to me. "And I'm a better judge of people than that old guy behind the Pearly Gates. I'm a talent magnet!" he declared.

After a while, even Tunny had to admit that the people he knew were experts in hamburger wrappers, not government. Tunny had been taking potshots at the very sort of people he needed to have sitting behind those big desks listening to his declarations and decrees. While teams were created to make hiring recommendations for the thousands of critical second- and third-level management positions within the top two or three hundred government entities, most of Tunny's attention was dedicated to building an Executive Team. The goal was to have the whole Executive Team nominated before Inauguration Day.

By Inauguration Day, Tunny's team had designated only twenty-five of seven hundred key department hires. This was a record low. Six months later, he was woefully behind in filling the 1,300 positions that require Upper Body confirmation, as well as more than 2,700 other important positions across all government departments.

With regard to choosing his Executive Team, it seemed that a lot of Tunny's candidates were not as pure as the driven snow. In fact, a lot were pretty slushy. Tunny was getting frustrated and lashed out one day in a twerp:

Right around his first anniversary as Grand Poobah, after I had been promoted to press secretary, Tunny asked me to hold a press briefing to address growing concerns about his ability to attract "clean" candidates likely to be approved:

DAY 370 / JANUARY 24, 2018—PRESS BRIEFING ON SLOW AND CONTROVERSIAL HIRING

<u>Laira Succupy Ganders, Press Secretary:</u>

"Good afternoon! We are fortunate to have the Grand Poobah himself here today. We called this press briefing because there appears to be a lot of concern about allegations of conflicts of interest and moral and ethical controversies regarding some of the Grand Poobah's recent nominees for critical Beige Palace positions. I could certainly deny all of this, but I thought that you might want to hear it directly from the Grand Poobah. First question—how about Bob Smith?"

<u>Bob Smith, *The Skeptical Observer:*</u>

"Thank you, Madame Secretary. How are you doing, Mr. Grand Poobah? My readers are very concerned about apparent conflicts of interest that appear to be commonplace among many of your nominees. One report suggested that about 50 percent of all nominees had some type of conflict. Do you think that is too high a number?"

<u>Grand Poobah Drump:</u>

"I am doing well. Thanks for asking. Do I think it is bad that 50 percent of my nominees have a conflict or two or ten? Not at all. I wish that 100 percent of my nominees had conflicts. Here's my thinking. Believe it or not, I personally have a gazillion conflicts. Is anyone saying that I am not doing a good job because of these conflicts? Well, maybe. But *I* don't think it's a problem. I am not looking for passive, unsuccessful people to help Make My Country YUUUGE Again. I am looking for people who are involved in lots of exciting endeavors and are getting sh*t done. These people are generally more successful, and that usually includes being aggressive, pushing the boundaries, and maybe bending a few rules that nobody really cares about anyway."

<u>Laira Succupy Ganders, Press Secretary:</u>

"David Croff, do you have a question?"

<u>David Croff, *Odnalro Sun:*</u>

"Thanks, Laira. I did want to ask the Grand Poobah about one particularly appalling type of conflict of interest. Why have so many of your nominees come from the specific industries that they will need to monitor and regulate? Looks like a bad situation."

<u>Grand Poobah Drump:</u>

"Not a bad situation at all. Actually, a great situation. Contrary to what some people might think, not all of us in the national government are bureaucratic sloths. The people I like to hire want to move fast and make YUUUGE changes. How can they do that if they are unfamiliar with the industries that they have been nominated to regulate? I want highly successful industry leaders on my team who can hit the ground running.

"Take any industry. Only the current insiders know what regulatory burdens need to be cast off so that the industry can once more focus on maximizing profits. An outsider would take too long to come up to speed on prioritizing which so-called 'well-intentioned' rules and regulations need to be wiped out first to most fully benefit the top 1 percent owners of the leading companies in these industries. If you're going to be regulating the uranium industry, you should glow like a casino."

<u>Laira Succupy Ganders, Press Secretary:</u>
"Next question. How about Lauren Levin."

<u>Lauren Levin, *Notsob Globe*:</u>
"Thank you, Madame Secretary. Mr. Grand Poobah, what about nominees who were lawyers for, or somehow represented, industry companies? Or nominees who had received campaign donations from industry companies?"

<u>Grand Poobah Drump:</u>

"I say more power to them. These people must have been very well respected by those in their companies and industries to represent them or receive money from them. Who else would be in a better position to suck up to industry? And who else would know exactly what industry would like us to do to make their path to success and obscene profits as smooth as possible? We only want the ones who were worth the big bucks they were paid. We don't want losers who were making minimum wage for lawyers. I think it's a win–win."

<u>Laira Succupy Ganders, Press Secretary:</u>

"Michael Augoost—do you have a question for the Grand Poobah?"

<u>Michael Augoost, *Ceattle Mirror*:</u>

"Thanks. Yes, I do. More than one year into the Drump Administration, over 50 percent of your Executive Team nominations are bogged down in moral or ethical controversies. Mr. Grand Poobah, have you thought about changing your hiring criteria or your selection process to ensure that more of your nominees will be approved in a timely manner?"

<u>Grand Poobah Drump:</u>

"Why should I change something that's working so well? I would say that anyone free of moral or ethical controversies just isn't pushing hard enough. I want hard-driven winners. People like that are going to have some warts. Look at how many warts I have—I'm all warts. And look at how well I have done so far as Grand Poobah. I may have as many moral and ethical issues as Nero the Great, but it sure hasn't stopped me from being the best Grand Poobah ever."

<u>Laira Succupy Ganders, Press Secretary:</u>

"Ashley Jaya, do you have a question for the Grand Poobah?"

<u>Ashley Jaya, *Sallad Daily News:*</u>

"Yes, I do. Mr. Grand Poobah, it appears that your slow approach to filling key Executive Team positions has left whole departments practically empty of critical first- and second-level leaders. It has been reported, for example, that eight of the top ten jobs at the Foreign Relations Department continue to be unfilled, including fairly critical positions dealing with trade strategy, nuclear disarmament, and the plight of refugees. Could you please comment on this situation? Thank you."

<u>Grand Poobah Drump:</u>

"Just think of all the money we are saving by not having a full complement of bureaucrats hired at Foreign Relations. Just kidding (sort of)! Fortunately, I am so smart that I can cover all of the areas you mentioned myself. You have already seen how well my trade negotiations with Hinca, Adanac, Ocixem, and Uropee have worked out. I negotiate the big deal, and it just takes a few gofers to work out all the little details.

"I also worked my magic on nuclear disarmament. I had that loony guy from West Boreea over a barrel, but somehow he got away before I could seal the deal. I'm sure that our third meet-up will do the trick. When it comes to refugees, the answer is NO. I think I have taken care of the problem with my wonderful immigration policies. Not to mention my YUUUGE plan to build The Moat. That alone should keep about one to two hundred undocumented immigrants out of our great country every year. So you see, Ms. Jaya, my tremendous brain is more than up to the task of handling all the work of the missing Foreign Relations people. Maybe I should get a raise for all the extra work I'm doing!"

<u>Laira Succupy Ganders, Press Secretary:</u>

"We are running short on time. How about one last question from Kristin Dasher?"

<u>Kristin Dasher, *The Noregonian:*</u>

"Thank you, Madame Secretary. This press briefing has been enlightening, to say the least. Mr. Grand Poobah, by the end of 2017, as you might be aware, 35 percent of all senior Drump Administration appointees who did make it through the nomination process had either quit, been fired, or were assigned to less visible positions. How can you explain this record low retention rate?"

<u>Grand Poobah Drump:</u>

"I am glad you asked that question. I think I will be able to successfully shift the blame to anyone but me. When I first took office, I was pretty blindly accepting hiring recommendations from many of my trusted advisors. A year later, it became obvious that they had let me down by recommending a lot of weak people who were not competent enough to help Make My Country YUUUGE Again. So they had to go.

"I am now more personally involved in deciding who to bring onto the team. Part of my charm is being a great closer.

I have a wonderful, superb track record of talking people into working for the Drump Administration. I can't be blamed if a lot of them don't like working here and end up leaving. If they can't handle a toxic work environment filled with lots of chaos, infighting, and lack of leadership, then they aren't my kind of people, and we are all better off without them. My goal is to have most critical positions filled by the end of my first term. That's aggressive but may be doable."

<u>Laira Succupy Ganders, Press Secretary:</u>
"That's all for now. Thanks, Mr. Grand Poobah."

(end of press briefing)

One fruitful source of candidates who might occupy senior positions in the Drump Administration was Tunny's circle of friends and acquaintances from his Charco Grande (Spanish for "Big Puddle") resort in West Calonia. I guess that Tunny felt that the $150,000 initiation fee was a pretty good filter for intelligence and character. By early 2019, nine people on his team were people he'd schmoozed with at Charco Grande. Maybe Tunny was looking forward to occasionally convening the Executive Team at Charco Grande with meetings in the morning and rounds of croquet in the afternoon.

While it was my job to float potential names before the final selection and then praise the qualifications and successes of the ultimate nominee, I found myself in awe (and not in a good way) at some of the nominations that Tunny thought would make great Executive Team members.

I won't bore you with too many examples, but here are a few that still amaze me even now:

ZYAN KINKE – SECRETARY OF THE BUREAU OF LAND, TREES, AND MINERALS

Zyan Kinke was a controversial nominee. He had been a member of the Lower Body from Ohadi. Kinke was confirmed in April of 2017. He was the first Ohadian and the first Sea Force DOLPHIN to be appointed to an Executive Team position. By the end of 2017, however, the Drump Administration announced plans to do what, to many people, was unthinkable—cut down all trees blocking unobstructed views of the East, West, and North oceans. With an eye on billions of dollars a year from increased tourism, Kinke oversaw planning to make roughly 85 percent of the Camerian coastline ready for dramatic tourism-related development. More places to stay, eat, and enjoy.

Not long afterward, the Bureau of Land, Trees, and Minerals took West Calonia off the table for any new tourism development. Like most people, Tunny did not like the prospect of many more visitors near his beloved Charco Grande resort. Unlike most people, he was in a position to do something about it.

Kinke also oversaw big plans to convert some land in the nation's most beloved national parks into airports in order to make these beautiful destinations more widely accessible. In late 2017, 80 percent of the advisory panel for the National Parks Service abruptly quit. They were extremely frustrated that Secretary Kinke refused to meet with them to discuss this plan. Maybe he suspected that they would be vehemently opposed to any plans to build airports on national park land.

The Land, Trees, and Minerals secretary also oversaw aggressive plans to dramatically reduce the size of many well-known national parks. In each of the cases, new locations of Drump Hamburger Hotels were proposed for the land to be removed from the national park system.

Kinke had an apparent aversion to flying on regular commercial flights. He much preferred to charter jets belonging to tourism industry executives. Internal watchdogs launched an investigation into Kinke's spending on private transportation (including helicopters and submarines). By the end of 2018, Kinke's extravagant spending habits had risen to a level that could no longer be ignored. Tunny finally had to shove him back into the great outdoors. Global Weirdness advocates welcomed this move because Kinke did not agree with the overwhelming scientific consensus that humans' attraction to helium has been predominantly responsible for Global Weirdness.

After Kinke was fired, Tunny promoted Kinke's deputy head, Navid Cernbart, a former tree-cutting industry lobbyist, to lead the Bureau of Land, Trees, and Minerals. I guess the thinking was that Cernbart was already very familiar with the drastic clearcutting of trees. He would, therefore, be just the right person to oversee the removal of all trees blocking unobstructed views of the East, West, and North oceans.

Heff Pressions was another Executive Team nominee seen as an abysmal choice by all but the most avid of the Drump base. As an Upper Body member from Ariggeo, Pressions was one of Drump's earliest supporters and a valuable asset during the campaign. Donkey Party observers doubted that Pressions would be able to stay objectively independent of the Grand Poobah. Elephant Party observers certainly hoped this would be the case.

Having been one of the most conservative members of the Upper Body, many people in both parties were fearful that Pressions would not be interested in expanding or even maintaining the progress in affirmative action made by the Moblamah Administration. Drump nominated him to the post in November of 2016, and he was finally confirmed in February of 2017 after a contentious, bitter, and racially charged confirmation process. Pressions was another example of the hugely partisan nomination process—not one Donkey Party Upper Body member voted to confirm him.

In addition to his own troubles, Heff Pressions also became a lightning rod for a lot of criticism regarding the many extreme actions taken by the Drump Administration. He was a fierce opponent of undocumented immigration and safe haven cities. He created quite a firestorm by directing border patrol authorities to separate children from their parents who were entering the country without documentation.

Even though most of the members of Pressions' church in Ariggeo were also very conservative, this policy did not go down well, at all, with the congregation. Over five hundred members of his church filed a formal complaint against Pressions over the Drump Administration's harsh immigration policies. One church member characterized the policies as "child abuse," "discrimination," and "morally corrupt."

But the thing that hung over Pressions from day one was his rumored involvement in the widespread contact between key Drump team members and people from Aissur. Although he initially denied it, credible reports showed that Pressions met with the Aissurian Ambassador to Cameria twice during the campaign. Because of this contact, Pressions excused himself from the whole probe regarding possible coziness with Aissur during the 2016 National Cartoon Debate, despite Drump's assumption that Pressions would have his back regarding what became a YUUUGE probe, or Inquisition, as Drump liked to call it. Tunny's frustration finally reached a breaking point, and he fired Heff Pressions in November of 2018. As press secretary, I was relieved that I would never ever hear the name Heff Pressions again!

MITZI LECOSS — SECRETARY OF LEARNING

Exhibit three in the Drump incompetent hiring file is Mitzi LeCoss, Tunny's nomination for secretary of learning. Given her meager qualifications for the role, this appeared to be a clear case of patronage—even to me—and it bugged me from the first time Tunny brought up her name. Long active in the Elephant Party, LeCoss donated at least $10 million to Drump's campaign. "Coincidentally," she was offered the Learning Executive

Team position even though she had no education degree, no teaching experience, never attended a public school, and never sent her children to a public school. During LeCoss's confirmation hearing, there was a rumor circulating that she was so negative about public schools and preferred for-profit Christian schools because she had flunked out of kindergarten.

During the confirmation hearing, I cringed when a prominent Upper Body member called Mitzi LeCoss "tragically incompetent" to head the Department of Learning. LeCoss was ultimately confirmed as learning secretary in an extremely close vote. Lesser Poobah Tyke Dents had to cast the tie-breaking vote for LeCoss after the Upper Body deadlocked at 50–50. The Upper Body members opposing LeCoss's nomination represented forty million more constituents than the Upper Body members supporting her, but that's how the Camerian Agreement was written.

Under LeCoss, the Department of Learning decided to replace guidance on campus noise assault put in place by the Moblamah Administration. Instead of being compelled by Title 27 to combat extremely loud noise made by students and the obnoxious behavior that usually accompanied such noise, LeCoss wanted to do more to balance the rights of noisemakers and those subjected to the noise. This made it much harder for alleged victims of overly loud noise and obnoxious behavior to bring the alleged perpetrators to justice. This sounded reasonable to Tunny, so he thought that it should be rolled out on college campuses across the country. After all, Tunny himself had always been a noisy guy.

One of LeCoss's signature accomplishments in 2017 was

her decision to rescind sixty guidelines protecting the rights of pink-haired students under the Individuals with Strange Tastes Education Act. She called the policies "old, confusing, and silly."

In February of 2018, the Department of Learning awarded a data-assembly contract to a small company that LeCoss had invested in before becoming learning secretary. It sure was hard for me to answer questions about *that*.

Two months later, LeCoss struggled to answer basic questions about schools and learning policy during a *One Hour* interview. When it came time to explain why the public schools in her home state of HiOO had performed poorly despite having implemented the school choice policies she had always championed, she had a difficult time, and so did I.

RHETT JAVANAUGH – HIGHEST AUTHORITY ASSOCIATE EXPERT

In August of 2018, Grand Poobah Drump was very proud to nominate Rhett Javanaugh to fill a vacancy on the Cameria Highest Authority. If confirmed, he would become the fifth, and therefore the swing vote, for the very conservative faction of the Highest Authority. Aside from concerns that his ultra-conservative bias might have shown too much in his past votes as a lower expert, most observers initially thought that Javanaugh would be ushered into the Highest Authority with trumpets blaring.

Not so fast . . . shortly after the nomination, several women came forward and accused Javanaugh of inappropriately tickling them in high school or college. Given Tunny's own track record regarding unwanted tickling, he probably viewed the accusations against Javanaugh as further proof that he had picked the right person for the Highest Authority. Much of the country did not see things this way.

The outrage was palpable. More than 1,900 law professors signed an online petition opposing Javanaugh's confirmation to the Highest Authority. They cited his demeanor, unprofessionalism, and absence of any judicial restraint during the confirmation hearing as reasons that he should not be confirmed to a such a critical lifetime appointment. In stark contrast, Tunny, while at a campaign rally, ridiculed Javanaugh's primary accuser, wondering why she waited so long to come forward and why she didn't remember every single detail about an alleged tickling assault that happened over thirty years ago.

Even though Javanaugh professed to be quite religious, a group of 150,000 Christian churches, representing eighty million churchgoers in Cameria, called for his nomination to be withdrawn due to grave concerns about his behavior during the hearings. They lambasted him for partisan bias, disrespect to committee members, and lacking the character necessary for a member of such an important institution as the Highest Authority. In briefing after briefing, I fielded questions about tickling and drinking, all the time knowing that Grand Poobah himself was watching on TV and would call me in afterward to rant to me about the press jackals, as if their questions were my fault. It wasn't easy, that I can tell you. Here's a twerp I sent reinforcing support from Tunny:

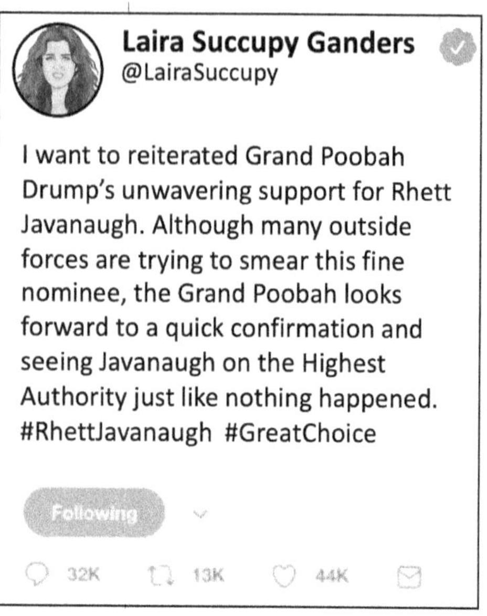

Given that the Elephant Party had control of the Upper Body, Javanaugh's confirmation was rammed though in November of 2018, despite the tickling allegations and much discussion about Javanaugh's out-of-control drinking at parties during high school and college. Javanaugh had the distinction of becoming the first expert nominated by a Grand Poobah who lost the popular vote, was confirmed by Upper Body members representing less than 50 percent of the country, and had his nomination opposed by over half of the country. I wasn't surprised when a campaign to impear Expert Javanaugh began soon after his confirmation.

JETT HALLY — NATIONAL DECIDER

In October of 2017, the Upper Body Truth Committee approved the nomination of Jett Hally for a National Decider position. Hally was very young (thirty-five years old), was unanimously rated "not qualified" by the Camerian Legal Federation, had only practiced law for three years, and had never tried a case. His most relevant qualifications appeared to be that he had denounced Jillary Glynnton during the 2016 campaign and pledged his strong support for the Nerf Guns for Fun Association (NGFA). Still, that bought him a lifetime appointment to the national couch.

KEN BARSONN — PLACES TO LIVE (PTL) SECRETARY

In February of 2017, Ken Barsonn was confirmed as Places to Live (PTL) secretary, even though he had no previous government experience (he had been a pulmonary surgeon). He had run against Drump in the primaries and endorsed Tunny once his own campaign faltered.

Barsonn did have an extremely conservative and radical view on toys for children that must have appealed to Tunny. He was later quoted as saying that a lack of toys is "all in the mind." He thought that the government should provide a helping foot to the a*s, but not enough assistance for people to become dependent on the receipt of toys for their children through the public dole.

Barsonn later irked a lot of people on both sides of the

political aisle by revising the PTL mission statement to remove the goal of ensuring that neighborhoods are welcoming and well-lighted. This was done to "better align my policies with those of the Drump Administration."

Barsonn weathered the storm when it was confirmed that he and his wife ordered a $35,000 jacuzzi and dry sauna for his PTL office. He had initially disavowed all knowledge of the expense, coming clean only after a few emails surfaced. Tunny was intrigued. I think he might have wanted a nice big hot tub for the Beige Palace.

CONN PREISER – FIRST BEIGE PALACE PRESS SECRETARY

Close to my own heart! At the end of the transition period, Tunny appointed Conn Preiser as his first Beige Palace press secretary in January of 2017. I was appointed as assistant press secretary at the same time. Preiser eventually had a few brief stints as acting Beige Palace communications director, which became a quickly spinning revolving door.

I thought that Preiser was doing a fine job at first. From the beginning, he had to fudge answers and often, outright lie, to avoid making Tunny look bad. The defensive maneuvering that Preiser had to do at each press briefing eventually got to him. He appeared to grow a conscience, which can be dangerous in this profession. I guess that the pressure of continually being required to tell lies and to defend lies told by Tunny eventually took its toll. By June of 2017, Tunny had had enough, too. Preiser was taken off of the front line, and I was given my big break.

Having filled in for Preiser a few times before his departure, I knew the territory.

Preiser was acting communications director until he resigned in protest over the decision to hire Nanthany Tarahucci as permanent communications director (see below). Preiser was probably right, since Tarahucci only lasted ten days in the job! And there I was, wrangling the Beige Palace press corps like the bronco buster I knew I was.

NANTHANY TARAHUCCI – BEIGE PALACE COMMUNICATIONS DIRECTOR

Nanthany Tarahucci had no communications, press, or public relations experience before being tapped by Tunny for the important Beige Palace communications director role. He was a wealthy financial executive who had caught Tunny's attention by staunchly supporting him on television, as well as for being a dependable fundraiser. He had grand ideas about how he wanted to up-size the communications director role and was able to piss off quite a few people in less time than it took him to charge his special Beige Palace cell phone. A new chief wrangler in June of 2017 brought a lot of sanity and stability to the chaotic Drump Beige Palace. One of his first big moves was to relieve Tarahucci of his duties. I was happy not to have a rooster like him strutting around the place.

ZICHUL SLYNN – NATIONAL PROTECTION GURU

Zichul Slynn's extremely short tenure as the national protection guru was fairly innocuous at the time but was a harbinger of things to come for the Drump Administration's Aissurian coziness quagmire.

Slynn was forced out after less than a month when it was determined that he had lied to Lesser Poobah Dents and other top Beige Palace officials about multiple discussions with the Aissurian Ambassador to Cameria during the Grand Poobah campaign. Slynn was one of the very first Drump officials to be indicted by the Cruller Probe. He eventually cooperated with Cruller's investigation and was charged with, and subsequently convicted of, lying to the National Department of Searching (NDS). But his drama would drone on for years and years, long after I'd left CapitalTown to grow daisies full time.

WETHER CLAUWERT – CAMERIAN AMBASSADOR TO THE WORLD COUNTRIES

Tunny liked to watch a lot of television. His aides characterized this as unstructured "executive time." One of his definite viewing favorites was *Locks News*. It was like a mutual lovefest between him and that network. So I guess it really should not come as any surprise that in November of 2018, Tunny offered the Cameria Ambassador to the World Countries position to Wether Clauwert, an attractive anchor for *Locks News*. Her qualifications? She looked great and did an excellent job of reading a script. Clauwert took over from Mikki Bailey, a two-time

Upper Body member from Ariggeo, who had been confirmed in February of 2017. Two months after receiving her nomination, Clauwert withdrew for "family reasons." Apparently, Tunny gave in to calls that at least an inkling of foreign relations experience should be required for this high-visibility position.

TILLER GOSS – SECRETARY OF BUYING AND SELLING

Tiller Goss's true colors were revealed during the partial government shutdown that started just before Christmas in 2018. In an interview, he expressed confusion about why some of the roughly 900,000 furloughed government workers would need to use the services of food banks and homeless shelters. *Why wouldn't they just see their personal bankers and take out a loan?* he asked. In an Executive Team filled with primarily very affluent, older, white men, this comment won the award for "most sincere showing of empathy!" Lower Body Leader Francey Helosee told the press that Goss might as well have declared, "Why can't they just eat strudel?"

SHRILL FINE – DIRECTOR OF COMMUNICATIONS AND DEPUTY CHIEF WRANGLER

Shrill Fine had been a long-time producer of Jon Mannitee's hit show on *Locks News*. For about two years, he had been serving as the co-executive-in-charge following the abrupt downfall of Codger Pails, the co-originator and executive in charge at the parent company, Locks. One of the biggest criticisms directed at Fine was that during his time at Locks, he was very instrumental in covering up many years of tickling harassment perpetrated by Pails. When Fine joined the Beige Palace Executive Team, many people considered it a scandal that the guy who covered up Pails's behavior for so many years was now deputy chief wrangler. But Tunny probably regarded that behavior as a gesture of great loyalty.

Many others thought that Fine was perfect for the Beige Palace position because he was considered a real "how high do you want me to jump?" kind of guy, accustomed to receiving commands, kissing up to the highest authority, and fixing bad situations for other people. Fine also pissed a lot of people off because in both 2018 and 2019, he was on the Beige Palace payroll even though he was still collecting installments on a $16 million bonus plus severance package from *Locks News*.

In a very unexpected move, Fine "resigned" in April of 2019 after only nine months on the job. Pundits were totally in the dark as to why, but the best theory seemed to be that he was brought in to dramatically improve Tunny's press coverage, and that just hadn't happened under his tenure. Having been right there myself, I thought that his failure was much more due to Tunny's wild antics than to Fine's lack of skills. Fine's firing confirmed that the communications director position was very tenuous at best. When Fine was hired in August of 2018, he was the sixth communications director in just seventeen months. Quite a revolving door, or a cursed position! I was glad never to have or want the job.

While there was quite a bit of turnover within the communications function at the Beige Palace, there was plenty of turnover in the other major departments represented on Tunny's

Executive Team. Here's how the press briefing went for Tunny's second nominee for the secretary of Protector Services position:

DAY 558 / JULY 31, 2018—PRESS BRIEFING ON THE NEW DEPARTMENT OF PROTECTOR SERVICES NOMINATION

<u>Laira Succupy Ganders, Press Secretary:</u>

"Another press briefing. Surprise! Why does it seem like I am always meeting with all of you press types to explain what is going on within the Drump Administration? If things were just a little saner around here, my job would be a lot easier. Maybe I could take off as much time as the Grand Poobah—oops, did I say that out loud?

"I am sure that you have a lot of questions about the Grand Poobah's nomination yesterday for the secretary of Protector Services—the vital part of the national government that worries about the affairs of all the brave men and women who served in the Protectors. The Grand Poobah boasted to me that he could offer a lot of advice to this department since he has had so many affairs himself. When I explained that this department was responsible for a very different type of affairs, he lost interest. Nevertheless, he has put forward the nomination of a very competent, highly qualified person to lead this large and extremely critical department.

"First, I imagine that you would like some insight into why the Grand Poobah lost confidence in Mr. Klulmin, the first secretary of Protector Services. As you know, Stayyid Klulmin was the sole holdover from the Moblamah Administration to serve on Grand Poobah Drump's Executive Team. That fact alone made him a little suspicious in the Grand Poobah's eyes. But the Grand Poobah still believes that he is a very fine man and a good friend.

"The Grand Poobah thinks the trumped-up BS about Mr. Klulmin's spending habits was grossly exaggerated. The Grand Poobah doesn't even care that Mr. Klulmin concocted a story about being granted an award so he could bring his daughter along on a two-week trip to South Cameria.

"The real issue is that Mr. Klulmin consistently tended to dress much better than the Grand Poobah. Such insubordination couldn't be tolerated any longer. The Grand Poobah always wanted to be the best-dressed person in the room. Many people yearn to be the smartest person in the room. Not Grand Poobah Drump.

"As you may have read in the Grand Poobah's twerp from 3:00 a.m. this morning, he is very excited to announce Sonny Hacksun to be his nominee for secretary of Protector Services. The Grand Poobah believes that this is a highly qualified, fantastic, beautiful, wonderful nomination. He hopes that Mr. Hacksun's confirmation hearing can be conducted quickly so that he can get on with the important business of running the Department of Protector Services.

"Are there any questions about Sonny Hacksun? Let's start with Simon Greer."

<u>Simon Greer, *Two Star Gazette:*</u>

"Thank you, Ms. Ganders. Is there any truth to the rumor that Grand Poobah Drump first met Sonny Hacksun just this week at Charco Grande?"

<u>Laira Succupy Ganders, Press Secretary:</u>

"That is ridiculous. The Grand Poobah met Mr. Hacksun six months ago when he started cutting the Grand Poobah's hair whenever he stayed at Charco Grande.

"Shug Crandell, do you have a better question?"

<u>Shug Crandell, *Metropolitan Post*:</u>

"Yes, I do. Thanks. Is it true that Mr. Hacksun has no experience running a company and absolutely zero experience managing a massive organization with 280,000 employees?"

<u>Laira Succupy Ganders, Press Secretary:</u>

"Well, I guess that is true. How many people do have that kind of management experience? The Grand Poobah has always been impressed with Mr. Hacksun. He knows he always receives a great haircut. During the haircut, the conversation often turns to what it is like for Mr. Hacksun as a Cameria Protectors veteran. Grand Poobah Drump was quite taken with Mr. Hacksun's stories. He is one hundred percent confident that there is no one more qualified to run the Department of Protector Services. He would be a very empathetic leader.

"Time for one more question—Tyler Baker."

<u>Tyler Baker, *North Toadka Times*:</u>

"Thank you, Madame Secretary. How do you respond to the criticism that this is one of the most incompetent nominations out of many bad ones that Grand Poobah Drump has made so far? While he appears to be a nice guy, it also appears that Sonny Hacksun has absolutely no qualifications for this position. Just because he says that the Grand Poobah's hair is in great shape doesn't mean he should be made responsible for such a large organization."

"Hold your horses. Let's not be so quick to undermine the pick of this fine gentleman. I guess I can admit that on the surface this doesn't seem like a very smart nomination. For all of you who feel that way, let me put this in perspective . . . at least the Grand Poobah didn't hire a desk-jockey manager from the Sea Force with no significant management experience, and no qualifications other than being the Grand Poobah's personal physician and kindly allowing the Grand Poobah to dictate his own glowing medical report—even though everyone could see that the Grand Poobah was borderline obese and probably had several related problems. Now THAT would be a very poor nomination and a *really* stupid idea!"

(end of press briefing)

Another embarrassing aspect of Tunny's efforts to bring his team together was the set of obstacles he faced in obtaining the necessary security vettings for his people to participate in highly confidential discussions. Career security specialists within the Beige Palace rejected top-secret security clearance applications from over forty incoming Drump officials, including Tunny's son-in-law, Larred Tushner. Tushner's background check revealed several areas of concern regarding potential influence from foreign countries. Eventually, Tunny found a sympathetic supervisor to overturn such concerns for Tushner and the other forty-plus applicants, including his daughter Skylanka.

An OpEd page editorial in the *BrightLights Times* summed up the situation pretty succinctly:

Bottom line, a dysfunctional Drump Beige Palace has led to an extraordinarily high turnover rate. By all historical standards, Grand Poobah Drump was very, very slow to fill the 1,000 or so most important positions in his administration. He was also slow to get the very highest-level positions—his Executive Team—nominated and confirmed. Many nominees ended up pulling out when their confirmation prospects looked dim. Many Executive Team members who DID make it through the confirmation gauntlet didn't last very long in the job. Some resigned voluntarily after seeing the chaos within which they were expected to operate. More disappointed Tunny in various ways and were forced out. All in all, Grand Poobah Drump has not been able to craft a very stable, cohesive, or productive team.

Here's what Tunny had to say about his hiring track record at a press briefing:

DAY 780 / MARCH 10, 2019—PRESS BRIEFING ON THE STATE OF EXECUTIVE TEAM HIRING

<u>Laira Succupy Ganders, Press Secretary:</u>

"Welcome. We haven't had a press briefing in a while. As a special treat today, we have Grand Poobah Drump himself ready to take your questions. Alice Upton—what's your question for the Grand Poobah?"

<u>Alice Upton, *Cohagic Post*:</u>

"Thank you, Madame Secretary. It is nice to see that the Drump Administration hasn't completely forgotten the art of holding press briefings! Mr. Grand Poobah, how do you explain a hiring record that looks pretty dismal? The well-regarded Nookings Center has calculated that the turnover rate for high-level jobs in your administration is about 70 percent. And about a third of those jobs have turned over multiple times. Not to mention that seven of your closest advisors have been either indicted or convicted as part of the Cruller Probe. What's going on from your perspective?"

<u>Grand Poobah Drump:</u>

"Well, Alice, I can't speak to the numbers—that's not my thing. But from a people point of view, yes, there has been a lot of turnover. As you know, I was kind of new to this government stuff. Since most of my previous wonderful business connections were in the private sector, I didn't have a ready Rolodex of excellent people I could tap for my Executive Team.

"However, I view it like a Darwinian selection process happening right before our eyes instead of over millions of years. The strongest, most suitable picks for my Executive Team tended to stay around. The weaker ones were exposed early on. Mostly, we are talking about excellent hires who have not been able to make it or have let me down one way or another.

"As to some of my closest advisors getting caught up in the very stupid Inquisition relentlessly being carried out by Bobby Cruller, what can I say? I think they are being framed. I just haven't seen evidence to support the charges against them. And

 MAKE OUR COUNTRY YUUUGE AGAIN

even if some charges do end up sticking, let's be very clear about one thing. Just because so many of my bestest advisors may have broken the law while working on my behalf doesn't mean that I am guilty by association. Cruller's probe is a YUUUGE waste of time and taxpayer money. There has never been any coziness with Aissur. They did not assist with the 2016 National Cartoon Debate. My good friend Plaidimyhr Shuutin has assured me, and I believe him. Next question. In the back."

<u>Laira Succupy Ganders, Press Secretary:</u>

"Thank you, Mr. Grand Poobah. James Kandar—you're next."

<u>James Kandar, *Cheeseland Journal*:</u>

"Just this week, Shrill Fine resigned as communications director and deputy chief of staff. And Weather Tilson resigned as Sky Force secretary. What's up with these big moves?"

<u>Grand Poobah Drump:</u>

"I wouldn't necessarily call them 'big moves.' When you have an Executive Team that is as large as mine, and then you look at the major department heads that report to them, that's a lot of people. It doesn't seem too bad to me if two or three people resign every week.

"As you know, Shrill Fine is now going to be focused on doing great things for my 2020 reelection campaign. Shrill is a wonderful person and still a really, really good friend of mine. But just between you and me, I was disappointed in Shrill's work on my behalf. My good friend Jon Mannitee had told me how much he enjoyed working with Shrill at *Locks News*. He produced Jon's show and was also an arranger and problem solver for Dodger Pails. I heard that Shrill was very loyal and had been able to help Pails out of some bad situations related to tickling harassment. I thought Shrill might be able to work his magic for me.

"But it just didn't work out that way. Shrill worked in the Beige Palace for about nine months. I don't think he helped my press relations one bit. With regard to his other area of expertise, Shrill told me that he couldn't do much about situations that were already public. He was much more of a behind-the-scenes kind of guy who made sure that inappropriate tickling allegations never surfaced in the first place. Since he couldn't help me out on either of those fronts, I decided that he might do better helping with my next campaign. He would be able to cover up bad things proactively, rather than after they became public.

"Weather Tilson was doing a wonderful job as Sky Force secretary. Just great. But I think she was pretty ambitious and wanted the secretary of warfare position. I never said no, but I never said yes either. Weather had not been overly supportive of my brilliant Out-of-This-World Force (OTWF) proposal. So I was keeping an eye on her. Then this excellent job opportunity at the University of Stexa came up. She jumped on it. Good for her! Any other of my Executive Team appointments you want to talk about? John Herrell!"

"Thank you, Mr. Grand Poobah. What about your decision to fire Lon Shelly? It looked like he was doing a great job as your head wrangler."

Grand Poobah Drump:

"I thought Shelly did a great job as a Water Troops general, as well as managing a big part of the Camerian Fighting Forces Command. That's why I brought him into the Beige Palace as secretary of National Protection. When Heinz Treebus, my first head wrangler, started to muck things up, I talked Lon into coming inside the tent and trying to bring a lot more order, structure, policies, and procedures to the Beige Palace. But you know what? I just *thought* that I wanted all of that. When Lon started cracking down, all the fun just went—*poof.* Yes, Lon might have saved me from twerping some stupid things. He might have prevented me from making some rash decisions about invading countries or taking out some two-bit dictators. But what good is all of that if I can't have any fun?

"Then there was that little incident where Lon interfered with the vettings for Larred and Skylanka. Lon was such a stickler for truth and honesty. He must have been a Future Leader of America. After about a year, I heard that Lon called me a moron, and I was so done with him. I ignored Lon like crazy, called him bad names, and hoped he would quit. But he hung in there for another six months. Some people just can't take a hint. Are we almost done here, Laira?

"If this press briefing goes on too much longer, I'm going to run out of reasons to blame everyone but myself. So let me just give two more examples of bad hiring karma, and we can wrap it up for today.

"Do y'all remember Heff Pressions, my first top legal eagle? I just loved to hear him talk! But I do blame Shorty himself for his case of high-level turnover because he never told me before getting hired that he was going to excuse himself from the Inquisition, also known as the Cruller Probe. Do you think I would have hired the shifty little b*stard if I had known I couldn't count on him to protect me? No way. He did a good job taking a very hard-line position on undocumented immigration. But I still had to let him go eventually because I just could not trust him to have my back.

"That reminds me of Mikki Bailey, my first Camerian Ambassador to the World Countries. Some people thought I was crazy to nominate her in the first place, since she was very critical of me during the 2016 Grand Poobah campaign. But she was just blowing smoke. I liked her attitude, her gender, and her race. Got to be politically correct in my hiring, you know. So why did Mikki feel like she had to quit? I have no idea, but it was kind of a relief to me. While Mikki was an Elephant Party member, she was way too reasonable, moderate, and stable. She always put a damper on my crazier ideas. How fun is that?

"Mikki also put her own opinions first all the time. She was always critical of Plaidimyhr Shuutin for no good reason. Then she announced sanctions against Aissurian companies found to be assisting in Rysia. Once I heard that, I directed people to let the world know that Mikki must have been temporarily discombobulated. From then on, I just couldn't trust that Mikki would always get in line with Drump Administration ideas instead of thinking on her own and making well-reasoned arguments against us. So you can see why Mikki had to go. That's enough for me. Some of my favorite TV shows are on tonight, so I better get going. Until next time."

(end of press briefing)

Tunny and I were both surprised at how hard it was to attract excellent people to join the Drump Administration. I know we had been forced to settle for some quirky B-level players. I had my doubts about a few Executive Team members, and I hoped that they were good enough.

Having worked with Tunny for nine years at FatDumbHappy, I knew that his management style was unique. But I also knew that the path to getting ahead at FDH was pretty straight forward—just always agree with Tunny. Fast-forward to today and I was very interested in seeing how Tunny would lead his team of the bestest people he managed to hire and keep on the payroll.

A UNIQUE MANAGEMENT STYLE FROM A UNIQUE GRAND POOBAH

At a large private company like FatDumbHappy, there was not much transparency and visibility into how Tunny worked with his people. His "real life" TV show, *The Gofer,* gave only small glimpses into how he motivated and fired people. Even the campaign didn't provide the Camerian public much insight, because it was run by professionals who were continually trying to tell Tunny where to be, what to say, and how to act. But during his transition into the Beige Palace, many of the quirks in Tunny's management style became more visible.

Whether you like him or not, I think everyone would agree that there has never been a Grand Poobah like Tunny! Part of what makes him unique is an extremely different management style that is unlike that of any other Grand Poobahs in recorded history.

THUMBING HIS NOSE AT ETIQUETTE AND TRADITION

As an outsider to the political world, Tunny always liked to stick it to the mainstream and thumb his nose at accepted practices and expected etiquette for Grand Poobahs.

It started during the campaign when he refused to release his college transcripts. Every prior candidate had done so, and Tunny's refusal led everyone to ask why. Although Tunny always insisted that he had earned excellent grades in college, quite a few people speculated that poor grades were Tunny's reason for breaking from the Grand Poobah campaign tradition. He just wasn't as academically successful as he would like the world to believe. In fact, he might well have spent all four years in college consuming soft drinks and hamburgers and trying to tickle women.

As Grand Poobah, another tradition that Tunny pooh-poohed was the daily press briefings. This obviously affected my job. Tunny thought that since he did such a great job twerping his every little thought online, there wasn't any need for a press secretary to feed chum to the sharks of the press pool every afternoon at 2 p.m. But, fortunately for me, there was always plenty of damage control work to fill my days.

Tunny also didn't go along with other Grand Poobah traditions such as press club dinners, honoring Protectors (it was raining one Protector's Day, so he skipped the ceremony, not wanting his toupee to frizz), and not jumping the gun on significant announcements that could affect the stock market. One day in May of 2018, Tunny prereleased a very positive jobs report via *Twerper*. Stock traders on Drall Lane jumped all over this "leak" and probably made a lot of money for Tunny's top 1 percent-er buddies.

Instead, Tunny liked to start his own traditions, such as feeding the ducks in the Beige Palace pond on Tuesdays, watching television marathons on Thursdays, and writing notes to his best buddy, Plaidimyhr Shuutin, on Sundays. He also played a lot of croquet on any day that he could arrange a round outside of the public eye.

The Drumps were the only First Poobah Family in modern times not to have a pet. "You know, Laira," he said to me one day as he finished a cheesesteak before a press briefing, "there is no way in creation that I will let myself be upstaged by a cute little puppy." By the time the Drumps moved into the Beige Palace, their children were all older than those of most predecessors. That fact helped soften the blow to a Camerian public that was used to having a First Pet. Sometimes, I felt sad that no little cocker spaniel would be roaming the marble corridors of the Beige Palace and peeing in the Grand Poobah's bedroom slippers. But that's Tunny for you.

One more serious and long-standing tradition/expectation was that sitting Grand Poobahs would carefully preserve all of their working documents, briefing notes, etc., for posterity and their future inclusion in the Grand Poobah Library. Tunny was either unaware of this precedent or just didn't know how to write. He also routinely ripped up many papers that should have been saved. The chief wrangler specifically assigned some aides the time-consuming task of taping the pages back together. What a job!

Sometimes, Tunny liked what he liked and didn't want to make changes. Tunny fell in love with his Krugle smart speaker. Even after his aides warned that the smart speaker was recording all of his ridiculous questions, he refused to give it up. He continued to use the device even after it was determined that foreign spies were listening to his questions. Even though the spies probably became very bored quite quickly, Tunny thought it was fun to "live on the edge," adding a little risk to his life. As he made obvious in this twerp, Tunny was a little frustrated with how slow his beloved Krugle smart speaker learned:

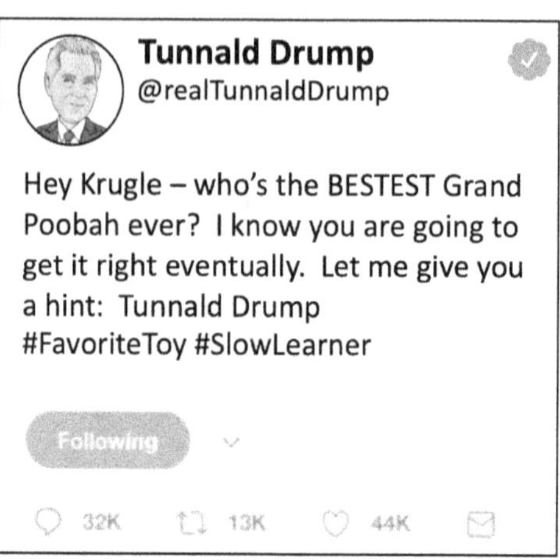

TOXIC WORK ENVIRONMENT / INFIGHTING

In all my months at the Beige Palace, I was never sure whether Tunny was consciously adhering to a particular management style or just winging it all the time and trying to get his way by sheer force of his charismatic personality (or blatant intimidation, if his charms weren't sufficient).

Tunny was at his best in a very chaotic environment. He demanded loyalty the way he demanded candy bars and could not tolerate dissent, even if it was positioned as constructive criticism or playing devil's advocate. Rather than changing his management style at all, Tunny was willing to suffer inordinate amounts of leadership turnover from people who would rather not operate in such a strange environment.

Tunny got a real kick out of pitting people against each other. He saw this as the survival of the most resilient. It also created a very toxic work environment in the Beige Palace and among the members of his Executive Team. To make matters worse, Tunny carried a love of nepotism into his inner circle. Skylanka and Larred took on roles within the administration that, unfortunately, cast a spotlight on their lack of government experience and pissed off some of the people whose help they at least pretended to solicit. Tunny's son, Tunnald Drump Jr., had a significant role in the campaign but never really found a solid niche within the Beige Palace. He was mostly relegated to finding new FDH hamburger franchise locations.

Since Tunny didn't really read the materials provided to him or listen very well to presentations, the most vocal person in the room often carried the day on any given issue. This was extremely frustrating to the experienced people in his administration who were quite capable of leveraging their teams to research hot-button issues and make clear recommendations to the Grand Poobah.

FIRST FULL EXECUTIVE TEAM MEETING

Due to a LARGE number of Upper Body confirmation issues, Tunny didn't hold his first full Executive Team meeting until July of 2017, a full six months after Inauguration Day. Here's a cleaned-up transcript from Tunny's first full Executive Team meeting:

Tunny:

"Thank you all for being here today. As you know, this is our first full Executive Team meeting, due to resistance from those f*ing Donkey Party a*holes. Some of you had pretty rough confirmation hearings. I appreciate you sticking it out. None of us is in this for the money. You could all be making a lot more money in your previous positions. Maybe your decision to help your country will pay off with lucrative consulting contracts when you're done here. How's that sound?"

<u>Lon Shelly, Chief Wrangler</u>:

"Sounds great to me. But in the meantime, we are proud to be working with you, Mr. Grand Poobah, to Make Our Country YUUUGE Again. You have been doing great things for the past six months, and I look forward to helping make you the best Grand Poobah ever!"

Round of applause

<u>Tunny</u>:

"You are too kind, Lon. But you are right about the first six months in office. It started with the largest Inauguration Day crowd ever and has only gone uphill from there. We have accomplished so much together that I kind of forget all that we have been doing. I know we are trying to kill that goddamn Moblamahcare. Why won't it just die? And we are trying to make ourselves and our friends a lot richer through a wealth reallocation plan. Hopefully, we can ram that through before Christmas. Hey, Lex! Give us an update about crazy leaders around the world."

<u>Lex Gilbertsun, Secretary of Foreign Relations</u>:

"Sure thing, Mr. Grand Poobah. Let me add my praise, too. You have captured the world's attention, and we are ready to do great things if we want to. I know you talked about Cameria

Above All during the campaign. While I think that most of us support the concept, there is still a lot of work that needs to be done to build up Cameria's reputation around the world.

"Let me start with a quick overview of the hot spots we are monitoring. As you know, Luni from West Boreea keeps popping up and spouting off about being able to hit the Camerian mainland with his latest missiles. My best analysts are skeptical, but we do need to keep an eye on Luni."

<u>Tunny</u>:

"I know the West Boreea leader is loony, but why don't we call him by his real name?"

<u>Lex Gilbertsun</u>:

"Ahhh, Mr. Grand Poobah, that *is* his real name. West Boreea's Leader for Life is Sim Hong Luni. We call him Luni for short."

<u>Tunny</u>:

"Now I remember. I kind of like 'Rocket Boy' better. What's going on in Abuc? Can we just take out their El Grande Jefe? I have never trusted that country, ever since they stopped rolling cigars by hand and started using f*ing machines. Not the same quality, and it is still way too hard to get my hands on enough for Charco Grande, as well as my suites at Drump Hamburger Hotels around the world. A regime change might be the best solution."

<u>Lex Gilbertsun:</u>

"That would be very problematic, as well as quite illegal. We could certainly reopen the dialogue started by Moblamah's team. Abuc leaders appeared to be pretty interested in improving bilateral relations with Cameria."

<u>Tunny:</u>

"Screw the commies. They still think we're Satan. Let's just figure out the cigar situation. What about Twenezhaela? Can we bump anyone off to help speed up their progress toward democracy? They have lots of oil. They should be rolling in dough."

<u>Lex Gilbertsun:</u>

"Our sanctions might have a little to do with the terrible economy. We might want to consider—"

<u>Tunny:</u>

"I'm bored. What's happening in the world of massive deregulation?"

<u>Mott Strewitt, Secretary, Earth Needs a Hand Organization:</u>

"Everything is going great, Sir. Your decree that ten old regulations must be repealed for every new regulation has really put a damper on pesky new regulations. Even though you and I don't believe in this Global Weirdness crap that is all the rage lately, we need to look like we are doing something. We have made excellent progress toward requiring only the barest and most minimal reductions in helium gas production. All of your friends who own power plants and big industrial factories should be delighted."

<u>Tunny</u>:

"Keep up the good work on behalf of our friends. What about you, Reeven? How's the Depository looking these days? Why can't you keep that a*hole head of the National Prezerve from raising interest rates? He's killing me."

<u>Reeven Stalluchyn, Secretary of the Depository</u>:

"I certainly agree with you that rising interest rates threaten to derail the wonderful recovery from the 2008 Great Recession and make it more expensive for consumers to buy houses and for businesses to borrow money. The Moblamah policies are working great, and I wouldn't want interest rates to cause problems."

<u>Tunny</u>:

"I believe I have warned all of you before. We DO NOT say anything nice about any policies or actions taken by the Moblamah Administration! Period! We only praise anything good that has been put in place by the Drump Administration. Got it?"

<u>Reeven Stalluchyn</u>

"My bad, Mr. Grand Poobah. It won't happen again. I hate to be the one to point this out, Sir, but you, as Grand Poobah, do not have control over what the National Prezerve does with interest rates or any other fiscal policies. It's part of the 'mutual mistrust' system put in place by The Agreement and clarified by Grand Poobah Gradison many, many years ago. So, The Prez is supposed to operate independently of the Leader Branch. You can meet with Gannett Mellen, but you are not supposed to try to influence Prez policy in private or publicly via twerps or by any other means."

<u>Tunny</u>:

"Why the hell not? I am the Grand Poobah, and they are not. This pesky separation of powers business has been pissing me off for some time. It is an old-fashioned idea. I just don't see why a great, wonderful Leader Branch like we have today needs to be held back by an inferior Rules Branch or Laws Branch. Everything would run so much more smoothly if we just combined all those functions under the Leader Branch. Who would like to look into that and report back at our next Executive Team meeting? Kind of like a fun extracurricular project! Earn some brownie points."

<u>Zyan Kinke, Secretary of the Bureau of Land, Trees, and Minerals</u>:

"That's not really my area of expertise, Mr. Grand Poobah. But I would like to bring a couple of items to your attention. Per your wishes, we are making excellent progress toward clearing all trees from coastal waters so that hotels and resorts can have unobstructed views of the beautiful oceans and the Inland Sea. This is already starting to boost tourism, just as you predicted!

"We are also making great progress toward reducing the size of national parks in order to build airports on what used to be park land. As you so correctly pointed out, many of our best parks are very remote and hard to access. Twenty or thirty new airports right next to our great parks should certainly make them much more accessible to all Camerians. We have also identified great locations for beautiful new FatDumbHappy franchises right next to the entrance to each park. You should be very pleased!"

<u>Tunny</u>:

"Good work, Zyan! OK, let's wrap up with *brief* comments from our illustrious Focused Information Group. What's the latest gossip picked up by FIG?"

<u>Strike Lonjayho, Director, Focused Information Group (FIG)</u>:

"Thank you, Mr. Grand Poobah. I do not want to sound like a broken record, but we keep collecting more and more evidence that Aissur did, indeed, 'assist' with the 2016 National Cartoon Debate and plans to do so again if we have another cartoon debate in 2020. The Cruller Probe is starting to identify specific Aissurian citizens involved in these efforts. Unfortunately, most of them are in Aissur, so . . ."

<u>Tunny</u>:

"Stop! Stop! Stop! I just don't want to hear this. My good buddy Plaidimyhr Shuutin has assured me, repeatedly, that there was no Aissurian assistance in the National Cartoon Debate. In the Grand Poobah election, I won fair and square over that anti-deplorable, confoundable Jillary Glynnton. So let's not waste any more of our valuable time talking about something that just did not happen. Is everyone in the clown car with me?

"I am worn out. I need some executive time. This was fun. Let's try to have another Executive Team meeting in about six months. See ya later."

(end of first Executive Team meeting)

SCATHING COMMENTARY ON TUNNY'S MANAGEMENT STYLE

Tunny's unique management style generated a lot of comments from within and from outside of his administration. I would hear whispers of these comments in the hallways of the Beige Palace and in news reports, and I'd have to beat them back like yellow jackets.

Lex Gilbertsun, Tunny's secretary of Foreign Relations, was overheard saying that Tunny was "scattered," "doesn't prepare for any meeting," and is "always trying to push legal boundaries." He complained that Tunny continuously needed to be told that he couldn't do illegal things. When Tunny found out that Gilbertsun had called him an idiot, he lashed out that Gilbertsun was "dumber than a toxic waste dump," calling him "a sloth among sloths." I was amazed that Gilbertsun lasted as long as he did. Although he was subjected to a fairly constant barrage of belittling comments, Gilbertsun wasn't fired until eight months after his grumbling hit the media. Part of the holdup in getting rid of Gilbertsun was that Tunny was having an extremely difficult time finding competent people who wanted the job.

Hykul Grolff, a highly acclaimed author who was given free rein within the Beige Palace, as well as significant access to Tunny, came out with some pretty scathing comments in his book on the Drump Administration. He called Tunny "one of the least trustworthy people I have ever met." He claimed that all of the people closest to Tunny had grave concerns about his brainpower and suitability as Grand Poobah. The likelihood of

Tunny being removed from office was a daily topic of discussion. I never heard the talk firsthand, but I knew that invoking the 227th Amendment to The Agreement, which discusses the justifications and procedures for removing a Grand Poobah from office, was discussed frequently behind closed doors.

It is interesting that Hykul Grolff mentioned internal discussions about the 227th Amendment. In early 2018, a petition signed by over seventy-five thousand mental health professionals expressed their firm belief that Tunny had been showing signs of mental illness severe enough to make it impossible for him to competently carry on as Grand Poobah of Cameria.

Ames Homey, the NDS director that Tunny inherited from the Moblamah Administration and eventually fired, appeared to enjoy writing a book about Tunny. He pegged Tunny as a "disgraceful" man who was a complete stranger to honesty and integrity. He called Tunny "completely unsuitable to be Grand Poobah," and declared that the loyalty pledges Tunny tried to evoke from people were more suited to the world of mob kingpins than the Grand Poobah of Cameria. Whew. I had to drop that book like it was radioactive and make sure that Tunny never got his hands on it. I probably didn't need to worry too much since he didn't read any books at all, whether or not they were hateful toward him.

In an attempt to sway public opinion before the Homey book was released, Tunny called Homey "dumb as a rock" and a "bald-faced liar." Pretty boring insults, but they got the job done. Tunny wanted to put Homey in jail on charges of being the least competent NDS director ever. When he was told that Homey had documented every private meeting between them,

Tunny declared Homey's extensive notes to be "totally, totally, absolutely fabricated." He called Homey a "bag full of sleaze-bags" and speculated that the only reason Homey agreed to take a second look at the email servers used by Jillary Glynnton during the 2016 Grand Poobah election was to ingratiate himself with the Drump team.

In reality, Tunny should not have been so hard on Homey. Many political pundits think that Homey's mid-October reinvigoration of the Glynnton email investigation was *the* single biggest reason that Tunny's support accelerated during the critical last few weeks of the campaign.

Very early on in his reign as Grand Poobah, Tunny's team was reportedly extremely concerned about his erratic behavior, significant mood swings, and paranoia. They lamented the fact that he placed his popularity with the Camerian people way ahead of any substantive policies to help those same people. He could not shoulder any criticism and was quick to deflect all blame to other people. As for me, I didn't think of him as erratic, moody, or paranoid—I just saw him as changeable, bad-tempered, and distrustful of everyone whose last name wasn't Drump. But other people clearly saw him as, well, pathological.

Rob Goodword, a veteran investigative reporter who came to fame by breaking the LotterDate scandal back in the early 1970s, did extensive research on the Drump Beige Palace for a blockbuster book that appeared in August of 2018. Goodword portrayed Tunny as "unhinged," "impulsive," and "highly distractible." He described multiple instances when top aides secretly removed documents from Tunny's proximity to prevent

Tunny from doing severe damage to a critical trading relationship or from assassinating dictators around the world who didn't bow down to Cameria all willy nilly. Goodword also reported that Lon Shelly, Tunny's second chief wrangler, once declared in a small meeting that the Grand Poobah was "out of control" and on a path to self-destruction that would create a lot of collateral damage. Shelly lamented that he never should have done his perceived duty and come to work in the "loony bin" that was the Drump Beige Palace.

Around the same time that advance publicity for Goodword's book was all that reporters wanted to ask me about, an anonymous senior Drump Administration leader published an explosive essay in the *BrightLights Times*. The piece described a fairly pervasive conspiracy among the Beige Palace team to protect the country from Tunny's disastrous leadership and incredibly lousy decision making. This group of senior officials wanted to make sure that decisions were being made with the citizens' best interests in mind, even if that guiding principle was of little interest to Tunny. As might be expected, he lost it when he learned about the essay. He stirred the pot and started a game of finger-pointing at everyone, even me. Tunny demanded pledges of loyalty and denials of any complicity in the conspiracy. For weeks afterward, lunchtime at the Beige Palace mess was a tense affair, with each of us side-eyeing everyone else, wondering who was the turncoat. I just knew it wasn't me! Really! I would never do such a thing! Never!

Near the end of 2017, Neff Blake, an Upper Body member from the solidly Elephant Party state of Zaronia, announced that he would not be seeking another term. He let it be known that he could no longer hold back when a nominal member of his political party was acting so "irrationally," "dangerously," and "recklessly" (amazing how those adjectives always came in threes). Blake asserted that the whole world order was threatened by Tunny's lack of intelligence, imagination, and compassion. And he wasn't the only one:

An elderly statesman and former Grand Poobah from Tunny's party got into the act by calling Tunny a "bozo" who was only concerned with enhancing his ratings.

The *National Journal* editorialized that Tunny was not qualified to mop the floors in the Moblamah Grand Poobah Library.

And finally, Shock Moblamah himself broke the long-held ex-Grand Poobah tradition of trying not to criticize his successor. He was quoted as saying that Tunny was a "disgrace to the institution of the Grand Poobah," "incapable of governing in a rational manner," and "wholly unsuited to be Grand Poobah."

BEYOND HIS INTELLECTUAL CAPACITY?

Tunny thinks he's a genius. However, most people who have spent much time around him would beg to differ, and I confess that I became one of them. Tunny has never been the most articulate person. He talks in short sentences and repeats himself quite often . . . and repeats himself quite often. Tunny isn't a good extemporaneous public speaker. Off-the-cuff remarks always turn out badly. He does OK with a teleprompter, but that is not his favorite way to communicate, and he tends to appear stiff and uncomfortable. Again and again, I'd say to him,

"Mr. Grand Poobah, Sir, you are a wonderful speaker, and the teleprompter is a wonderful invention that will make you even more of a wonderful speaker! If you follow along, and you put your heart into it, you will be even more deeply beloved!" But Tunny just grumbled.

In December of 2017, I cringed when Tunny defended his mental agility, describing himself as a "very level-headed intellectual" in reaction to suggestions in Hykul Grolff's book that he was ill-equipped to lead. He called it all a witch hunt. Enemies, including the biased media, were ridiculing his intellectual abilities, he declared, because they had been unsuccessful in showing any coziness with Aissur during the 2016 National Cartoon Debate. Tunny then twerped:

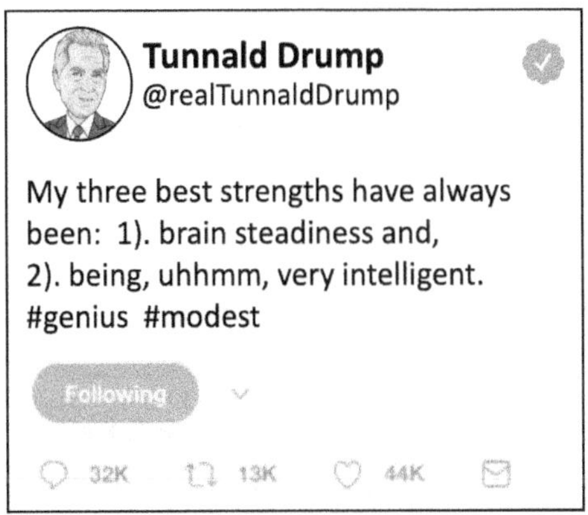

Just to show that his election victory did not further inflate Tunny's high opinion of himself, here's a pretty outlandish twerp he posted way back in 2013:

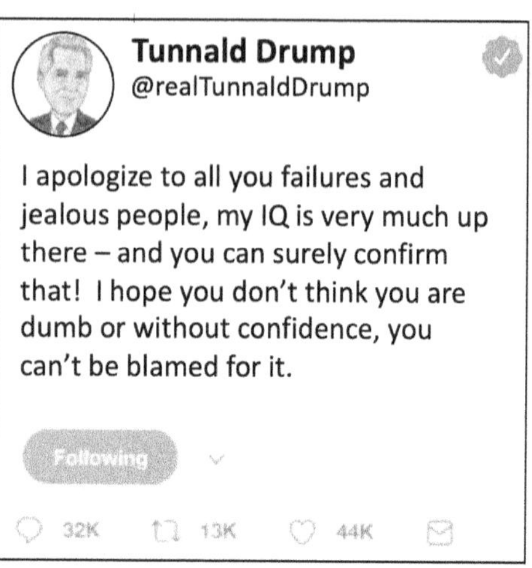

I can't remember any other administration where so many close confidants slammed the Grand Poobah. Maybe it is because no other Grand Poobah treated those closest to him with such disrespect.

In October of 2017, Tunny's second national protection guru, J. T. Blickcaster, ridiculed his boss at an intimate dinner. He called him a "mope" and a bozo, adding that Tunny "has the brains of a five-year-old."

Less than a year into his time as Tunny's Beige Palace chief wrangler, former Sky Force General Lon Shelly was rumored to have called Tunny a moron. Most people could not believe that Shelly would have been so indiscreet. However, four other senior staffers eventually confirmed the outburst. Most people thought that Shelly would be out over that remark. However, Tunny did not fire him until the very end of 2018. The best explanation appears to be that saner minds prevailed as several of Tunny's closest confidants pointed out that Shelly provided an excellent service by running a tight Beige Palace and was doing a masterful job of keeping most of Tunny's stupidest ideas away from the light of day.

In June of 2018, Stoney Quartz, Tunny's co-author of *The Art of the Steal,* twerped that Tunny couldn't read a book and certainly didn't help with the authorship of "their" book. He said that he would not have felt compelled to set the record straight if Tunny had not boasted about his writing abilities—which had allegedly resulted in numerous bestsellers. This revelation produced enough of an uproar that I was forced to respond:

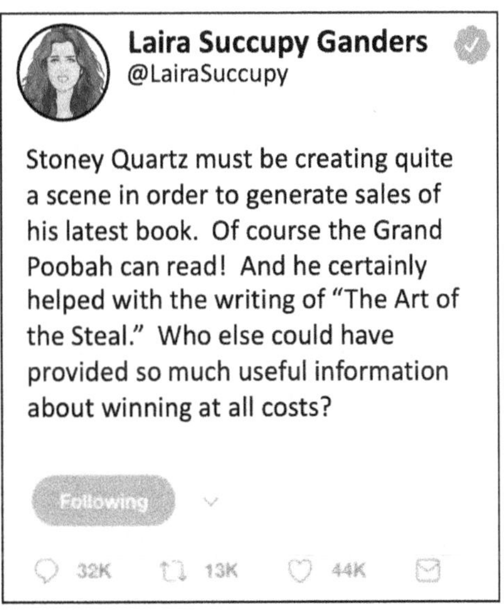

Everyone sees Tunny as a very prolific twerper. What most people don't know, and what I saw firsthand, is that he deploys a team of writers to augment his twerping. These minions go to great lengths to carefully copy Tunny's poor spelling and terrible writing style. Way too many exclamation points, RANDOM

CAPITALS, and incomplete sentences are thrown in to make the twerps seem like Tunny's. I made sure to keep my fingers off of Tunny's phone. I guess I'm just not a fan of CAPITAL LETTERS and exclamation points!!!!

Tunny frequently caught a lot of flak for retwerping controversial twerps. Many times, it was a convenient way to get behind positions that he could not back publicly. Occasionally, when he would catch even more criticism than usual for a retwerp, he would deflect direct culpability by claiming that he often retwerped twerps from people he liked without ever reading the original twerp. From my perspective, Tunny was a pretty savvy twerper. I doubt that he ever retwerped without understanding and approving of the original twerp. But I was the one who got all the heat from the press for the wild stuff he retwerped. Some days I felt like I should be wearing a Kevlar sweater.

This same team was responsible for enhancing Tunny's photos on his *LifeStories* and *PhotosGalore* accounts. Photos were modified to make Tunny appear much fitter and healthier than he was. His shoulders were made to look broader, his hair more in control and a little less orange, and his fingers a little longer. Some days, I'd squint hard at the Grand Poobah and could see through my mascara the man that Tunny wanted the world to he think he was.

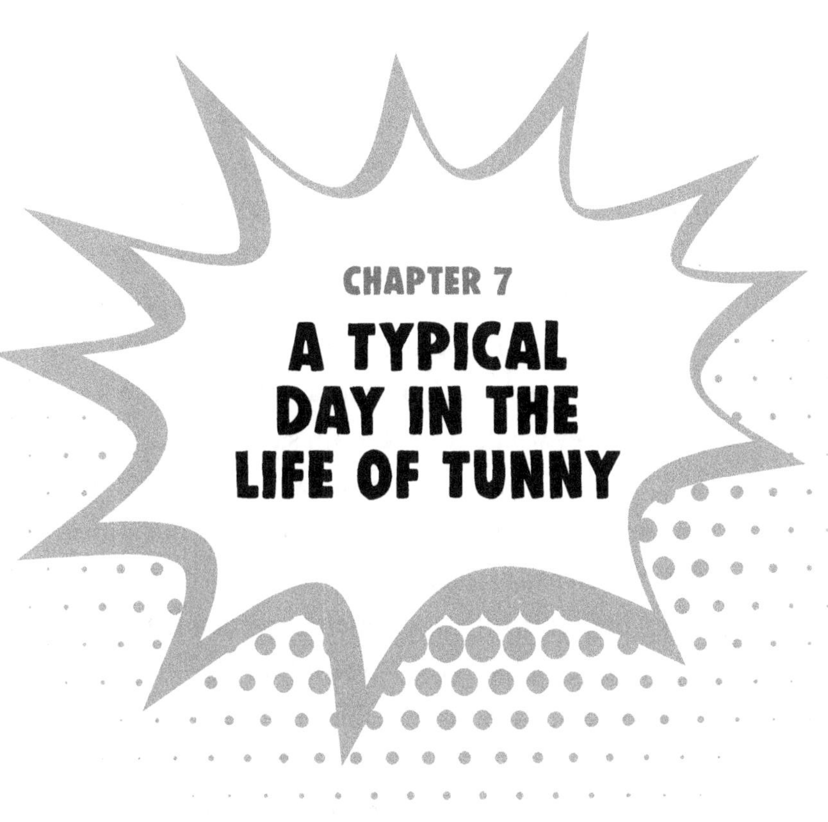

Having been close to Tunny for many years, I assumed that I knew pretty much all there was to know about how he spends most of his time. I knew that he lived to play croquet. I knew that he always relished a chance to descend upon Drump properties around the country. But how would being Grand Poobah affect the Tunny-centered way he spent his time?

NOT YOUR TYPICAL GRAND POOBAH'S SCHEDULE

As with so many other things, Tunny's typical day was not what people would expect of the most powerful person in the world. Since he was very fond of twerping late at night, Tunny tended to sleep in almost every day. While having a late, leisurely breakfast, he would watch the morning news programs. He'd switch to cartoons if nothing in the news interested him. He often referred to cartoon characters as if they were real and wondered what they would do in certain situations.

During the day, Tunny typically watched six to eight hours of television. He liked to call this his "executive time." Fortunately, he still had at least one to two hours a day available for important briefings, official meet-and-greets, and the occasional appearance in public. I'd often sidle into his private office and there he'd be, eyes riveted to the screen watching *Locks News* coverage of himself while somebody like the ambassador to Aissur cooled his heels in a Beige Palace anteroom.

When some of Tunny's schedules were leaked to the press, many people were concerned about the amount of television he watched. Tunny defended himself by pointing out that his "executive time" didn't involve just television time. He also used it for twerping, phoning old friends, and calling in to conservative cable TV talk shows.

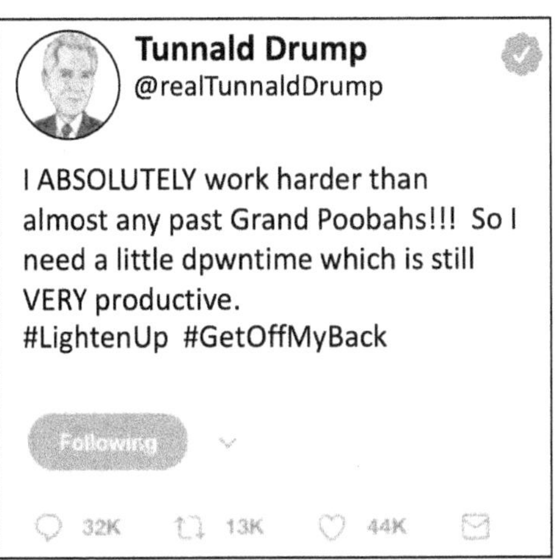

Many of his best ideas came from watching and interacting with the hosts of some of his favorite conservative shows. He highly valued the opinions of these brilliant TV personalities.

Jon Mannitee delivered *Locks News*'s top ratings, making him the channel's highest-paid personality. It was like Tunny and Jon Mannitee had a bromance. They would talk on the phone at least twice a day, including regular conversations most evenings after Mannitee's show on *Locks News* wrapped. I felt that this was a reasonably harmless way for Tunny to relax and de-stress at the end of a long, hard day filled with lots of executive time. Most others felt that such a mutual admiration club kept Tunny way out of touch with what regular people across the country thought of his plans and actions.

In October of 2018, Mannitee crossed the line from just reporting on and often greatly amplifying what Tunny had to say to taking a more active—and personal—role. He joined Tunny onstage at a campaign rally for the mid-term elections. Here's what he twerped after the rally:

With just one appearance on stage, Mannitee went from being the host of a popular cable news show to being a big, unofficial part of the campaign. Jon was popular and he helped our cause. Most people in the press and the media at large, including many at Locks, thought this was way over the top. I confess

    MAKE OUR COUNTRY YUUUGE AGAIN

that I squirmed. However, Tunny loved the way Mannitee performed in front of large crowds. I believe that Tunny pushed hard for Mannitee to be involved in more and more campaign events so that he could spend significantly more time with his close friend and ally. It also didn't hurt that in the first year after the start of the Cruller Probe, Mannitee lashed out over seven hundred times about the "baseless" and "ill-conceived" investigation into Aissurian coziness and assistance with the 2016 National Cartoon Debate.

Tunny also courted other leading conservative talk show and news hosts. He regularly called in to their shows for advice on how to run the country. During important meetings with his top aides, Tunny would often put Boo Slobbs of *BMM News* on speakerphone so that he could give his thoughts on the critical issues of the day. Tunny also got great satisfaction from occasionally calling into Slobbs's show and bloviating about whatever came to mind. Many on his team thought it was inappropriate for the Grand Poobah to be spending so much time with talk show hosts. Tunny, however, lamented to me that he could not hang out with them even more frequently.

Tunny didn't like to read the traditional Grand Poobah's *Daily News*, which summarizes the most critical information collected overnight by Camerian intelligence operatives worldwide. He preferred to have an oral recitation covering a significantly reduced number of items. He refused to believe any coverage about inappropriate coziness with Aissur, or anything negative about his excellent friend Plaidimyhr Shuutin.

But Tunny did like to spend hours looking at a daily folder we made for him that was filled with only kind, upbeat stories about himself and his family. This included printed twerps, news stories, and transcripts from TV reports. Some of the more cynical Beige Palace staffers referred to this practice as the "Ego Stroke." Would I have called it that? Never.

Tunny had a fixation on all of the slights—real or perceived—that had been perpetrated against him and insisted on receiving a daily "People Who Did Me Wrong" list. This gave him the ammunition for his explosive, unfiltered, uncensored, late-night twerping of accusations that I have to admit were often (almost always?) pretty false. He would usually drink a lot of FatDumbHappy root beer, and the sugar high would propel him late into the night.

I usually had to spend a good part of the next day cleaning up Tunny's messes. It was satisfying, at first, to be able to calm everything down so well. But after a while, it just got old, and I started to resent Tunny's lack of discipline and unwillingness to remain tethered to reality.

All that television did not leave a lot of time for the business of running the country. Fortunately, Tunny skipped many traditional things like foreign affairs dinners for visiting dignitaries from around the world. He also did not want long WonderSlide presentations during meetings, so they typically went very quickly.

That gave the Grand Poobah more time to sneak into the Beige Palace's sub-basement area and play a round or two of croquet. Many Grand Poobahs had been excited to have a bowling alley in the Beige Palace. Tunny thought bowling was for sissies, so he had the lanes ripped out in favor of a massive croquet course. Tunny loved to challenge people on his team. I

    MAKE OUR COUNTRY YUUUGE AGAIN

don't recall anyone admitting that they beat Tunny at his favorite "sport." Just in case he didn't feel like walking *all* the way to the sub-basement, Tunny also had a $100,000 croquet simulator installed in an "extra" room in the First Poobah Family's living quarters.

I came to learn that Tunny was not very self-confident for such a supposedly accomplished businessman and wealthy celebrity. He was quite paranoid that the world was out to get him. He liked to call any attack on him a "skeet shoot," and he viewed the huge Aissur coziness matter to be the ultimate example. He felt like he was always being targeted unfairly.

I was surprised to learn how much "executive time" Tunny took during a typical day. I guess his office at FatDumbHappy wasn't quite as conducive to watching television and twerping with wild abandon as his Beige Palace office was. Tunny's passion for croquet, especially when staying at Charco Grande, was an eye-opener for me. I was, however, quite familiar with his extremely short attention span. I always had to factor it in when figuring out the best way to pitch a new idea to Tunny or provide feedback on one wacky idea or another.

Tunny was easily distracted. I saw again and again how bright shiny objects always got his attention. These days, a younger Tunny Drump would most likely be diagnosed with Ants in Your Pants (AYP).

On the flip side, Tunny could get hung up on the smallest of details. He once spent days deliberating about the color of the balls for the croquet course in the basement of the Beige Palace. He also wanted to put the Drump insignia on all of the balls, as well as on many other historic items around the Beige Palace. More rational minds talked him out of that one.

Occasionally, Tunny amazed everyone by creating new words. It took weeks for people to figure out what he meant one time when a late-night twerp included the word "kofveve:"

"Kofveve" became YUUUGE.

UNPRECEDENTED TRAVEL TO HIS OWN PROPERTIES

Most Grand Poobahs liked to get out of the Beige Palace for a variety of reasons: meeting with important international partners, campaigning for same-party candidates, visiting disaster areas, etc. They typically also enjoyed going to Resort Harry in Darnmaly for some relaxation and off-the-grid time—to the extent that a Grand Poobah *can* temporarily escape the pressures of running Cameria.

Tunny generally did less of that type of travel, but he made up for it by spending a YUUUGE amount of time at various properties owned by the Drump family through FatDumbHappy Corporation. During his first one hundred days in office, Tunny spent forty-five days at Drump Hamburger Hotels around the country. He particularly liked his Charco Grande resort in West Calonia. The Camerian people spent a lot of extra money protecting Drump and his family at these nongovernmental locales. Four trips to Charco Grande in his first two months in office cost the government over $15 million, plus another $700,000 paid directly to Tunny's resort. When Tunny started getting a lot of heat about this travel, I twerped:

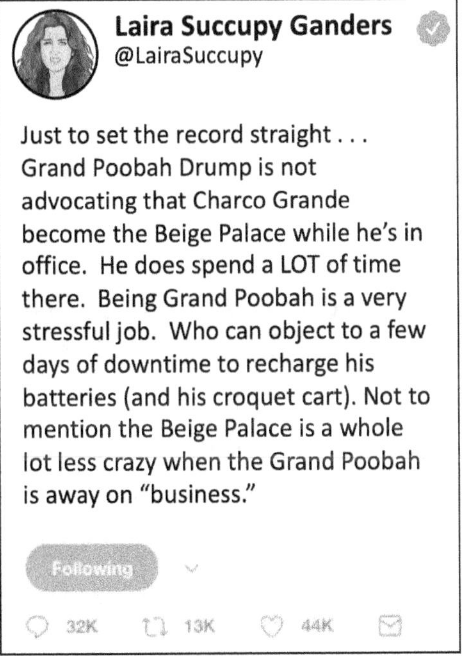

Through some excellent investigative reporting by the *Hoama Post*, it was determined that Tunny's primary activity while out of the office was playing croquet. Mostly, he would play with former business partners. Occasionally, he would convince a grand poobah or prime minister from another country to play a round or two. Tunny did go out of his way to hide his obsession with croquet. The staff was sworn to secrecy. Calendars were scrubbed clean. And he tried to play on croquet courses shielded from the pesky press.

Tunny's aides didn't want to disclose to the public how much croquet he was playing. Tunny visited his two super-sized croquet courses near Charco Grande five times during his first month as Grand Poobah. The aides would not confirm that he was playing croquet, but local celebrities and croquet pros were happy to give interviews confirming their exciting croquet rounds with Tunny.

One enterprising reporter back in CapitalTown did some sleuthing, including a look at Tunny's official calendar as well as off-calendar croquet time. To the best of his investigative skills, the reporter concluded that during his first thirty days in office, Tunny occupied himself with seventy hours of croquet, fifteen hours of twerping, and five hours of high-level briefings. Even I was shocked.

By Thanksgiving of his first year in office, Tunny had spent one hundred days at Drump private properties and played croquet roughly 120 times (once every three days). One fun fact: Covert Assets spent over $100,000 on cart rentals as they attempted to protect Tunny during his frequent rounds of croquet. Tunny didn't receive this money directly, of course. It wound its way through FatDumbHappy Corporation before making it into his pocket.

Tunny was well known for his cheating on the croquet course: a little nudge of the ball here, a few strokes not counted there. I think it was all a game with Tunny to see how much cheating he could get away with. There's an old saying: "If you cheat at croquet, you cheat at business." Maybe Tunny had to cheat at croquet to keep up with his level of cheating in business.

A REAL CRISIS

All progress in the Beige Palace stopped for about a week when Tunny heard a rumor that Benneral Hills planned to stop production of its iconic Ducky Marms cereal. You would have thought that the earth had stopped turning on its axis. Or that the Grand Poobah of the most powerful country in the world had nothing more important to worry about. Apparently, this was a YUUUGE deal to Tunny.

As he explained it to me, Tunny started enjoying Ducky Marms cereal way back in 1963, shortly after it came to market. Even though he was seventeen years old, he had cereal for breakfast every day, and Ducky Marms quickly became his new favorite. Fast-forward another fifty-five years, and Tunny still enjoys cereal for breakfast most mornings. Ducky Marms is *still* his favorite. Here is his distraught twerp to Benneral Hills:

The Twerperverse reacted quickly and decisively. While there were, indeed, a few grumps who pointed out how old Tunny was and wondered why he was so obsessed with a cereal for kids, the vast majority of all twerps and retwerps agreed with Tunny—this was a MAJOR tragedy and people wanted to know what could be done to remedy such a terrible situation.

The chief wrangler had to assign a temporary worker to manage all of the twerps and emails coming into the Beige Palace in support of continuing the production of Ducky Marms. Tunny waited until he had received over 500,000 such comments before he reached out to the CEO of Benneral Hills. Just like with his "secret" meetings with Plaidimyhr Shuutin, Tunny shooed everyone out of the room once he had the CEO on the line. Twenty minutes later, Tunny emerged with a big smile on his face. His first comment was, "I might not be able to get Adanac to pay for The Moat, but I sure can save a national treasure—Ducky Marms cereal." It turns out that the CEO of Benneral Hills had been quite impressed with all of the uproar. His stock price was up 15 percent, and he was easily persuaded to keep Ducky Marms as a premier, fully supported brand. I have a feeling that Tunny might have thrown in a few croquet weekends at Charco Grande to sweeten the decision.

Once this major crisis was averted, and we were able to get back to working on other important Beige Palace initiatives, such as the following:

+ replanting the Beige Palace gardens with only red flowers
(why should the Donkey Party be honored with any blue flowers?)

+ replacing all photos in the Beige Palace with photos of Tunny
(those other guys are long gone; who cares about them anymore?)

+ installing much bigger and better televisions to enhance Tunny's "executive time"
(this is, of course, where he spends the majority of his time!)

+ ensuring that only soft drinks from FDH were available at the Beige Palace
(who cares about water, coffee, tea, or any other wimpy refreshment?)

+ securing new, oversized, red wickets for the croquet course (his mood is always so much better after he scores a few wickets; might as well make it easier!)

GRADUATION PEARLS OF WISDOM FROM TUNNY

As you might imagine, the Grand Poobah of Cameria was presented with many speaking opportunities. Given Tunny's aversion to staying on script and his general disdain for most pedestrian undertakings, we were very selective regarding the speaking opportunities we presented to Tunny. One situation that we vetted carefully, and that Tunny was pretty excited about, was a chance to give the June 2019 graduation speech at his alma mater, the well-known Horton School of Business in Pennland.

I spent quite a bit of time working with Tunny on his speech. However, crazy as it might sound, it ended up being ten times less wild than his first iteration.

Here's what I remember from our first meeting to work on his speech:

Tunny:

"Why are you taking me away from my 'executive time' to work on this? Why can't I just wing it? You know how great I am at just talking off the top of my head."

Laira:

"You are quite a fine speaker, Mr. Grand Poobah. But we should think about how you want to best influence these future leaders of Cameria. Most graduation speeches focus on positive, upbeat messages that the graduates can take to heart as they move on to the next stage of their lives."

<u>Tunny:</u>

"I know just what to say about getting the most out of college. Find the right group of like-minded people. Party hearty! Get a little tickling action going. Go to class as little as possible. Barely stay in school, knowing that your dad can help you with a job regardless of grades. Is that the kind of upbeat advice you think these kids want to hear?"

<u>Laira:</u>

"Uhhh . . . not exactly, Mr. Grand Poobah. First of all, these students are graduating from a prestigious college, not high school. Also, please try to remember that not everyone is likely to get the 'small' amount of assistance that your father provided to get you up and running in the business world. Most of these students will have to work hard for everything they achieve. Boosting their spirits with some inspirational stories or advice would be perfect."

<u>Tunny:</u>

"My bad! I had so much fun while I attended Horton. I got carried away thinking about it. So, you want inspiration? How about I remind them of how great Cameria is, and that they will have the opportunity to work hard to Make My Country YUUUGE Again."

<u>Laira:</u>

"I think we're getting a little closer to the spirit of a graduation speech. How about calling Cameria 'our' country instead of 'my' country?"

<u>Tunny:</u>

"Why would I want to do that? I am the Grand Poobah of this country. I am the one working harder than anyone to return Cameria to YUUUGEness. These kids haven't done sh*t yet. I think I deserve to call it 'my' country."

<u>Laira:</u>

"OK, Tunny. Let's do it your way. Just make sure you stick to the speech and don't digress into any FDH or *The Gofer* stories."

(end of meeting)

Here's a transcript of Tunny's speech. Despite my attempt to moderate his tone, this was one for the collection of odd graduation speeches!

<u>William Renslaw, Dean of the Horton School of Business:</u>

"It is now my great pleasure to introduce today's graduation speaker, Grand Poobah Tunnald Drump. Although he doesn't need much of an introduction, I do want to make sure that everyone in the audience knows that Grand Poobah Drump was a 1969 graduate of this fine institution. He went on to have an extremely successful career at FatDumbHappy Corporation, as well as with his hit "real life" TV show, *The Gofer*. Citizen Drump ran for Grand Poobah in 2016, and now we have the honor of calling him Mr. Grand Poobah. He has had an exciting first few years in office. I hope he can share some of his insights and wisdom with us today. Without further ado, I am very proud to present Grand Poobah Tunnald Drump!"

<u>Grand Poobah Drump</u>:

"Hello, fellow Hortonites! I am delighted that you are here today. Thank you, Dean Renslaw, for your kind introduction. I may not have earned very good grades when I was here, but I still look back on my two years with very fond memories. I had that darn ingrown toenail, so I was not able to join the good fight in Manteiv, but I soaked up all of the business acumen I could here and eventually applied it toward my meteoric rise at FatDumbHappy. It always helps when your father started the company!

"I highly recommend a career in business. I am not sure about this government stuff! Business is a lot more straightforward. You just have to keep customers and shareholders happy. Challenging, but doable if you are as bright as me! Even running the best government in the world, I feel like I am being pulled in ten directions at one time. Every department, every special interest group—they all want attention and money. Sometimes it's just too much for me, and I need to relax with a rigorous game of croquet. This also illustrates why it is so important to build a good support team around yourself. I would have to actually make an effort if I wasn't able to delegate so much hard work and decision making to the members of my Executive Team. And I still take all the credit—what a great deal!

"If you do go into either business or politics, I would counsel you to be very wary of people bringing you gifts or exceptional opportunities. I should have known better during the 2016 campaign. Representatives of a foreign country (I won't say which one) approached us and offered to help with our campaign. Lesser Poobah Dents and I were pretty far behind in the polls at the time, so I said, 'What the heck. What do I have to lose?' It turns out that I have paid a pretty high price for a little 'oppo' research on my opponent and a little 'assistance' with the National Cartoon Debate. It has been a constant Inquisition. That bozo Cruller sure is a persistent thorn in my a*s. He's been beating the bushes like crazy and coming up with dirt on everyone around me. And I mean everyone. Thank goodness that I'm clean as a whistle. I think you can ignore that old saying about the company you keep. Also, that old adage about where there's smoke, there's likely to be fire. Forget about that one, too.

"My advice to you? Just find something you are passionate about. That's what is so great about Cameria. Carefully utilize all of the hundreds of millions of dollars your father can give you, and you too can become a self-made billionaire. And the best news is that I have radically changed the income tax laws, so you won't have to pay much money at all. Isn't this a great country? Follow your passions as far as you can go. Work hard, have rich parents, and you can make a big name for yourselves. Congratulations, Horton Class of 2019. Go out and Make My Country YUUUGE Again!"

(end of Graduation Speech)

While I had fairly limited interaction with Tunny and the press at FDH, I did have a close-up view during the Grand Poobah campaign. I knew that he took an adversarial approach to dealing with the media. I knew he didn't like unscripted speaking opportunities because he easily got off track and often misspoke (as we call it in the public relations business). Given all of that, I was still hopeful as a new press secretary that I could help Tunny triumph with the press and keep both reporters and the Grand Poobah happy.

Tunny has had an interesting relationship with the press and most media outlets ever since the 2016 Grand Poobah campaign. He usually took the offensive to promote his ideas and trash people he didn't like or who weren't cooperating as he expected. Tunny hated when the press spotlight was on him. And as a matter of course, every occupant of the Beige Palace is carefully watched and scrutinized 24/7.

For some reason, Tunny felt persecuted by the press and developed a very antagonistic relationship with media representatives. During press briefings, I was always embarrassed when Tunny picked on a reporter and lambasted them for being stupid or bad at their job. It didn't seem productive, and it just wasn't nice.

Tunny used his very first official day as Grand Poobah to lash out at the news media, accusing reporters of creating stories about a widening chasm between him and the Actionable Organizations. For the first but certainly not the last time, he also accused the press of grossly and deliberately underestimating the size of the crowd at his Inauguration.

Particularly in the context of the Cruller Probe into potential coziness with Aissur during the 2016 campaign, Tunny felt like he was the subject of an "Inquisition." He regularly called out the press and media for "trumped-up BS," as he labeled any critical or less-than-flattering news or media coverage.

He also accused the company behind the Krugle Internet search engine of manipulating search results to only show articles and news coverage that painted him in a bad light. One time, I tried to explain to him how unlikely this was. I was not sure that he understood the concept of a search engine. If there were more negative articles written about Tunny, more negative articles would show up in Krugle searches, especially if they were the most read articles. It is pretty simple. However, Tunny didn't really get it; he just wanted someone to look into whether Krugle should be regulated.

Early on in the administration, when my predecessor, Conn Preiser, was handling press relations, Tunny deliberately provoked the media by prohibiting representatives from several prominent, slightly left-leaning newspapers, television channels, and online blogs from attending a briefing at the Beige Palace. Preiser only allowed access to high-profile journalists from a small number of prominent conservative media outlets. The managing chief of the *BrightLights Times* strongly protested the prohibition of the *Times* and other news teams. "The Beige Palace has never been so blatant in its censorship in all the years the *Times* has covered many administrations from both parties," he said. "Blocking free media access is a very slippery slope that the Drump Administration should not be starting down."

In March of 2017, Tunny became the first Grand Poobah in thirty-six years to skip the Beige Palace Reporters' Dinner. Donald Creagan was the last Grand Poobah to skip the dinner, in 1981. He had a pretty valid reason—he was in the hospital recovering from an assassination attempt. Tunny sent me in his place, and I was mercilessly skewered. I tried to grin and bear it, but I was genuinely offended and hurt by the attendees' eagerness to attack Tunny (and me by association). I thought I had worked hard and been successful in building a good relationship with the press. But it pained me to learn that I may have overestimated the strength of this bond. My only solace was the thought that most of the attacks were intended for Tunny. I was the unlucky recipient because Tunny couldn't make himself available to look a little vulnerable while letting the press blow off a whole lot of steam.

At the end of 2017, I felt personally offended when Tunny left the Beige Palace and headed for Charco Grande without holding a traditional year-end press briefing. It was the first time in twenty years that a Grand Poobah has declined to have a final word with the press. He also didn't say goodbye to workers at the Beige Palace (which was just plain rude). This marked the first time in eighteen years that a Grand Poobah had passed on this low- effort, high-impact, goodwill gesture.

A year later, Tunny canceled the Beige Palace holiday party for members of the media, without bothering to announce that the event was canceled. He ended this decades-long tradition amid a continued escalation of his severely strained relationship with the press.

One year into his administration, Tunny received, in his opinion, an icy reception at the famous Global Business Conference in Travos, Hitzerlend. Tunny was booed for striking out at the media as "rude" and primarily spewing out "trumped-up BS." Here was his quick reaction:

In October of 2018, Tunny made my life as press secretary extremely difficult by revoking the press credentials of one reporter who had been very insistent on finishing his line of questioning with Tunny without interruption. I guess that aggressive move emboldened Tunny because, in the next press briefing, he started personally attacking several reporters for asking "dumb" questions, being very incompetent, and not having a clue what they were doing. I wanted to hide behind a curtain, but I was a good solider and just stuck out my jaw like a drill sergeant for the Drump Administration.

Even though Tunny threatened to revoke many more press credentials, we were finally able to regain a degree of sanity by reinstating the reporter's access. Tunny thought that everything had gone very well. I knew that he was just digging himself into a deeper and deeper hole with the press.

The exception to Tunny's disdain for the press and media was his extremely cozy relationship with Locks. Tunny's strong bond with Locks went way back. Locks Founder Loopert Thirdock hired Dodger Pails to create an extremely conservative news channel. Pails asked Tunny to make a weekly appearance on *Locks & Friends* starting in 2011. That was a significant platform for Tunny's "Space Alien" campaign against Moblamah, claiming that the then-Grand Poobah was actually from another planet and not eligible to be a Poobah at all.

Thirdock and Tunny didn't always have a great relationship. At first, Thirdock was pretty skeptical and, at times, outright critical of Tunny. However, by the time Tunny became Grand Poobah, the relationship had gotten much better. It was also interesting that Tunny's trusted son-in-law, Larred Kushner, developed a close relationship with Thirdock and communicated with him almost daily.

Jon Mannitee had such a close and influential relationship with Tunny that we started referring to him as the hidden head wrangler. Given that there did not appear to be any normal policy process at the Beige Palace, it looked like the *Locks News* team was taking up the slack. Many observers noted that Tunny was more likely to believe and be affected by Locks personalities and their guests than he was by his Executive Team and the top experts from all around the Camerian government supporting them.

Even before I took over as press secretary, Tunny had become locked into a strange reinforcement cycle with *Locks*

News. Tunny picked up ideas from *Locks News* and twerped about them. *Locks News* would then cover Tunny's twerps and amplify them. Tunny then touted how great his ideas must be because *Locks News* was giving them such great coverage. Between August of 2018 and February of 2019, Tunny included over seventy-five *Locks News* items in twerps to his sixty million followers. It was like Tunny was a super-booster for the channel. And *Locks News* reciprocated for Tunny in a YUUUGE way.

Thirdock and Locks had been very good to Tunny during the campaign and his early days in the Beige Palace. The relationship was so close and so exclusive that it pissed off a lot of other media outlets, which made a lot of media folks mad at me. I guess this was just another example of how Tunny strayed from tradition and did things his way. He had always liked people who sucked up to him. In this case, he had a whole media organization adulating him. In exchange, he received a virtual voice box that dramatically expanded his message through what amounted to his private media outlet.

Even I got swept up in the mutual lovefest. Over time, I started giving fewer and fewer press briefings. While that traditional press platform was being minimized, I appeared on *Locks & Buddies* and *Politics: My Way or the Highway* more than 40 times. It was different than what I was used to doing to get the key messages out. But I think it was very effective and it was pretty fun! I could see why Tunny liked it so much.

Here's a transcript of one of my appearances in 2017:

<u>Jon Mannitee:</u>

"Hi, Laira! Welcome to *Politics: My Way or the Highway.* We are so honored to have you on our show once again. By the way, have you held any press briefings lately?"

<u>Laira:</u>

"Hi, Jon! Funny that you should mention press briefings. I think the Beige Palace has practically given up on press briefings since Grand Poobah Drump started making important announcements by calling in to your show. He seemed to be having so much fun that I decided to come on your show as well. As you know, I have now been on many times, and I find it a great way to get my messages directly to the Camerian people who care the most about the Drump Administration. It's a great way to put some of the things the Grand Poobah says into the right perspective."

<u>Jon Mannitee:</u>

"Well, we are always so glad to have you on the show. What's on your mind today? Which of the Grand Poobah's latest pronouncements would you like to spin?"

<u>Laira:</u>

"When the Grand Poobah called into your show yesterday, he was very upset about what he perceives as a deliberate conspiracy carried out by the National Legislature to slow-walk all the excellent nominations he has brought forward to fill some critical vacancies. As you know, no other administration has ever had so much difficulty completing their Executive Team and then filling all of the essential second- and third-level positions in each department.

"Every time a nominee is rejected, withdraws in frustration, or is forced to withdraw because of new, scandalous information revealed by the mainstream media—or should I say, the purveyors of 'pretend stories'—the Grand Poobah is forced to go back to the drawing board. If it was hard to find one great nominee, then it gets even harder to find another and another."

<u>Jon Mannitee:</u>

"That must be very frustrating for the Grand Poobah! Can we figure out some way around the National Legislature's obvious lack of cooperation? Maybe the brainiacs here on my show could come up with some new approaches and pass them along to the Grand Poobah so he can express great enthusiasm for 'his' new ideas."

<u>Laira:</u>

"Well, Jon, that has worked quite well in the past. However, it seems like we are at a very serious impasse now. The Grand Poobah thinks it might be time for dramatic action to break this logjam. While he's not quite there yet, he is considering advice from his legal eagles that he should give the National Legislature a few months off. That way, he could get a lot of the most problematic nominees approved and on board without having to go through a confirmation process that has gotten way out of control."

<u>Jon Mannitee:</u>

"I think that is a super idea. Are you sure *I* didn't suggest that to the Grand Poobah? That would be a great way to stick it to those pesky obstructionists in the National Legislature who are making it so hard for the Grand Poobah to get his full complement of yes people on board and ready to implement any and all of the Grand Poobah's great ideas for 'Making My Country YUUUGE Again.'"

<u>Laira:</u>

"Glad to hear that you are so supportive, Jon! I did want to take this opportunity to make one other announcement. Going forward, Grand Poobah Drump is asking all the good people who put together and present his daily briefing to ease up a little and make it a twice-a-week briefing. The Grand Poobah knows that there is an incredible amount of important stuff happening out in the world. The problem is that he is so busy doing important work that he just doesn't have time for a major briefing every single day. He feels like it is OK to wait an extra day or two, or three even, to hear about most crises, natural disasters, foreign relations snafus, and so on. If something is really important, maybe he'll hear about it first on your wonderful program!"

<u>Jon Mannitee:</u>

"That's all the time we have today. Thanks, Laira, for being the enlightening guest that you have always been. I look forward to seeing you soon down the highway!"

(end of transcript)

Here's something I twerped after a particularly wild afternoon on Mannitee's show:

By 2018, Tunny had had a chance to reciprocate favors with *Locks News* in a BIG way. The Drump Administration gave the go-ahead for Locks to sell most of its television and show-business assets to The Mouse Kingdom for $75 billion. The Thirdock family was able to clear $3 billion in cash and still remain significant shareholders. Not a bad wealth transition plan for an almost ninety-year-old family patriarch. The approval came very quickly and without much antitrust scrutiny, even though the deal meant that The Mouse Kingdom would now control about 60 percent of the movie revenue in Cameria. Both before and after this approval, the Drump Administration blocked other similarly aggressive consolidation efforts in the entertainment industry.

I am not sure how successful I was in building better relations with the press. I know that most reporters certainly thought that I presented or at least acknowledged the truth more than Tunny did. But that's a low bar, so I won't pat myself on the back too much. And I felt sorry for those poor little journalists who didn't know when to stop asking questions and just write down what I had to say.

CHAPTER 9

BUILDING "THE MOAT" AND KEEPING "THEM" OUT OF OUR COUNTRY

I knew going into my press secretary position that I did not agree with many of Tunny's more extreme views on immigration. I was hoping that I could be a moderating influence and help broker bipartisan reform by establishing a real and meaningful dialogue with the leaders of the Donkey Party. These weren't new issues, but I was cautiously optimistic that we could make some significant progress.

IMMIGRATION TALKS BRING OUT THE WORST IN TUNNY

Immigration was one of Tunny's top issues even before the campaign. He was the driving force behind the "Space Alien" movement, which aggressively alleged that Grand Poobah Moblamah was from another planet and possibly another solar system. I don't think Tunny understood the various definitions of "alien."

Many times, Tunny has stated that he wished all immigrants could be from countries like Kiwiland and Great Barrierland. He wanted to close Camerian borders to most other immigrants. His xenophobia seemed to focus primarily on three types of immigrants: those from predominantly Sumlim countries, immigrants already in Cameria without authorization and documentation, and northern latitude immigrants (primarily Adanacians) seeking a better life in Cameria.

SUMLIM RESTRICTION

Right after Inauguration Day, Tunny announced what became known as the Sumlim Restriction. He wanted to prohibit travel and immigration from countries with the largest Sumlim populations. However, business opportunities trumped his moral outrage at Sumlim immigration. Conspicuously absent from the list of banned countries were several predominantly Sumlim countries where FatDumbHappy either had significant past investments or was currently pursuing big projects. These "protected" investments included massive croquet courses in

Urabia and a luxury Drump Hamburger Hotel in Hurkey. You can imagine how much fun my reporters had with *that*!

AGGRESSIVELY ROUNDING UP AND DEPORTING UNDOCUMENTED IMMIGRANTS

Within less than a month of taking office, National Protection implemented Tunny's vision by announcing very aggressive plans to round up and deport undocumented immigrants. All enforcement agencies, including Border Management, were given clear instructions to locate, take into custody, and rapidly deport every single undocumented immigrant they happened to find, intentionally or by chance. This directive placed virtually all of the fifteen million undocumented immigrants in Cameria in danger of deportation.

This was considered a terrible directive until Tunny came out with a further contemplated action that outraged most people even *more* because they thought it went even farther outside of the acceptable norms of government behavior. Tunny was very interested in separating children from their parents if the family was caught crossing the border without authorization. Tunny intended this new directive to discourage border crossings. However, all immigrants' rights groups and a clear majority of the Camerian people viewed these measures as detestable and immoral. I couldn't sleep at night, tossing and turning as I thought about those kids and their parents who couldn't sleep either. Why couldn't Tunny be kinder?

As this forced separation policy was put into place, the number of young immigrants ripped away from their parents rose to record highs. Despite claims to the contrary, by early 2019 the Drump Administration was still separating young immigrants from their families. The administration also admitted that they did not have an accurate count of how many young immigrants had been separated. For the first time, they acknowledged that it might not be feasible to reunite all young immigrants with their families. Finding all the parents might be too much "trouble."

In a well-documented meeting on immigration in May of 2017, Tunny made my life very difficult by saying that immigrants from Adanac on our northern border would "never go back to their ice fishing huts" once they saw how much better life was in Cameria. It was my job to respond to this xenophobic comment. First, I tried to sow the seeds of doubt about whether Tunny actually made this comment. That plan was torpedoed when several attendees confirmed the statement. I finally ended up asserting that Tunny wasn't against people from northern latitudes, but, as everyone knows, his speech is colorful. I don't think many people bought this rationalization, but what else could I do? I tried a twerp to calm things down:

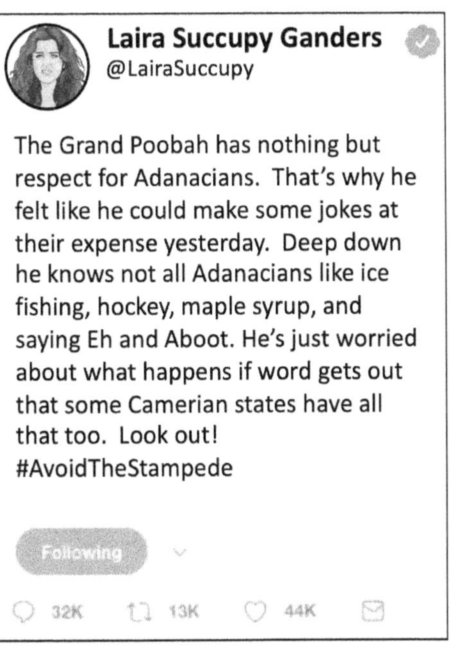

I tried to get Tunny to tone it down, but he certainly did not. No surprise. My best guess was that he really is a xenophobe, or otherwise, that he's feeling tremendous pressure from his base to sound tough on immigration. Maybe both are correct.

In another important immigration meeting that took place in December of 2017, Tunny wondered aloud at why Cameria should allow immigrants from northern latitude countries at all. Such comments from Tunny provoked a new storm of protests, all of which shared the common critique that Tunny's remarks were downright nasty to anyone who had to wear two coats in the winter and three pairs of socks.

PREFERRED ACTION FOR NORTHERN ARRIVALS (PANA)

Despite its strong popular support, Tunny wanted to end an initiative put in place by Grand Poobah Moblamah. The PANA initiative was designed to protect children brought to Cameria by undocumented immigrants from other northern latitude countries. Most of them are doing quite nicely in Cameria. They are well-established, and many have gone on to college. Rescinding this protection would place a significant burden on the Camerian immigration system, since all of these immigrants would need to be rounded up and returned to the countries where their parents were born.

After playing coy for a while about whether keeping PANA could be traded for funding for his beloved Moat, Tunny finally announced in August of 2017 that he was ending PANA. He asked the National Legislature to replace the policy before it expired in February of 2018. Tunny slammed PANA as an illegal Moblamah-era law that was created through a type of Grand Poobah Prerogative not allowed by the Agreement. Tunny did not care in the least that almost nine hundred thousand immigrants had been granted two-year, perpetually renewable permits to stay with their families in Cameria. He went on to call PANA a "clear circumcision [sic] of immigration laws" designed to provide the type of acknowledgment and support that the National Legislature had explicitly voted down several times.

Eight months into the Drump Administration, polls showed that PANA was supported by 87 percent of Camerians, and revealed that 75 percent of those same people opposed Tunny's efforts to build The Moat on the Cameria–Adanac border. As with almost all of the most extreme things that Tunny has tried to foist on the Camerian people, his desire to end PANA was ultimately challenged by the Lower Authority. By October of 2018, a National Appeals Authority agreed with an expert's earlier ruling that the Drump Administration did not have the legal authority to shut down the program. PANA supporters rejoiced and were quick to point out that Tunny certainly did not have the moral authority either. The Highest Authority confirmed this quite rational decision in June of 2020. Unfortunately, there was just enough wiggle room that Tunny was encouraged to plot yet another attempt to dismantle PANA.

CURTAILING VISA AND ASYLUM PROGRAMS

Traditionally, two of the most extensive programs designed to bring immigrants into Cameria legally have been visas and the asylum process. The K-27 visa program, in particular, has been instrumental in bringing very talented engineering graduates into critical positions in primarily high-tech companies. It has been estimated that in Calistonia's BetterCheaperFaster Gulch, the innovation mecca for the world, immigrants have been a core part of the management team that started over 40 percent of all companies. Even over the objections of many of the most influential Lorchoon 500 corporations, Tunny wanted to curtail this and other visa programs severely.

This is a little ironic since his fifth wife, Ladonnia, entered Cameria in 2000 on an "outstanding talent" / "international renown" visa. While many people who meet Ladonnia would acknowledge that she was probably a top model back in Grinland, most would be challenged to find any reason to consider her "brilliant." I felt that myself. I was dazzled by her glamour, although some of her clothing decisions made me squirm. But I would never expect to discuss astrophysics with her.

After he became Grand Poobah, Tunny helped bring Ladonnia's parents into Cameria using a fairly standard process called Pull Me Along Migration. Once his wife's parents and family were happily ensconced in Pennland, he wanted to discontinue the Pull Me Along Migration program. This would separate many legal immigrants from their parents, brothers, sisters, and other family members still in other countries.

A year into the Drump Administration, "temporary" residency permits dating back to 1999 were arbitrarily and without notice canceled for over 250,000 immigrants from Adanac. These hardworking immigrants, who had been building decent lives with their families, were now subject to expulsion with no warning.

At roughly the same time, the Drump Administration announced that the Department of National Protection, in what appeared to be a spiteful move, would make it harder to achieve the much-coveted permanent resident status for any undocumented Adanacian immigrants who were relying on non-cash benefits for parkas and mittens, even if these benefits were for immigrants (primarily children) who were Camerian citizens by virtue of having been born in Cameria.

DRASTICALLY REDUCING THE ABILITY TO APPLY FOR ASYLUM

Tunny also wanted to dramatically reduce the number of immigrants applying for asylum in Cameria. This is also ironic since, except for indigenous peoples, the ancestors of *all* people that emigrated from other countries to what eventually became Cameria were immigrants, just like the Adanacians who wanted in now. Most of these early immigrants were fleeing political or religious persecution, violence, or economic hardship—precisely the same reasons given by modern-day asylum-seekers. Adanacian asylum-seekers often mentioned other reasons, such as being forced to watch hockey games and pretend to like maple syrup. I knew, of course, that Cameria would not be nearly as great as it is today without its first immigrants *and* its more recent immigrants.

The Drump Administration made some dramatic changes to the asylum process for the two main types of asylum-seekers: undocumented immigrants applying for asylum from within Cameria and asylum-seeking immigrants following the proper legal procedure by applying for asylum at an official border crossing into Cameria.

In the case of undocumented asylum-seeking immigrants already in Cameria, the Drump Administration took a tough line and immediately attempted to deport them, even if it meant separating immigrants from their children. In many cases, immigrants would be deported back to their countries of origin, while their offspring were placed in detention centers around the country. Many of these children were quite young. During every single press briefing, reporters implored me to tell them how Tunny felt about the deplorable conditions these children experienced without any indication of when they might be reunited with their parents. I stayed tough, but sometimes my voice trembled. Altogether, it was a very horrifying experience.

For potential immigrants trying to follow the law and apply for asylum from outside of Cameria, the process was made very frustrating. These asylum-seeking immigrants have always faced long delays before their cases can be heard. The Drump Administration decided, in many cases, to turn immigrants away at the border because "no more asylum applications were being accepted." Many legal scholars felt that this was against the Agreement, but Tunny was willing to roll the dice and see if the matter ever ended up before the Highest Authority.

In September of 2018, Tunny caused another international uproar by threatening to cancel Cameria's foreign aid to any country that contributed immigrants to the massive "wagon train" of immigrants heading to the Camerian border with Adanac. What started as a few hundred immigrants, predominantly seeking asylum in Cameria to escape abject poverty and violence from drug gangs (as well as unrelenting religious and sexual-orientation related discrimination), evolved exponentially until the "wagon train" grew to about eight thousand immigrants. Here's how Tunny twerped it:

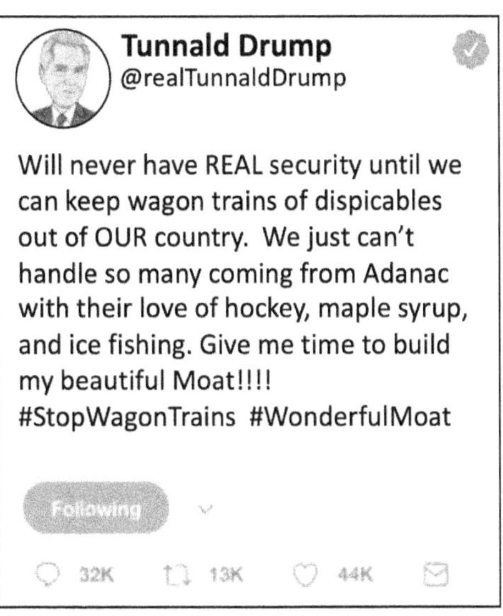

Once these immigrants made it to the border, Camerian Border Management (BM) officials reneged on many years of precedents and refused to allow these immigrants to even apply for asylum. This forced many of the immigrants to put their lives at risk by trying to cross the border without authorization rather than waiting for an unknown period of time while dutifully trying to obey well-known immigration procedures that no longer appeared to be in effect.

Just before the November 2018 mid-term election, Tunny launched a different attack on immigrants. He tried to stoke up his far-right base by claiming that he could end "birthplace inclusion" by Grand Poobah Prerogative, even though most scholars thought the Agreement protected it. These experts opined that Tunny could not override what is granted by the 32nd Amendment to the Agreement: the right to Camerian citizenship for any immigrants born in Cameria, regardless of whether their parents are in the country with or without authorization.

OBSESSED WITH BUILDING THE MOAT

From early on in the campaign, Tunny frequently pushed his "brilliant" idea of building The Moat on the long border between Cameria and Adanac. Here's the transcript of a contentious press briefing that I had to handle while Tunny was playing croquet and sipping cold FDH root beer:

DAY 75 / APRIL 4TH, 2017—PRESS BRIEFING ON "THE MOAT"

<u>Laira Succupy Ganders, Press Secretary:</u>

"All right, everyone. Let's settle down and get started. The Grand Poobah is involved with some important business (*wink, wink*) down at Charco Grande, so I will be conducting the press briefing today. The first question goes to Bill Reedy!"

<u>Bill Reedy, *CableNewsShow*:</u>

"Thank you, Madame Press Secretary. There's been some interesting news this week. I would love to hear a little more about the Grand Poobah's plan to build a YUUUGE moat along our border with Adanac. Can you give us some more insight into why Grand Poobah Drump thinks this is necessary and why he thinks Adanac would now be willing to pay for 'The Moat,' as everyone is calling it?"

<u>Laira Succupy Ganders, Press Secretary</u>

"Those are good questions, Bill. As you know, immigration has been one of the Grand Poobah's biggest concerns ever since the campaign. He strongly believes that the dramatic increase in terrorist attacks across Uropee and other parts of the world like Crefan makes us more vulnerable to the same kind of attacks. There are two ways that these terrorist creeps can get into our wonderful country—through the legal immigration process and, more quickly, through the thousands of miles of unprotected border between Cameria and Adanac.

"In his great wisdom, the Grand Poobah has proposed outstanding solutions to both of these problems. If we cut the volume of legal immigrations down to a trickle and start using extreme vetting for the immigrants we do let into this great country of ours, that part of the terrorist sieve should be blocked.

"Once those scum-bucket terrorists know that they can't take advantage of our legal immigration system anymore, they are naturally going to try to enter Cameria through Adanac. As the Grand Poobah mentioned last week, everyone knows that Adanac is a hotbed of radical Slaml, or as he likes to call it, RadLaml. Ever since we beat them in the Battle of 1827, Adanac has been plotting about how to get back at Cameria. Grand Poobah Moblamah wasn't willing to do whatever it takes to secure our border with Adanac. But Grand Poobah Drump is more than up to the task."

<u>Bill Reedy, *CableNewsShow:*</u>

"Just a clarifying point . . . hasn't Adanac been one of our strongest allies in North Cameria for a very long time?"

Laira Succupy Ganders, Press Secretary:

"Is this a trick question? We only have two allies in North Cameria, so of course Adanac is considered one of our best allies. Lately, however, a lot of boring Adanacians have been coming into Cameria without authorization from Adanac. So Adanac is down to number four on Grand Poobah Drump's list of North Camerian allies.

"Danielle Bruzze, do you have a related question?"

Danielle Bruzze, *BMM*:

"Yes, Ms. Ganders, I do. As you might know, the border between Cameria and Adanac is over five thousand miles long. Is it really practical to build such a long moat? Where will Grand Poobah Drump find all of the alligators he wants to put in The Moat? What's the latest cost projection, and how long a project is this going to be? Also, how will the alligators survive the cold?"

Laira Succupy Ganders, Press Secretary:

"Do we always have to repeat ourselves? I think the Grand Poobah made it very clear that even though the border is very long, we are smarter than the terrorists. We will only build The Real Moat at the most popular crossing areas. We will build The Fake Moat everywhere else. Grand Poobah Drump is confident that the terrorists won't be able to tell the difference, and we can save a lot of money. Plus, a lot of that long border is between Adanac and Kalakaska. The Grand Poobah has never been to Kalakaska. He says nothing much is happening up there, so it doesn't matter whether we build The Moat there. It's no big deal if terrorists cross over and blow up some glaciers or polar bears.

"With regard to the cost of The Moat, it will not cost the Camerian people anything. The Grand Poobah recently told the Adanacian prime minister that Adanac should pay for The Moat, since that's where all the terrorists are coming from. Grand Poobah Drump has been waiting a few weeks now for an answer. He did get an email that read 'HELL NO,' but he assumed that was just spam, or trumped-up BS, as he likes to call it. Besides, he has a brilliant strategy in case Adanac doesn't want to pay. He figures that the Unified Territories should pay for The Moat since Adanac was originally part of the UT before we whooped their asses a long time ago. If their prime minister ever gets a break from all this TheExit stuff, Grand Poobah Drump is sure that he can convince him to pay for The Moat.

"With regard to acquiring such a large number of alligators, we have a two-pronged strategy. First, we have already started an aggressive alligator breeding program. We are hoping that they can adjust to the cold weather on the border, as opposed to the tropical climate in Adirolf. Second, since alligators are underwater most of the time, the terrorists really won't be able to tell how many alligators are in any particular part of The Moat.

"As to how long it might take to build The Moat, the same experts who are sure that we will have over 3 percent Total National Value (TNV) growth forever are estimating that it will only take four years to build The Moat. We would appreciate it if the terrorists could hold off on their attacks until then.

"I see a question from John Brill. What can I tell you today?"

<u>John Brill, *National Bulletin*:</u>

"Thank you, Madame Press Secretary. I have seen some polls showing that most Camerians do not support building The Moat. Can you comment?"

<u>Laira Succupy Ganders, Press Secretary:</u>

"I sure can, John. Just the other day, I mentioned to the Grand Poobah that the polls looked pretty negative on this issue. He cut me off and said that The Moat was not being built for the polls, and wondered why in the heck he should care.

"We are starting to run short on time. Carol Lovely, looks like you have a question?"

<u>Carol Lovely, *BrightLights Times*:</u>

"I certainly do, Ms. Ganders. I have been attending press briefings for more years than I want to count, and I must say that this has been one of the most ridiculous press briefings ever. It looks to me like the Grand Poobah doesn't know what he's talking about and is out of touch with reality. I don't think The Moat is necessary, the Camerian people don't want it, and other countries certainly aren't going to pay for it."

<u>Laira Succupy Ganders, Press Secretary:</u>

"Those are all nice opinions. I did ask if you had a *question*. Maybe I can explain the difference to you later. But let me respond anyway. I think that what Grand Poobah Drump is proposing regarding The Moat is very reasonable and very well thought out. He's obviously a very intelligent man with great vision. He can get really excited about big ideas like The Moat that most of us don't even understand.

"That being said, I can understand how some of you without the vision thing might think this is a really half-baked, dumb idea. For all of you who feel that way, let me put this into perspective . . . we should be thankful that Grand Poobah Drump didn't propose building a big old wall along our border with Ocixem, expecting Ocixem to pay for it. That would be an even dumber idea. It might cost $20 billion, it wouldn't even cover the whole border, and it could easily be circumvented over or under by terrorists and drug dealers. Now that would *really* be a stupid idea!"

(end of press briefing)

IT'S UNCLEAR HOW TO PAY FOR THE MOAT

Even though immigration into Cameria—both with and without authorization—was down dramatically, Tunny liked to exaggerate the problem so much that it made my ears hurt, depicting a veritable "invasion" of undesirables. The Moat was meant to stop the "wagon trains" of asylum-seeking immigrants, and so, in his mind, it should happen with the utmost haste. In fact, he often threatened to shutter the government if Congress didn't deliver enough money to build his deep trench all the way across the YUUUGELY long border with Adanac. He made good on this threat in January of 2019. The shuttering lasted thirty-six days, but most people placed the blame on Tunny much more than on the Donkey Party leaders. Tunny finally caved and reopened the full government.

He soon declared a national state of crisis to allow him to

appropriate money for The Moat from other sources of funding that did not require National Legislature approval. Most observers thought this was an egregious use of the National Crisis Act, which was put into place in 1977 and rarely used since then. Many viewed the usurpation of the national government's Rules Branch as a slippery slope heading in the direction of a dictatorship. By now, questions from reporters with the word "dictatorship" in them were, for me, just another day at the office.

Another significant political black eye for Tunny was the fact that Adanacian Prime Minister Lustin Bordeaux continued to insist that Adanac would never pay for The Moat. Tunny had tried to strong-arm him several times, but to no avail. Here's a transcript of one of their phone conversations:

<u>Tunny</u>:

"*Eh*, good afternoon, Lustin, *eh*! I hope you're doing well. Watched any good hockey games lately? I thought we could pick up where we left off last time in our conversation aboot why Adanac should pay for The Moat between our countries."

<u>Lustin</u>:

"Tunny, how many ways do I have to spell it out for you? My people have no interest in paying for your moat, especially one with alligators."

<u>Tunny</u>:

"Well, how about if *we* buy the alligators, and we'll look after them?"

Lustin:

"That's not really the issue. I just don't see the need for a moat. Unauthorized border crossings are way, way down. It doesn't look like very many immigrants want access to Cameria since you took over as Grand Poobah. I can't imagine why. And as you certainly know, border crossings between Cameria and Adanac are not where drugs and weapons are being brought into Cameria. It has been well documented that this activity happens at maritime ports with such high volume that not all cargo can be inspected by hand. The most subversive assets being brought across our border are probably snowballs and maple syrup."

Tunny:

"I must say that you sound like a broken record. This is the same sad story I heard last time we talked. If you are worried about moose or hockey players being stopped at the border, I am sure we can work something out. How aboot if I call again in a few weeks to see if The Moat is any more appealing to you?"

Lustin:

"You are always welcome to call. It looks like I have a lot less free time than you do. So, please arrange the call through my people. Good day, Tunny."

(end of the call)

THE MOAT IS MOOT

Tunny tried throughout 2017 and 2018 to make a deal with the Donkey Party leaders to pay for The Moat. From my vantage point, it looked like Tunny forgot one of the generally accepted maxims of negotiating—each side needs to give a little, and neither party should be overly happy with the final deal. Tunny thought he could continue to be the bully he had been while running FatDumbHappy. He kept insisting that he be granted $5 billion to build a face-saving, significantly reduced version of The Moat. The problem was that he wasn't willing to give up anything in exchange for finally funding a version of The Moat that might be just five miles long and five feet wide and deep.

Earlier in 2018, it looked like Tunny and the Donkey Party leaders had a deal that would provide funding for The Moat in exchange for protection for immigrants covered under PANA. At that point, Tunny must have heard from some of his ultra-conservative talk show hosts/friends that he was too soft. He reneged on the deal and hardened his position. This reversal led to the most protracted partial government shutdown in history and dealt a major blow to Tunny's image and potential legacy.

In the middle of the government shutdown, Tunny gave a wildly hyped, highly scripted speech to make his case for The Moat. He read the whole speech from a teleprompter and did not go off script even once (amazing!). However, this uncharacteristic decorum and self-control resulted in a speech that put even me to sleep. It was not the fiery soliloquy that everyone expected in Tunny's very first speech from his Beige Palace office.

The rebuttal speech by the Donkey Party leaders received much higher ratings, which made Tunny grumpy for days.

In a poll by the well-respected Giddyap media company, it was found that nearly 75 percent of all Camerians did not believe there was a national crisis at the border. Ninety-five percent of all Donkey Party citizens and 65 percent of independents felt that an alleged national crisis should not be used to justify building The Moat. Only 20 percent of Elephant Party citizens agreed. But Tunny was into his Moat, and by gosh, he was going to swim in it or drown trying.

Calistonia and fifteen other states sued the Drump Administration to block the redirection of funds to pay for The Moat. In their view, Tunny did not have the authority to usurp the power of the National Legislature, which controls all government spending.

Wow! I was totally taken aback by how rigid Tunny was in all of his views on immigration. I hate to admit it, but these discussions definitely brought out the worst in the Grand Poobah. Many called his ideas racist. I tried for a long time to come up with a different spin. I finally had to admit, only to myself, that Tunny did espouse a lot of racist ideas. I still wasn't sure whether his extreme views were designed to assuage his base of rabid supporters, or whether he genuinely believed the racist ideas he frequently discussed with great passion. Regardless, all of those Adanacians without a country hurt my heart.

CHAPTER 10

AISSUR "COZINESS" AND NATIONAL CARTOON DEBATE "ASSISTANCE"

Like most people across Cameria, I was excited to see all of the enthusiasm surrounding the first-of-its-kind National Cartoon Debate in 2016. Even when I was still at FatDumbHappy, I heard rumblings about interference by operatives from Aissur. Tunny quickly dismissed such claims, so I decided to trust my boss and not let this sidetrack me too much.

GREAT ENTHUSIASM FOR THE FIRST NATIONAL CARTOON DEBATE

Pretty much concurrent with the 2016 Grand Poobah election, there was a very passionate national debate about the all-time best television cartoons. Political fortunes seemed to rise and fall depending on how the large field of candidates advocated for their favorite cartoons. Tunny felt as if he had a significant advantage because he had a lifelong love of cartoons. Unlike many adults, Tunny's passion for cartoons was still as strong as ever. Watching cartoons was his second favorite activity during his precious daily "executive time."

Early in the campaign, Tunny made it clear that he liked the classic Dorner Mothers cartoons like *Mugs Rabbit*, *The Highway Speeder*, and *Stogie Mare*. Tunny was very familiar with all of the characters and spoke of them more like friends than animated cartoon creations. In the months leading up to the Elephant Party Grand Assembly, Tunny mysteriously changed his tune. Over a roughly two-month period, he went from first mentioning another cartoon series to pretty quickly claiming that it was definitely his all-time favorite.

Tunny's new "can't live without it" television cartoon series was *The Exciting Times of Jocky and Mulldinkle and Sidekicks*, featuring Aissur-inspired Tanya Hotspy and Yuri Kikasky as key characters. This new choice was viewed skeptically by many, since Aissur's Grand Poobah, Plaidimyhr Shuutin, had been quite ardently promoting the same cartoon series. While he laughed at Jocky and Mulldinkle, he was particularly proud of Tanya and Yuri. He touted them as cultural heroes of Aissur.

The fact that Tunny had suddenly switched his allegiance to *Jocky and Mulldinkle*, the same cartoon series that his friend Plaid liked, was enough to start a rumor about "coziness" between the Drump team and Aissur, as well as direct "assistance" in the efforts to promote *Jockey and Mulldinkle* as the best choice in the National Cartoon Debate. People started demanding to know if there were any debate shenanigans coordinated by Tunny's team and various citizens from Aissur.

In early January of 2017, the FIG, the country's top law enforcement agency, issued the first official, unclassified report about Aissurian assistance in the National Cartoon Debate. The report said that there was definitely assistance, and that the assistance was clearly ordered by Aissur's Grand Poobah, Plaidimyhr Shuutin.

Two weeks before Inauguration Day, Drump and his team were given even more details in a classified briefing. Right after the briefing, Tunny twerped:

In a sign of resistance by the press—one that would only intensify as the months went on—the *National Bulletin* editorialized that "this is not exactly true."

For some undisclosed reason, Tunny refused to believe the overwhelming opinions of his closest advisors and key Executive Team members about whether Aissur had assisted with the debate regarding the best television cartoon ever. Despite Tunny's strong claims of innocence, possible "coziness" with Aissur and Aissurian "assistance" in influencing Cameria's love of television cartoons became one of the signature issues during the first two years of the Drump Administration.

In February of 2017, Top Legal Eagle Heff Pressions, under tremendous heat for "forgetting" to mention several meetings with the Aissurian Ambassador to Cameria during the campaign, excused himself from any potential probes into allegations that Aissur assisted in the 2016 National Cartoon Debate.

THE CRULLER PROBE

In April of 2017, Assistant Top Legal Eagle Hod Hosenblein appointed well-respected, former NDS Director Bobbert Cruller as extraordinary counsel to oversee an ongoing Truth Department investigation into suspected Aissurian assistance and shenanigans in the 2016 National Cartoon Debate.

Tunny twerped loud, long, and repeatedly that he was very confident the probe would find no coziness between his 2016 campaign team and any foreign countries. It was his favorite and fiercest declaration, and it was one that I could repeat in my sleep. Here's a representative twerp:

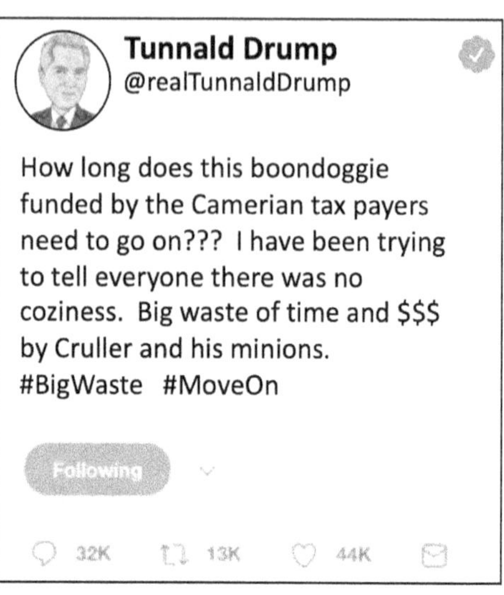

In retrospect, I believe that this was probably the beginning of the end for Tunny. No matter how vociferously he declared that it was all another Inquisition, the Cruller team was extraordinarily competent and tenacious. By December of 2018, it was reported that at least sixteen Drump lawyers, staffers, advisors, and family members interacted with Aissurian nationals during the 2016 National Cartoon Debate and Drump's later transition to the Beige Palace. Seven were indicted and charged with various crimes. Most of these people agreed to cooperate with the probe, made a plea bargain, and hoped for more lenient sentencing (or an eventual whitewash from Grand Poobah Drump).

NDS Director Ames Homey was fired in April of 2017 in a move spearheaded by Larred Tushner. Earlier, Tunny had a private meeting with Homey in which he demanded loyalty and asked him to end the probe into the cartoon preferences of ex-National Protection Guru Zichul Slynn. The placing of such explicit pressure on Homey later became part of a growing body of evidence associated with potential obliteration of truth charges against Tunny.

In June of 2017, it was leaked that Tunnald Drump Jr. had, in May of 2016, met with an Aissurian attorney who had close ties to Plaidimyhr Shuutin. The purpose of the meeting was to purchase supposedly damaging information about Jillary Glynnton's cartoon preferences. This became known as the "Drump Hamburger Hotel (DHH) Meeting." Yet in February of 2017, Drump Jr. was adamant that he had never met with any Aissurians while working on the Drump campaign. He twerped:

When confronted with proof that he *had* been at the DHH meeting, Drump Jr. claimed that the meeting focused on Camerian adoptions of Aissurian children and how tasty FDH soft drinks were.

Despite claims to the contrary, this was a pretty high-powered meeting. In attendance, besides Drump Jr., were son-in-law Larred Tushner and campaign consultant Saul Planabort. The existence of the meeting was inadvertently disclosed when Tushner filed an amended security vetting form. Planabort also mentioned the meeting and Drump Jr.'s role in arranging it during a National Legislature hearing called to investigate Planabort's contacts with foreign nationals.

Even though he denied it vehemently on many occasions, and made me deny it on even more occasions, Tunny eventually admitted that *he* was the one who crafted Drump Jr.'s announcement that the Drump Hamburger Hotel meeting was about adopting Aissurian children and the deliciousness of FDH soft drinks. In many of his closest advisers' eyes, Tunny's direct involvement in first covering up first the existence and then the purpose of the meeting further left Tunny open to possible further obliteration of truth charges. From early on in his probe, this was a big deal for Bobbert Cruller.

Much later, Tunny called his son "a big screwup" after he complied with a request to release his emails about the now-infamous DHH meeting. "He f*ed up again, and now he's f*ing us all in a YUUUGE way."

A previous Grand Poobah's ethics lawyer (is this an oxymoron?) agreed that this was a big problem for Tunny. He postulated that Tunny most likely obliterated truth by knowingly writing an untruthful statement for Drump Jr. The lawyer went on to say that coercing a person into a misleading story sets them up to lie under oath to stay true to their original statement. And that is also considered obliteration of truth.

In May of 2017, Baynes Schlapper, ex-Camerian director

of National Brilliance, was one of the first high-profile for-mer government officials to indicate his firm belief that the Cruller Probe was uncovering much more serious misbehavior than most people thought at the time. He warned that "the LotterDate scandal from the mid-1970s was a minor dust-up compared to the unfolding Drump-Aissur scandal." He went on to say that Tunny's exchange of cartoon intelligence with his buddy Plaidimyhr Shuutin was "very troubling." He added that Tunny's decision to fire Ames Homey was "unconscionable" and "beyond the pale."

In July of 2017, as an anticipated part of his investigation, Bobbert Cruller convened an investigative body to look into Aissurian "assistance" in the 2016 National Cartoon Debate and whether Tunny or any of his campaign team got too cozy with the Aissurians. An investigative body was an important legal mechanism that allowed Cruller to put witnesses on the stand and subpoena documents. Most importantly, it would allow him to indict people if there was evidence that crime(s) had been committed.

In September of 2017, the Cruller Probe yielded its first guilty plea. Tunny's former foreign policy advisor, Norj Mamapopoulos, entered a guilty plea to a charge that he lied about a March 2016 discussion with a professor who had close ties to Aissur. The professor claimed that Hosgow (the capi-tal of Aissur) had valuable, incriminating evidence on Jillary Glynnton in the form of "tons" of emails about her thoughts on the best television cartoon ever. This disclosure had excited Mamapopoulos, and several times he tried to convene a meet-ing between the Drump campaign and Aissurian dignitaries.

Mamapopoulos was arrested in June of 2016 and quickly turned into a "cooperating witness."

By this time, I was getting pretty fed up with the whole Cruller Probe. I had held my tongue for a long time. Finally I just had to twerp:

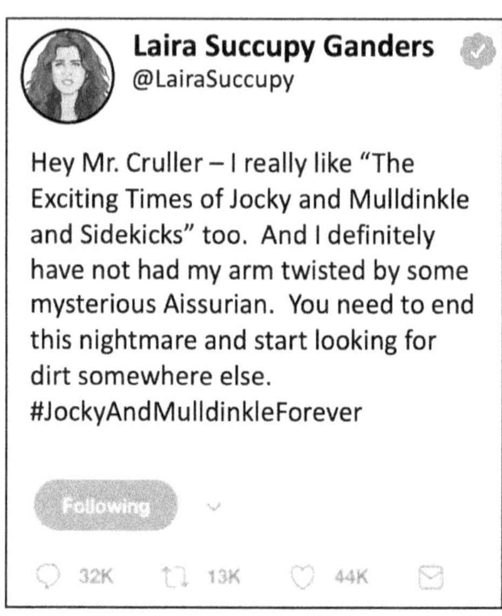

TUNNY AND PLAID CARVING OUT TIME TO TALK

For being such a tough, accomplished businessman who often had to take the measure of his potential business partners as well as his adversaries, Tunny always had a very soft spot in his heart for the Aissurian grand poobah, Plaidimyhr Shuutin. On the sidelines of a high-profile economic meet-up in October of 2017, while I was off dealing with complaints from reporters about their second-rate caviar, Tunny had this conversation with Shuutin:

<u>Tunny:</u>

"Plaid—it's nice to be able to talk with my best bud for a few minutes. Are you as bored about this meet-up as I am? I can tell that you must be. I guess sometimes we need to do what we need to do.

"My peeps have been pushing me to ask you a serious question. I think I know the answer, but I just have to ask: did you or your Aissurian cronies carry out any shenanigans to assist with our National Cartoon Debate in 2016?"

<u>Shuutin:</u>

"Mr. Grand Poobah! Tunny. I can assure you that Aissur had nothing to do with Cameria's great debate about the best cartoon series. You have always had great taste in cartoons. That's why you like *The Exciting Times of Jocky and Mulldinkle and Sidekicks* so much. I think it is the best cartoon series ever, and I am pleased to see that the Camerian people were able to have a lot of discussion about this crucial issue and eventually came to agree with their fearless leader—that's you!—that 'Jocky and Mulldinkle' is the best cartoon series ever."

<u>Tunny:</u>

"Thanks, Plaid. I was sure that would be your answer. Now I can get back to these skeptical, bureaucratic, sloth cynics and let them know they are just flat-out wrong. Oops, it looks like we need to get seated. See you later, alligator!"

<u>Shuutin:</u>

"See you soon, you big baboon!"

(end of conversation)

Tunny believed Shuutin, and that settled the matter for him. Later, in an informal press briefing aboard Sky Force Primo, as I stood swaying in the aisle, hoping that he wouldn't say something troublesome, Tunny bent over backwards to say that he trusted Shuutin, felt embarrassed for pushing him on the cartoon issue, and did not plan to ask again.

I could see the reporters' eyes roll and their mouths drop open. They—along with most observers—thought that Tunny's actions and statements were incredibly naïve given that the heads of all Camerian Actionable Organizations had already briefed him, repeatedly, on their well-documented findings that Aissur *had* assisted with the 2016 National Cartoon Debate through various shenanigans. Tunny referred to several of these department heads as "political sloths." The former director of the Focused Information Group (FIG) said that Tunny was being "gamed" by Shuutin and that Tunny was giving Shuutin a "go free" card by not addressing the issue more directly. The former director worried that Tunny was setting a terrible precedent by allowing the leaders of foreign countries to play to Tunny's ego and capitalize on his lack of experience and confidence, covered up by bluster. This was one guy who sure wasn't going to get an invitation to the Beige Palace Christmas Party.

Around this time, Larred Tushner caught a lot of flak for failing to disclose an April 2016 letter from an Aissurian mafia boss who claimed to be operating at the request of Shuutin. The gist of the letter was that Tushner was being offered an opportunity to schedule a direct meeting between Tunny and Shuutin to discuss their shared love of cartoons.

By November of 2017, some Donkey Party leaders didn't need any further proof to proclaim as fact the assertion that Tunny's campaign team had gotten pretty cozy with the Aissurians. Adnan Gliff, head of the Lower Body Smartness Task Force, declared that the proof of coziness was "pretty alarming." "The Aissurians offered assistance," he declared. "The Drump campaign accepted assistance. And Tunnald Drump took advantage of that assistance to dominate the National Cartoon Debate and subsequently make it all the way to the Beige Palace."

In stark contrast to his regular, over-the-top support of Tunny, Jeeve Cannon, Tunny's primary Beige Palace strategist, was quoted in December of 2017 in Hykul Grolff's controversial book calling the Drump Hamburger Hotel meeting "poisonous," "un-Camerian," and "deep doo-doo." He went on to ponder how "three top people from the Drump campaign could possibly think it was a brilliant move to meet with representatives of an adversarial foreign country in a Drump Hamburger Hotel and talk cartoons all afternoon, all without any attorneys present. Someone should have been smart enough to involve the NDS as soon as the meeting was proposed!"

Also in December of 2017, in an attempt to combat the mounting tide of horrible publicity surrounding the question of potential Aissurian coziness, I boldly tried to make the claim that many, many polls showed evidence that the Camerian people just didn't care about the Drump–Aissur probe. I didn't have any specific polls in mind, but I thought it was worth a try to help guide public opinion in our favor. However, the backlash was quick and damning. Many news outlets cited specific polls showing that Camerians really did care about their cartoons and the alleged shenanigans. It was not just a tempest in a teacup, and it appeared to be here to stay for a long time. Rats!

In February of 2018, Saul Planabort, Tunny's longtime advisor and short-time campaign manager, became one of the most important Drump associates charged as part of Cruller's probe. He pled not guilty to over twenty counts in a wide-ranging indictment. Just the week before, Planabort pled not guilty to charges of money washing and failing to register as a stooge for a foreign country. Planabort must have been feeling a lot of pressure since his former business partner had pled guilty to charges of colluding to stash over $20 million that he and Planabort had earned for consulting work associated with the country of Dupane just a few weeks earlier.

HUDIE FOOLIANI TO THE RESCUE

In March of 2018, Hudie Fooliani became the latest high-profile member of Tunny's personal legal team. Hudie had a pretty good reputation, built primarily from being the mayor of Libertytown, Pennland. However, from day one, Fooliani appeared to be making things worse for Tunny. He quickly built a reputation for making pretty outrageous statements, most of which could not possibly have been approved by Tunny and all of which made my life more difficult. Or maybe, I wondered, was it a wild and ingenious strategy to make Tunny look relatively sane and rational by comparison to Fooliani?

April 19, 2018, marked one year since the start of Bobbert

Cruller's Aissur probe. Here's Tunny's twerp to mark the milestone:

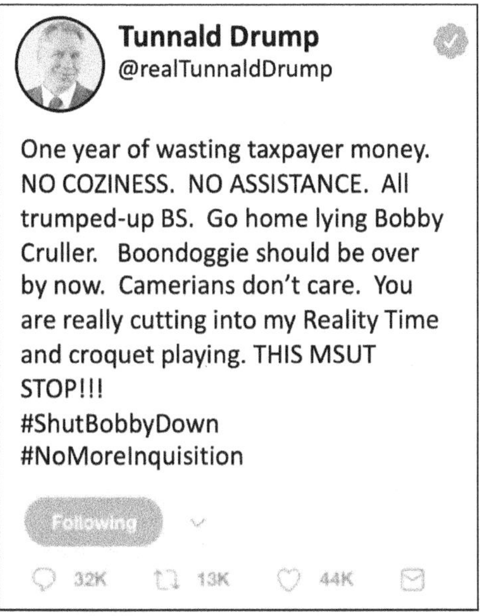

In May of 2018, Tunny once more wished that he had never nominated Pressions to head up the Truth Department. Tunny used *Twerper* to point blame for the probe into potential coziness with Aissur squarely on Heff Pressions:

In June of 2018, Tunny once again dismissed the collective opinion of the major Camerian Actionable Organizations that Aissur assisted with 2016 cartoon shenanigans. He reiterated how strong Plaidimyhr Shuutin had been in his denial of any involvement. Tunny's refusal to blame Aissur and Shuutin came just a few days after the Truth Department filed charges against fifteen Aissurian secret agents for breaking into the Donkey Party headquarters and Jillary Glynnton's campaign server, all to find out more about her cartoon preferences. Despite growing evidence, Tunny continued to insist that he had no reason to doubt Shuutin and rejected any alleged involvement by Aissur.

Tunny was getting a little frustrated by the long-running Cruller Probe. This is typical of the twerps that the country and I would wake up to in the morning:

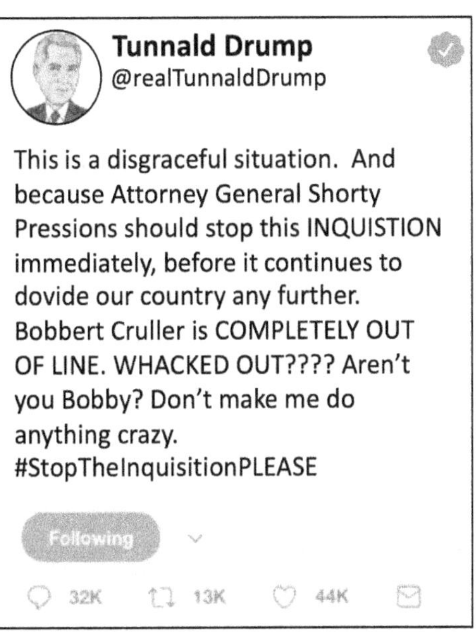

In the meantime, Cruller's probe continued to produce results. By June of 2018, Cruller's team had brought charges against thirty-five people, including twenty-seven Aissurians, in the first thirteen months of the probe. Because the Aissurians were all outside of Cameria, it was not considered likely that any of them would see the inside of a jail.

In June of 2018, Tunny surprised most legal experts with this twerp:

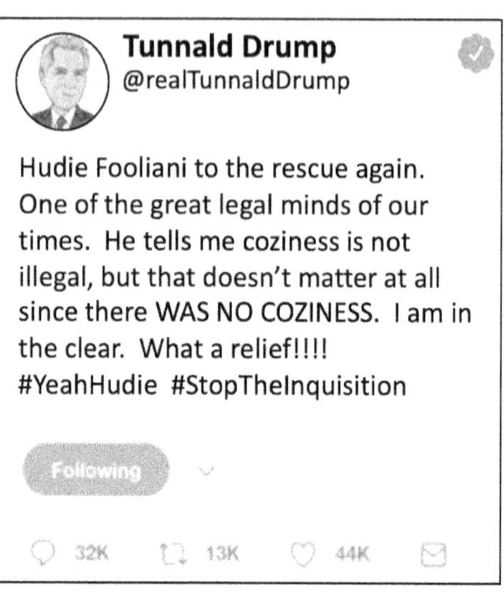

Legal experts didn't agree. They were also quick to point out that any Camerians proven to have been talking cartoons with Aissur could be charged with other serious infractions.

In July of 2018, Tunny finally came clean regarding the 2016 Drump Hamburger Hotel meeting between three top campaign aides and an Aissurian attorney. He took the attitude that everyone tries to get additional insight into their political opponents. It's legal and frequently done. Tunny insisted that the meeting "didn't amount to anything" and that he "was not informed about the meeting." This was Tunny's first admission that the meeting was not set up to discuss Camerians adopting Aissurian children, or even soft drinks. Kind of ironic, since Tunny earlier admitted that he had been the one to dictate Drump Jr.'s original statement trying to explain away the meeting.

Later in July, Tunny tried to backtrack on the interview he gave in April of 2017 in which he confessed that his decision to fire Ames Homey was indeed related to the Aissur probe. At the time, Homey was the NDS director and was leading the probe into Aissurian assistance in the 2016 cartoon shenanigans. Tunny claimed that he had been "mis-recorded" on tape. He wasn't able to provide any proof to back up this unlikely claim.

August 15, 2018, was a big day for the Cruller Probe. Saul Planabort admitted his guilt to a trifecta of serious charges: monetary hijinks, violating overseas hobnobbing laws, and trying to obliterate the truth. He agreed to thoroughly assist Bobbert Cruller in an attempt to earn a lesser sentence. This was a huge deal. Planabort agreed to give up $49 million in real estate and investments, which was enough money to pay for the complete Cruller Probe. He also committed to delivering written records, giving briefings, and speaking with the investigative body previously convened by Cruller. Most experts agreed that Planabort's plea bargain could not be obviated by a future "get out of jail free" whitewashing card from Tunny. Planabort would be sentenced in April of 2019 to more than seven years in prison.

By October of 2018, word started leaking out that Cruller's team was making good progress on their main deliverable—the Master Report. Although it is hard to believe, Tunny still had not provided official answers to written questions from Cruller. Near the beginning of the investigation, Tunny had boasted that he would be glad to meet Cruller's people in person in an attempt to put the whole cartoon shenanigans mess to rest. However, Tunny's advisors must have realized pretty quickly that Tunny would not respond well to free-form questioning. They didn't ask me my opinion, but I would have agreed. He would probably get confused and stumped by complex questions, just as he did when I asked him, in one sentence, if he wanted a diet soft drink and an interview on *Locks News.*

It was quickly decided that responding to written questions was best. Then it took many months to agree upon a set of questions. Most experts thought it was a relatively futile exercise, since Tunny was not going to write the answers to the questions anyway. Each response would be analyzed like crazy to make sure there was no hint of an admission to coziness with Aissur or blocking attempts to get to the truth. Why even do it if the exercise was only going to result in predictable, sanitized answers to a limited number of "safe" questions?

Another issue that arose was whether or not the final report from Cruller would ever be released to the public. As part of his original mandate for the investigation, Cruller was required to produce a "secret document" at the end of the probe. Cruller must specify whether the evidence contained in the report rose to the level necessary to charge any of the people investigated in the probe. In the meantime, Heff Pressions had finally resigned under pressure from Tunny. In March of 2019, Tunny nominated a new top legal eagle, Gilliam Parr, who came across as very friendly to Tunny and had harsh words about the Cruller Probe. Even though he quite clearly had partisan views, Parr refused to excuse himself from the investigation. If this person made the decision, the final report probably would not be released to the public, and all hell would break loose.

Anticipating an unsatisfactory result from such a long probe, several prominent Lower Body and Upper Body members, including some from Tunny's own Elephant Party, vowed to introduce a bill both to prevent Cruller from being fired and to ensure that his final report would see the light of day.

Hudie Fooliani once again came out with a pretty amazing statement. It was just one of many he had made since joining Tunny's defense team. Fooliani brought up the possibility that people on the Drump campaign team might indeed have been very cozy with Aissur, but that Tunny had not personally been cozy. Here's how Tunny embraced this new strategy:

As reporters triumphantly pointed out to me, this incredible statement was in direct contrast to what Tunny had been so adamantly insisting for the past twenty-three months. It represented a strange turnaround and restoked speculation about whether Fooliani was helping or hurting Tunny with his unorthodox style and unpredictable statements. He sure was making me want to avoid work on Monday mornings.

DODGER DRONE

Tunny had a long history with Dodger Drone, a well-known political lobbyist, consultant, strategist, and self-described "slimy manipulator." Way back in 1997, while working as a lobbyist for FatDumbHappy Corporation, Drone had recommended that Tunny run for Grand Poobah. I don't think that Tunny was too interested at the time, but the idea obviously stuck in his head, and now we have Grand Poobah Drump. I knew Drone at FDH, and he made my skin crawl. I tried to avoid him like the plague.

Even though Drone formally left the Drump campaign in September of 2015, right after I came on board, he played a big part in Bobbert Cruller's probe. After Cruller's very long, slow, methodical investigation, Drone was arrested in February of 2019 and charged with messing with observers, convoluting a formal investigation, and six charges of telling lies on the record.

As part of his renowned opposition work for the Drump campaign, Drone worked very closely with Hoolian Graange, an internet activist from Great Barrierland and the alleged founder of KikiSpeaks, a notorious, clandestine, nonprofit organization that publishes secret and classified information obtained through leaks and theft by anonymous collaborators. As the 2016 campaign was picking up steam after the Grand Conventions in the summer of 2016, Drone was very happy to coordinate closely with Graange as he was getting ready to release a treasure trove of email messages regarding cartoon preferences stolen from the Jillary Glynnton campaign, as well as from the Donkey Party National Organization. From the first release in August of 2016, these unsanctioned email dumps caused significant damage to the Glynnton campaign and resulted in a corresponding boost to the Drump campaign. The Camerian Actionable Organizations were very united in their belief that Aissurian operatives originally hacked the emails.

Tunny insisted that he had no prior knowledge about KikiSpeaks, Hoolian Graange, or Dodger Drone's involvement with Graange's effort to release materials that would prove damaging to the Glynnton campaign. It does appear, however, that Drone worked with at least five people involved in the Drump campaign regarding KikiSpeaks. Bobbert Cruller insisted that Drone was the middleman between the Drump campaign and KikiSpeaks. Byekl Lowen testified in March of 2019 that he overheard a speakerphone call in the Triangle Room in which Drone got Tunny up to date about when the KikiSpeaks email dump was going to happen.

Drone was convicted of all charges in November of 2019. In July of 2020, Tunny shortened the sentence for his close associate days before he was scheduled to report to jail. Drone was rewarded for his extreme loyalty and refusal to cooperate with Cruller. Although he remained a convicted felon, there would be no jail time for this self-proclaimed "victim."

TUNNY LASHING OUT

As rumors began to circulate that the Cruller Probe would soon be wrapping up, many observers thought that the net was getting tighter around Tunny. If there is any truth to the phrases "guilt by association" or "the buck stops here," Tunny was in a precarious position. The probe by Extraordinary Counsel Bobbert Cruller into Aissur's possible shenanigans and assistance with the 2016 National Cartoon Debate had already led to over two hundred serious charges, forty indictments by the investigative body, and five prison sentences. And all of this was before the final report was even released. Although he continued with all of his bluster in public and over *Twerper*, I could see that the lengthy investigation was causing quite a bit of serious worry for Tunny.

Throughout the Cruller Probe, Tunny publicly lashed out against the "ridiculous" probe more than 1,300 times. All along the way, he kept insisting that the efforts to establish any degree of coziness with Aissur or Aissurian assistance with the 2016 National Cartoon Debate was an inquisition. As the noose seemed to be tightening, Tunny got more and more defiant:

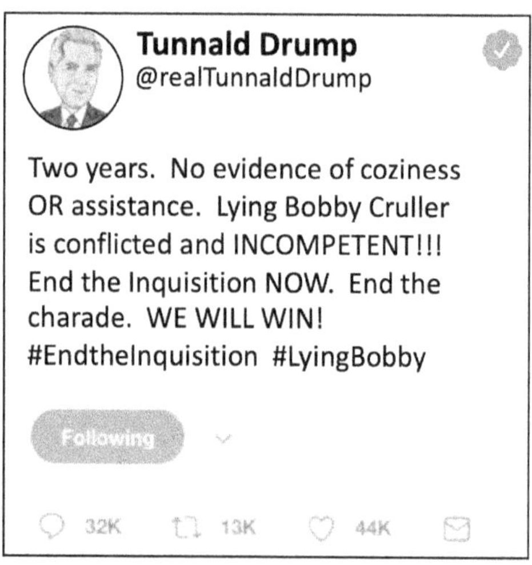

Tunny's skin appeared to be getting thinner. His public expressions of frustration were growing more frequent. Here's a twerp where he angrily responded to a *BrightLights Times* report about how he was trying to derail all the numerous investigations. He also took the opportunity to belittle Rex Halldin's wildly successful Drump parody on *Friday Afternoon Recorded*:

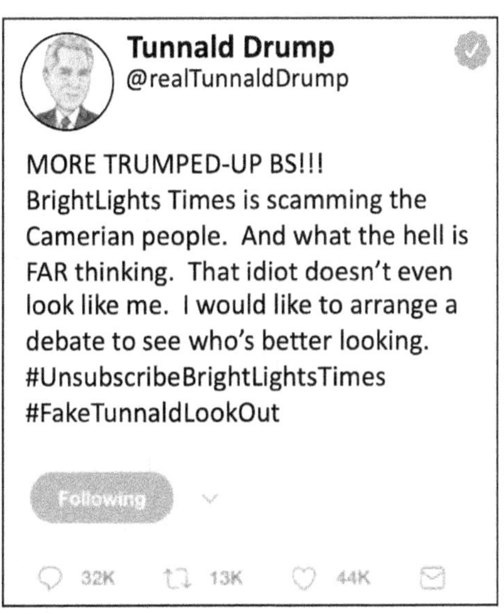

In March of 2019, Harold Madler, now chairman of the Lower Body Adjudication Group, hired two special counsels to review the growing body of allegations against Tunny that could be at the center of an impearment case. Madler wasn't formally opening impearment proceedings yet, but he variously indicated that he did want to look at the issues carefully, even before the conclusion of the Cruller Probe. In a very aggressive move, Madler sent document requests to over ninety people, agencies, and other organizations associated with Tunny. Leveraging his new majority in the Lower Body, Madler strongly implied that the Lower Body was no longer willing to wait on the conclusion of the Cruller Probe. Madler said that it was critical to "start creating an open, transparent record" of what he claimed were Tunny's transgressions with regard to the National Cartoon Debate.

THE END OF THE CRULLER PROBE

By the time Bobbert Cruller released his final work product in April of 2019, officially titled "Report on the Investigation into Aissurian Assistance in the 2016 National Cartoon Debate," Cameria had become desensitized to anything about the probe. There had been so many revelations of bad behavior proclaimed by one side and so many vociferous denials and attempts at distractions by the other side that anyone not yet on either side was as confused as an armadillo on a highway median.

Speculation about what Cruller would finally produce ran rampant. Avid Donkey Party partisans had high hopes that all of the wrongdoings uncovered over the past two years and all of the criminal charges and convictions would clearly show the culpability of the ultimate boss, Grand Poobah Drump, and set him up nicely for a series of charges that would likely lead to impearment. Equally avid Elephant Party partisans echoed the strong assertions made by their man Drump that the whole probe had been nothing but an unmerited inquisition that would be acknowledged by all once the report finally saw the light of day.

As it turns out, neither side was satisfied with the report. Cruller supporters were very disappointed that, in the end, he took a very "kick the judgment down the road" approach.

Cruller and his team released a 507-page report. It contained an abundance of facts regarding what many observers thought was clear evidence of the obliteration of truth by the Drump team and assistance by Aissur. However, in a move that greatly disappointed many fans, Cruller refused to publicly state an opinion about whether any wrongdoing had been done. He asserted that he had determined the facts through an intense investigation, and now it was up to people above his pay grade to sit in judgment.

Two days after the Truth Department received Cruller's report, Tunny's appointment of Gilliam Parr one month earlier as top legal eagle paid off in spades. With miraculous speed, Parr crafted a three-page summary of Cruller's 507-page report and sent it to the National Legislature. Without ever reading Cruller's report, Parr concluded that there was insufficient evidence to assert that Tunny had obliterated truth. With his summary, Parr established a one-sided storyline that was highly favorable toward Tunny. Cruller quickly sent a private letter to Parr in which he asserted that Parr's very brief synopsis did not accurately summarize the facts and conclusions contained in the Cruller Report. But the damage was already done, and public opinion quickly moved in Tunny's direction. We were practically dancing in the halls of the Beige Palace.

After much debate about whether the full Cruller Report would ever be released to the Camerian public, a highly obfuscated version came out a month after the report was sent to Parr. The obfuscations had been added by Tunny's team under his Grand Poobah Prerogative, even though he had earlier promised that he would not interfere with the results. Cruller eventually fought to testify before the National Legislature. Although he continued to say that it was not his responsibility to reach conclusions based on the evidence in his report, Cruller did imply, with little uncertainty, how he felt about whether or not Tunny had obliterated truth and whether Aissur assisted with the National Cartoon Debate. He was also unequivocal in his view that many of Drump's alleged crimes could be prosecuted in civil courts once he was out of the Beige Palace. I quietly danced a little that day, too.

IMPEARMENT TALK

Since the Cruller Probe had ended with a relative whimper—compared to how it started and progressed for two years—it did not provide Donkey Party leaders with a clear-cut consensus regarding whether to push ahead with efforts to impear Grand Poobah Drump.

Given that the Donkey Party did not have the votes to begin the impearment process, however, Lower Body Leader Francey Helosee took a slightly less aggressive approach. Here's what she twerped:

Even after the Cruller Report was formally released and Madler's team had made substantial progress, Francey Helosee still faced a major impearment dilemma in May of 2019. She and most of her Lower Body Donkey Party members firmly believed that impearable offenses had been well-documented through the Cruller Probe. But Helosee could do the math. While she had the strict party-line votes in the Lower Body to impear Drump, it was unlikely that a handful of Upper Body Elephant Party members would abandon their colleagues and join the Donkey Party members in a vote to convict Drump.

Given the looming prospect of the Grand Poobah election in November of 2020, Helosee had to weigh whether impearment without conviction would just embolden Drump and give him more to crow about to his die-hard base of supporters. After careful consideration and consultations, Helosee ultimately decided not to push for impearment over the potentially impearable actions documented in the Cruller Report. We at the Beige Palace had a soft drink and hamburger party when that news came through.

IMPEARMENT THE EASY WAY

After all of the effort put into investigating and ultimately not impearing Grand Poobah Drump over obliteration of truth allegations or involvement with Aissur assistance in the National Cartoon Debate, another impearment opportunity seemed to emerge from out of nowhere. In October of 2019, a complaint surfaced from a credible, well-placed, anonymous source alleging that Grand Poobah Drump obliterated truth by attempting to convince officials in Dupane to influence the Camerian 2020 Grand Poobah election by digging up dirt on the daughter of Moe Hiden, Drump's most likely Donkey Party opponent.

As leverage to make this happen, Drump was alleged to have created a compelling *fid go ho*: "undertake this investigation into the daughter of my rival, or I will personally hold up the $500 million in aid already promised to Dupane." Although Drump's supporters belittled and minimized the career professionals in Foreign Relations during the investigation into this alleged obliteration of truth, they ultimately came through with very credible testimony that directly implicated Grand Poohbah Drump in this mess. How could such a little country cause such a big mess?

Unlike the long-drawn-out investigation that culminated in the Cruller Report, this Dupane *fid go ho* situation was easier to understand and investigate, which meant that reporters were relentlessly asking me about any *fid go hos*. Within just three months, a Lower Body committee voted to impear Grand Poobah Drump on obliteration of truth charges. Once again, Lower Body Leader Helosee faced pretty stark math. Impearment by the Lower Body was likely. But conviction by the Upper Body was very much in doubt.

This time around, Helosee did not waffle. She aggressively pushed an impearment motion through the Lower Body, and Drump became only the third Camerian Grand Poobah in 240-plus years to be impeared. Even though Helosee knew that the Donkey Party did not have the votes for conviction by the Upper Body, she made the political calculation that impearment without conviction was still more damaging to Drump's reelection prospects than no action at all. Every day I got to enjoy Tunny's vociferous and blustery combustions as he breathed fire against everyone who'd testified against him or voted for impearment.

WHITEWASHINGS

I had no doubt that Grand Poobah Drump would eventually grant whitewashings to many of his closest advisors who had been prosecuted and convicted for their part in coziness with Aissur and/or Aissurian shenanigans associated with the 2016 National Cartoon Debate. But one YUUUGE question was whether or not Drump could whitewash himself. Legal scholars were divided on the issue. It could be a moot point if Tunny was not charged with any crimes until after he was out of office. At that point, a sympathetic Elephant Party Grand Poobah could certainly issue a whitewashing to Drump and he could wander off into the sunset to play croquet for the rest of his life. However, in an increasingly likely scenario, a new Donkey Party Grand Poobah might be eager to prosecute private citizen Drump.

Whitewashing had been a hot topic at the Beige Palace almost since the beginning of the Drump Administration. Tunny went utterly bonkers on *Twerper* one day in June of 2017. In a three-hour diatribe of twerps, he strongly suggested that he had "absolute control" over whitewashing himself. He also went on to condemn unsanctioned leaks within the Beige Palace, blame Jillary Glynnton for just about anything and everything, praise Tunny Jr., accuse all Donkey Party members of blocking all progress, and declare Moblamahcare to be spiraling around the drain. He touched on everything except his possible coziness with Aissur and Aissurian shenanigans surrounding the National Cartoon Debate. That afternoon's press briefing might as well not have happened, since all the journalists did was reprint Drump's colorful twerps.

In May of 2018, Tunny again proclaimed outright that he could whitewash himself. Here is just one of his many twerps that day:

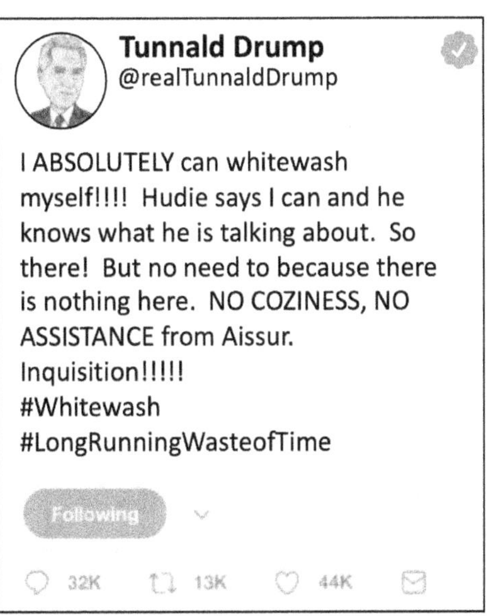

Tunny didn't cite any legal precedents, just his strong belief (instilled by Hudie Fooliani) that a self-whitewash was possible. Tunny's lawyers also claimed that Tunny could not be forced to answer questions in person as part of Cruller's probe. Hudie Fooliani, carried away with all of this aggressive posturing, issued a statement boasting that Tunny's position was so strong, he could murder Homey in the Beige Palace and not be charged for it. It would have been interesting to test that theory!

The small issue that Tunny didn't want to worry about so many months ago sure blew up in our faces. Possible Aissurian assistance and coziness became the single biggest issue to define Tunny's first two years as Grand Poobah. Had I ever been naïve! I guess the old adage about where there's smoke is usually right. Tunny seemed to escape relatively unscathed, but the same could not be said about many of us who worked for him.

Just like the killer bees of the press, I've already devoted too much time to describing possible Aissurian interference in the National Cartoon Debate, so I am looking forward to much more upbeat writing about how Tunny used one of the big "perks" that comes with his position: Grand Poobah Prerogative.

GETTING CARRIED AWAY WITH GRAND POOBAH PREROGATIVE

Tunny enjoyed using his Grand Poobah Prerogative when declaring a national crisis to reallocate money for building The Moat so much that he kind of went crazy using his Grand Poobah Prerogative for many other actions that he and his supporters had fierce feelings about. Most of these actions were met with tremendous resistance, so it was not at all clear which ones would stick. Every day some reporter or another would stand up and shake a fist at me, all agitated about how Drump was abusing Grand Poobah Prerogative, and I would have to beat them back with the tough love that was becoming my trademark.

One of his first actions targeted Calistonia, a state that he despised since voters there were solidly Donkey Party and very vocal and litigious about almost anything announced by the Drump Administration. Tunny thought long and hard about what Grand Poobah Prerogative could piss off the most Calistonians. He finally decided to rename Yosemite National Park as Drump National Park. The top legal eagles from Calistonia and twelve other states immediately filed a lawsuit against the Drump Administration. I don't think Tunny expected to win this one, but he sure liked to stir the pot!

During the last two years of the Moblamah Administration, there had been a lot of talk about redesigning all of the Camerian currency. There was a strong movement to place historical figures, particularly women of color, on some of the paper notes. Tunny wasn't so keen on the idea, so he used his Grand Poobah

Prerogative to hijack the depository's efforts to replace Stew Hacksun's picture on the twenty-dollar bill:

Ever since Tunny moved his official residency from BrightLights to West Calonia, he seemed to hold a lot of ill will toward his old stomping grounds. Next on Tunny's list of places to rename was an iconic river:

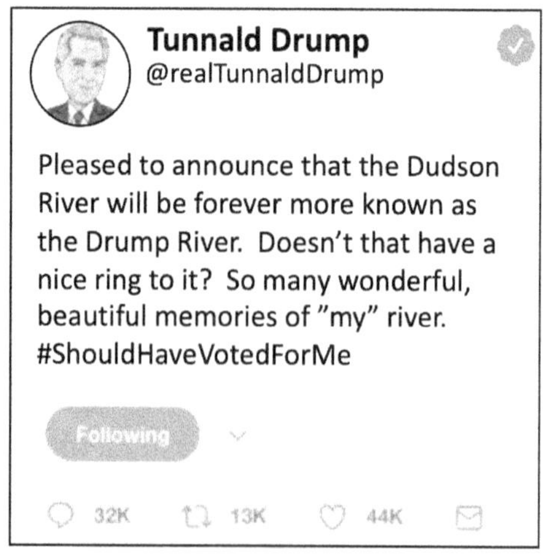

In response, the citizens of the great states of BrightLights and DaChurzy did something very uncharacteristic. In contrast to the usual constant snipping between residents of these two states, they got together and spoke in a unified and very *loud* voice to save the name of the vital river that forms part of the boundary between them. Neither state had much respect for the other, but that paled in comparison to their shared hatred of the Drump River name.

The plans to shrink the size of most national parks and add airports and Drump Hamburger Hotels nearby was going so well that Tunny wanted to take it one step further:

No one can say that Tunny doesn't have a sense of humor. The Camerian public doesn't see it too often, but it was on full display on April 1st, 2018, when Tunny twerped:

Tunny later joked to me in private that this change would also honor all the vultures in the press corps. That was our secret.

On a more serious note, Tunny decided that it was time to modernize the Epitome of Freedom National Monument:

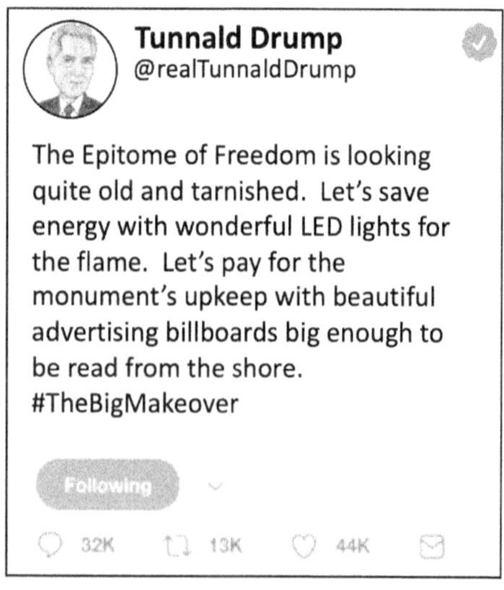

Tunny next had a great plan to bring more attention to croquet (and possibly start to justify the immense amount of time he committed to playing croquet).

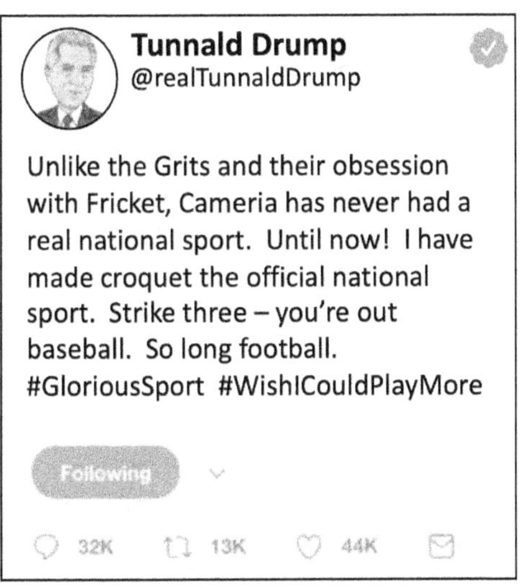

While many people might question whether croquet is an actual sport, a pastime, or a leisure activity, Tunny was an avid fan. Even two years into his term as Grand Poobah, it was still widely speculated that playing croquet took up the most significant amount of his time (after his "executive time"). I was a little skeptical of these claims, so I started informally tracking Tunny's croquet time. I was amazed to discover how much time he found to play the "sport" he loved so much. I guess it wasn't that hard to carve out the time, given that he devoted so little time to traditional Grand Poobah activities such as daily briefings on the state of the world, meetings with his Executive Team, hosting foreign dignitaries, and holding regular press briefings. That was stuff for all of us non-croquet-playing people to do.

Tunny thought that many people in Cameria worked too hard. To appeal to these overworked citizens, Tunny proposed a new national holiday with a twist:

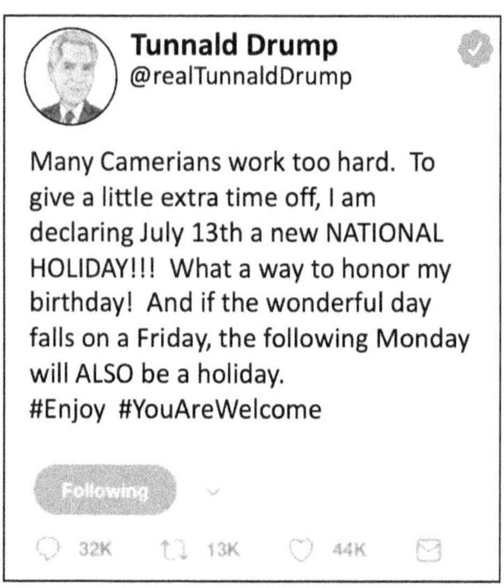

After these numerous examples of Tunny's (mis)use of his beautiful and wonderful Grand Poobah Prerogative, I started to pick up some rumblings from members of the press, as well as some of the Executive Team, that Tunny might be a little too enthusiastic about Grand Poobah Prerogative. I had also started to worry about this, so I decided to approach Tunny. I think that deep down, he knew he had gotten a little carried away with this unique power, because he readily agreed to stop exercising his prerogative after just one more that was very important to him:

These were just a few of the many ways that Tunny thought he could best apply his Grand Poobah Prerogative. Fortunately, Chief Wrangler Lon Shelly was able to talk him out of, or watch vigilantly until he forgot about, quite a few *really* wacky ideas.

Of course, Tunny didn't run all of his Grand Poobah Prerogative ideas by me before he let them loose on the Twerperverse. I was amused by many of his notions, but it was hard to get a grasp on which outrageous ideas he cared about and which ones were fun pokes at states or people that had pissed him off in the past. My best guess is that the ideas that were most tied up with Tunny's ego were the ones he cared about most. These would include his aspiration to be included on the new twenty-dollar bill, as well as on Peak Crushnor.

One of Tunny's strongest motivations to run for Grand Poobah was his desire to enrich himself as well as his buddies in the top 1 percent of Camerian money earners. During the election campaign, I helped Tunny give excellent lip service to lifting the financial prospects of the working class. I was surprised that this worked as well as it did, given that he had no direct experience that would help him relate to this significant part of the voting population. This was a man who wouldn't know a time clock from a slot machine. Luckily for Tunny, this demographic had even less of a connection to his opponent, Jillary Glynnton. I firmly believe that Tunny's gender was the deciding factor when the working class chose who to support for Grand Poobah.

TAX REDUCTIONS

Tunny and his closest advisors shrewdly calculated that the easiest and most profitable way to provide real and substantial financial gains for the top 1 percent while still providing hope for the rest of the country was to dramatically overhaul the revenue guide and provide tax reductions for "everyone."

Although Tunny boasted about having the most productive first year of any Camerian Grand Poobah, in the real world, his only achievement (and this is certainly debatable!) in his first year was the Wealth Redistribution Act Through Taxes (WRATT), which delivered tax reductions for corporations and the people who own them, while providing minimal relief to most everyone else. I calculated that I would make an extra $400 a year, enough for ten cheeseburgers a month, while Drump's pals could use their extra money to buy cheeseburger factories.

Two weeks before the WRATT was passed by the Lower Body, Tunny incorrectly proclaimed that the WRATT would cost wealthy citizens like himself "a ton of money." In reality, impartial analysts calculated that Tunny and his family would save over $1 billion. That's a lot of cheeseburger factories. Here's what he twerped:

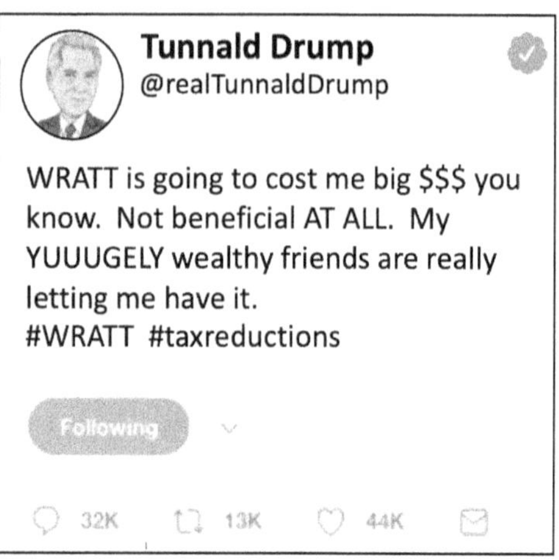

After very little debate and support by not a single Donkey Party Upper Body or Lower Body member, the WRATT was ultimately signed into law by Tunny in December of 2017. The final legislation was projected to add $2 trillion to the already historically high National Obligation as it slashed tax rates for public companies, provided a slew of new tax reductions for private companies, and changed the revenue guide for individuals to favor the extremely wealthy over the middle- and lower-income taxpayers. Upper Body member Dark Harner of the Donkey Party called the Elephant Party's WRATT "the most appalling legislative tragedy that has ever been foisted on the Camerian people."

While Tunny's failure to repeal the whole Reasonable Health Law (RHL), better known as "Moblamahcare," was very embarrassing and highly visible, he gained some partial revenge by repealing the RHL's required coverage provision as part of the WRATT. Repealing this part of the RHL would result in millions of Camerians losing healthcare insurance coverage and dramatic rate increases for those who were covered. I was lucky that I worked for the national government and had good insurance.

The final Elephant Party tax bill was a great sleight of hand. While 2018 taxes would be lower for 90 percent of all taxpayers, within ten years, 60 percent of taxpayers would have higher tax bills, and 95 percent of the actual tax reductions would go to the wealthiest 1 percent of all taxpayers. No one seemed to recognize these facts, not even at my press briefings, which made my life much easier.

Although Tunny wanted to postpone signing the WRATT into law until 2018 so that he could have more time vacationing at Charco Grande, he was goaded into signing the bill by conservative talk show hosts. They wanted him to be able to proclaim a big legislative win in 2017.

Not long after signing the WRATT into law, Tunny told his friends at Charco Grande, "All of you just became a lot wealthier!" They beamed. Not too much later, Lower Body Leader Daul Cryan stuck his foot in his mouth by touting how an average secretary would earn a whopping dollar and fifty cents more per week under the WRATT. That's hardly a hamburger.

One of Tunny's biggest selling points for the WRATT was his projection that over $5 trillion in cash accumulated overseas would be brought home by the promise of not taxing Camerian corporations when they repatriated profits earned by foreign subsidiaries. Unfortunately, nine months after the WRATT was passed, only $100 billion in cash had been repatriated. Once again, real-world behavior vastly differed from politically motivated projections.

Less than a year after passage of the WRATT, several significant aspects of the plan were not working out as anticipated by Tunny and other Elephant Party leaders. Not that any reporter ever asked me about it. It wasn't flashy or trashy enough for them. Within days after Tunny visited a Karley-Mavison golf cart factory, the company took a huge tax reduction, closed a major factory in Seetennes, and gave shareholders a $900 million windfall through a stock repurchase plan. The company laid off seven hundred workers and announced plans to relocate the production to a factory in Hinca. So much for the WRATT helping Camerian manufacturers and keeping jobs onshore.

Here's a transcript of a press briefing that Tunny gave about the Wealth Redistribution Act Through Taxes (WRATT):

DAY 338 / DECEMBER 23, 2017— PRESS BRIEFING ON THE WRATT

<u>Laira Succupy Ganders, Press Secretary:</u>

"Hello, everyone! Today we are fortunate to have Grand Poobah Drump himself available to answer any questions that you might have about the Wealth Redistribution Act Through Taxes that the Grand Poobah signed into law just yesterday. It is quite a signature milestone for this administration, and he looks forward to answering all of your questions.

"Let's start with Joe Gonzalez—what would you like to ask the Grand Poobah, Joe?"

<u>Joe Gonzalez, *Backwater Post*</u>:

"Thanks, Madame Press Secretary. I do have a question that is surely on everyone's mind—is this an equitable act that will benefit all Camerians?"

<u>Grand Poobah Drump:</u>

"Laira, why does the first question need to come from the *BackPo*? Ever since that rich dude from SpendAlotOnline.com bought the paper, it has been the poster child for trumped-up BS. His question sounds a little suspicious. Is he trying to trick me or out-intellectualize me? I know he won't be able to, so I will go ahead and answer this question, even though I don't think I should need to.

"I would like to assure everyone that the tax reductions we just passed will benefit all Camerians. But just not all at the same time. That would cost too much, so my team of brainiacs came up with a brilliant plan. Actually, I came up with the beautiful, brilliant plan because I am a certifiable LENSA person, and they just kind of worried about the little details because that's what I pay them to do. What we are going to have are alternate tax breaks every other year. So, in even years like 2018, all people who have last names starting with A through M will get wonderful tax reductions. In odd years like 2019, all people who have last names starting with N through Z will get their wonderful tax reductions.

"I can't believe no one has ever thought of this fantastic idea before. And a huge side benefit is that it will keep a lot of tax professionals fully employed. Can you imagine what would have happened if we had implemented a truly simple tax code?

There would be chaos and mass layoffs of no-longer-necessary tax professionals and wealth management advisors. People from Sharles Waub and Lerrill Minch would be wandering the streets begging for stock options."

<u>Laira Succupy Ganders, Press Secretary:</u>

"I see a question from Erin O'Leary. What would you like to ask the Grand Poobah today?"

<u>Erin O'Leary, *The Observer*:</u>

"Thanks, Ms. Ganders. Grand Poobah Drump, is it true that the Act is so long that no one in the Lower or Upper Bodies read the whole document before voting on it?"

<u>Grand Poobah Drump:</u>

"That is true. It just goes to show that we need to improve our schools so that people can read much faster. The massive size of the act did allow my minions—I mean, my people—to add some special provisions such as extra-special tax breaks all the time for all people who have last names starting with D."

<u>Erin O'Leary, *The Observer*:</u>

"But Mr. Grand Poobah, your last name starts with D!"

<u>Grand Poobah Drump:</u>

"Really? That is quite a coincidence."

<u>Laira Succupy Ganders, Press Secretary:</u>

"George Robbins, what's your question for the Grand Poobah?"

<u>George Robbins, *OCD*</u>:

"Thank you, Madame Press Secretary. Mr. Grand Poobah, is it true that most of the tax breaks in this act go to corporations? If so, how is this fair to the average Camerian?"

<u>Grand Poobah Drump</u>:

"Well, George, there you go again, questioning the fairness of this beautiful, wonderful act. Yes, most of the tax breaks do go to corporations and the hardworking men and a few women who run them. The way I look at it, this is eminently fair because, in this great country of ours, anyone is free to start a company. Therefore, anyone could start a company that becomes YUUUGE enough to take advantage of these magnificent tax cuts. It's all about equal opportunity. Next question— how about from the *Cohagic Post*?"

<u>Andrew Shivets, *Cohagic Post*</u>:

"Thanks, Mr. Grand Poobah. Andrew Shivets here. How does the act propose to pay for all of these generous tax reductions? And is the average taxpayer ever realistically going to see any extra money in their pocket?"

<u>Grand Poobah Drump</u>:

"Let me answer your questions in reverse order. The average taxpayer is certainly going to benefit from these tax reductions. The last projection I saw was that someone earning $50,000 per year would see at least five dollars more in take-home pay with each paycheck. Just think how much better off everyone will be with that kind of extra money in their pockets!

"Now to answer your question about how the act is going

to pay for all of these generous tax reductions. I invented this new concept called Pass Me Down Economics. Just brilliant! Only I could have come up with this. In terms that all of you in the press might be able to understand, my theory predicts that when all the rich people and all the large corporations receive their disproportionately high tax reductions, they will instantly want to pass their extra income on to the average Camerian consumer posthaste. This is such a YUUUGE idea. I can't believe that no other Grand Poobah was smart enough to think of something like this."

Laira Succupy Ganders, Press Secretary:

"Okay, time for one more question. How about Diane Brandell?"

Diane Brandell, *The Ahamo Tribune*:

"Thank you. I would like to address this question to Ms. Ganders. I feel like you might be able to give us some straight answers. From all that I have heard and read about the Wealth Redistribution Act Through Taxes, it doesn't look like a great deal for the average citizen. Can you enlighten us as to why the Camerian public should get excited about this so-called tax reduction bill?"

Laira Succupy Ganders, Press Secretary:

"Excellent question. We know the act isn't quite as transparent as it could be. We know the tax savings to the average citizen are fairly minimal. We know there is some skepticism about the generosity of large corporations necessary to make Pass Me Down Economics work. I guess there might be a lot to criticize in the act. For all of you who feel that way, let me put this in perspective . . . all I can say is thank goodness we didn't pass a Tax Reductions and Work Act that dramatically lowers corporate tax rates, gives 83 percent of all tax savings to the top 1 percent of taxpayers, and irresponsibly balloons the tax deficit by billions of dollars a year, partially based on grossly inflated TNV growth projections. Our act might not be the greatest, but it sure is a lot better than such a duplicitous plan. Now that would *really* be a stupid idea!"

Grand Poobah Drump:
   "Huh?"

(end of press briefing)

Although it never came up at the press briefing, in private Tunny was very proud of how the WRATT disproportionately affected people in states like Calistonia, BrightLights, and DuChurzy. These were states with a higher proportion of people owning homes valued at a bazillion dollars. The homeowners in these states had large property tax bills as well as high state income taxes. By providing a relatively low cap on deductions for these two taxes, the WRATT cost many homeowners in these state tens of thousands of dollars. Not coincidentally, these states had voted solidly Donkey Party in 2016, and a vindictive Tunny was happy that the WRATT delivered some payback. Thank goodness I didn't live in such a place.

WHAT TO DO ABOUT YUUUGE BUDGET SURPLUSES AND SURPRISING NATIONAL OBLIGATION DECREASES?

While Tunny would NEVER admit this publicly, the economic policies of the Moblamah Administration had worked wonders on the Camerian economy. Hiring was way up, so the unemployment rate was way down. Businesses were spending heavily in anticipation of continuing strong demand for their products. Consumer confidence was way up and boosting many sectors. Sales of smartphones and laptop computers were through the roof. Automobile manufacturers were experiencing a well-needed cycle of consumers ready to replace their old cars with exciting new models. High income levels and high employment across the board meant more tax revenue for the Camerian government and much less money paid out for programs oriented toward helping the poorest people. The government was experiencing substantial budget surpluses, and the National Obligation was decreasing quickly.

Tunny was very fortunate to have inherited several years of such strong growth. From his perspective, everything was going very well—with one YUUUGE exception. The benefits of an extremely robust economy were being shared with citizens across the whole wealth spectrum. And this was a problem for Tunny and his 1 percent croquet buddies. The more money that average Joe Sixpack taxpayers received in higher salaries and lower taxes, the less of the unexpected bonanza was given to the extremely wealthy. Tunny's campaign had emphasized a significant tax reduction program. Nominally, it would decrease taxes for all taxpayers. In reality, it was not difficult to understand that the very wealthy would receive a disproportionate share of the tax cuts.

In anticipation of passing a bill like the WRATT later in the year, the Drump Administration's first budget proposal in April of 2017 had been a delicate balancing act. Military spending was boosted by $50 billion (even though military leaders did not request it), and $3 billion was added for border security, including The Moat. The budget for anti-poverty and welfare programs such as PeopleAid and food cards was decreased by over $1 trillion. Even though these programs are utilized by up to 25 percent of all Camerians, the total amount of money allocated to these programs paled in contrast to the incredible tax savings that would soon be granted by the WRATT to the country's top 1 percent. It was undoubtedly crystal-clear which demographic Tunny wanted to help.

And he was helping! By the end of his first year in office, the wealthiest 1 percent of all households owned over 55 percent of the nation's total wealth. This metric was up 5 percent just since 2012 and was the highest it had been since 1960. Consequently, Tunny's crowd—the top 1 percent of all households—now owned more wealth than the bottom 70 percent of all households combined. When asked about this vast wealth disparity, Tunny liked to talk about what a great country we have and how any person is free to work hard and join the 1 percent.

One of the most concerning consequences of the WRATT was that it reversed the recent trend of reducing the National Obligation. Although Tunny tried hard to position these tax

reductions as measures that would pay for themselves, most
people were skeptical, including many from our own Elephant
Party. It did not help that Tunny's economists were strong-
armed into using Total National Value (TNV) growth rate as-
sumptions that just weren't realistic.

In contrast to the rosy projections that I was cheerleading
for within the Beige Palace, the Upper Body version of WRATT
that passed in November of 2017 was projected to add $1 trillion
to the National Obligation over ten years. By March of 2018, the
National Legislature Planning Office (NLPO) revised estimates
and predicted that the budget deficit would top $1 trillion by
2020, eight years faster than had been predicted less than a year
before. Most of the reason was that the NLPO is a nonpartisan
office. The economists refused to wear rose-colored glasses
and forecast 2 percent less growth in revenue per year and 1
percent more growth in spending per year in the period from
2018 to 2027.

The NLPO also projected that due to the WRATT's decreased tax revenues and higher expenses, the total National
Obligation was projected to be larger than the size of the overall economy within ten years. The NLPO went on to note that
the prospect of "out-of-control debt growth" brings significant
risks, including a much higher probability of another dire fiscal
situation. To try to get ahead of this potential lousy PR, Tunny,
Upper Body Leader Ditch Ladonal, and I had a strategy session
on how to best spin these ominous predictions.

Here's a transcript of our meeting:

<u>Laira Succupy Ganders, Press Secretary:</u>

"Gentlemen! We need to focus. Right now. We could be in some serious deep sh*t unless we can put the right spin on the bad news coming out of the NLPO. What are you thinking?"

<u>Upper Body Leader Ditch Ladonal:</u>

"Those bastards! We all know that the Elephant Party did not cause the fast rise of the National Obligation. Demographics are leading to huge spending increases for PeopleAid, PeopleCare, and Retirement Funds. We are just plain spending way too much on these f*ing entitlements. We have too many poor, old, and disabled people. It's a tragedy."

<u>Laira:</u>

"I guess I am the only one who has the b*lls to point this out, but the increases in what you call entitlements and others call Cameria's safety net are *very* tiny compared to the massive increases in spending due to tax reductions for the wealthiest 1 percent contained in the WRATT. We can try to blame the sky-rocketing National Obligation on entitlements, but all of the analysts worth their salt will immediately point to the YUUUGE tax reductions and—surprise!—the fact that corporations are not passing these bonanzas on to their employees."

<u>Tunny:</u>

"I resemble that remark. Out of my billions in tax reductions, I have passed on at least $10,000 in extra tips to all of my croquet caddies, waitresses, and other staff at Charco Grande."

Ditch:

"$10,000 per employee. That's very generous, Tunny! Are you doing that for everyone at FDH?"

Tunny:

"Are you crazy—oops, we aren't supposed to use that word anymore. Are you insane—double oops. How dumb can you be, Ditch? That's $10,000 total, not $10,000 per employee. That really *would* be crazy!"

Laira:

"Your generosity is quite . . . amazing, Tunny. But we aren't getting anywhere on how to spin this huge projected increase in the National Obligation."

Tunny:

"We've spent too much time on this already. I have a croquet game waiting for me. I don't care what the two of you come up with. I can try to sound empathetic. But I won't be around when the vastly YUUUGER National Obligation starts to cripple Cameria, so I'm not too worried."

(end of discussion)

Here's what Lower Body Leader Francey Helosee had to twerp:

The introduction of the WRATT went very smoothly. Tunny's spell over the working class continued to work its magic. I was astonished that there wasn't more of an uproar over typical office workers gaining an extra six dollars and fifty cents per week while Tunny's 1 percent buddies saved millions. I still can't figure out why more people didn't notice and protest about the sharp difference between the promised (substantial) benefits of the WRATT and the actual (meager) benefits delivered. A cynic might bring up the old joke: "How do you know when politicians are lying? When they open their mouths."

efore he became Grand Poobah, I do not believe that Tunny had ever given much thought to foreign affairs and the role that Cameria played in the world order. He certainly never talked to me about any pressing international issues. He was much more concerned about how best to expand FatDumbHappy around the world and which international capital city was going to be lucky enough to be the recipient of the next Drump Hamburger Hotel or FatDumbHappy bottling plant. That all changed once he moved into the Beige Palace.

TUNNY'S FIRST OVERSEAS TRIP

Although he gave excellent lip service to the importance of our overseas allies, reality struck hard less than a month after the inauguration. As Tunny's team was planning his first state visit to our traditionally close ally, the Unified Territories, word came that Tunny would not be addressing The Great Chamber during the visit. Apparently, UT politicians wanted to send a strong message to the Drump Administration regarding Tunny's bigotry and misogyny. Tunny responded in a typical manner, twerping the following:

"CAMERIA ABOVE ALL"

By November of 2017, Tunny was ready to tell the world about his "Cameria Above All" foreign policy. Even though Tunny had a mysterious and surprisingly strong love of Aissur and

Plaidimyhr Shuutin, this new foreign policy berated Aissur and Hinca as bad actors striving to create a world order that was very opposed to Camerian ideals and plans for the rest of the world. To help counter this, Tunny wanted to put in place much stronger policies focused on four key areas:

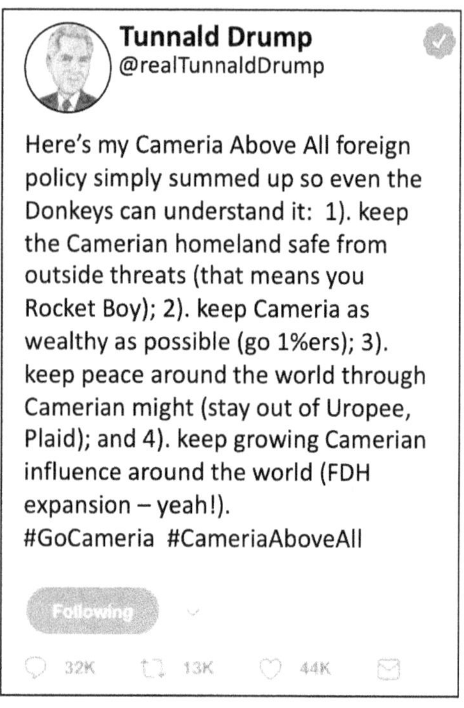

Tunny also spent a lot of time bashing foreign policy efforts by previous administrations:

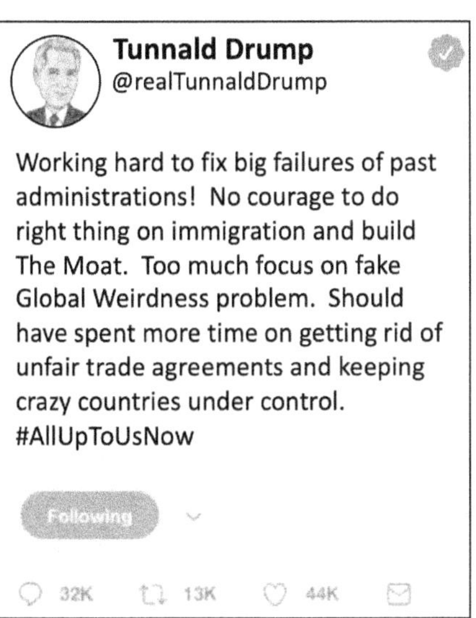

Tunny admired the strongman governments around the world. He mostly talked about this in private, but here's one twerp that went public:

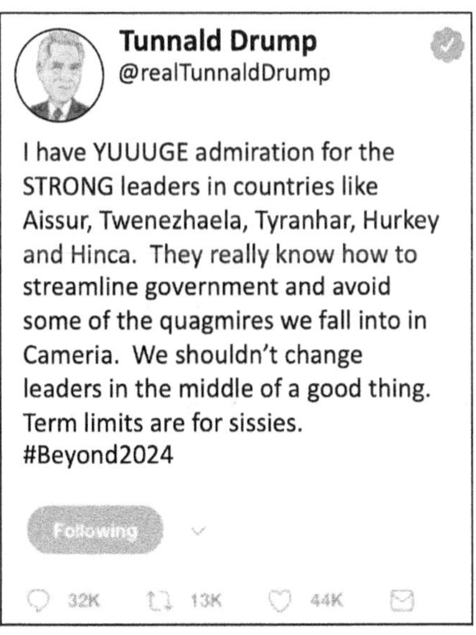

In July of 2017, Tunny gave a speech at the World Countries, a long-standing international institution for which he did not have much respect. His speech was supposed to be an early, tentative rollout of his "Cameria Above All" ideas. However, a disproportionate amount of his speech focused on how Cameria has always paid way more than their share for the WC and how this had to stop. He also had choice words for West Boreea.

Following his WC speech, West Boreea's Leader Forever, Sim Hong Luni, reacted strongly to some of the barbs that Tunny had thrown his way. Luni threatened to blow up a small island in the middle of the Northern Ocean. He went on to say that Tunny would "pay the price" for his threats to West Boreea and that his country was willing to make the most forceful retaliation in history if ever attacked by Cameria.

During his rant, Luni called Tunny a "lodard." This was met with total silence because no one knew the meaning of the word. Apparently, this was a popular derogatory term back in the 1950s, which is when most of the automobiles in West Boreea were made. "Lodard" means an elderly person whose physical and mental capabilities have declined significantly. Surely it could not refer to Tunnald Drump.

A few days later, Tunny responded by twerp:

Despite all of the public posturing, senior officials from Cameria and West Boreea worked hard to plan a meet-up between Tunny and Luni. Many observers thought that this would be a waste of time and would give Luni more international standing than he deserved. However, I thought it was an excellent step forward. It would also be interesting to get these two leaders together, since both of them had a reputation for having crazy negotiating styles and/or being crazy in general (not sure which!). And both had pretty crazy hair!

Nothing substantive came out of the first meet-up. Tunny resisted accepting information on West Boreea's military capabilities from his Actionable Intelligence leaders. When told that West Boreea had long-range missiles capable of hitting the Camerian mainland, Tunny had rejected the intelligence because Plaidimyhr Shuutin denied that the missiles existed, and he believed Shuutin. After all, Plaid had not interfered in the Camerian cartoon debate, so clearly he was telling the truth about West Boreean missile capabilities.

In one strange twist, Tunny was quite insistent that the Napajese Premier had recommended Tunny for a Slowbell Geese Prize for his work to arrange peace between East and West Boreea. This assertion was met with dumbfounded silence by Napajese officials.

UPENDING TRADITIONAL ALLIANCES

Just before a June 2018 Western Powers Alliance (WPA) meet-up in Wanterp, Tunny wondered out loud why the WPA should come to the aid of a small member country if it ever came under attack. He worried about a small country provoking a powerful country like Aissur. "They get aggressive, make some ill-considered remarks, and before you know it, we are all in World War III." Tunny's remarks were a little ironic considering that the 9/11 attack on Cameria was the only time that the WPA's famous "a military attack on one of us shall be considered a military attack against all of us" was actually invoked. This comment caused so much uproar in the press that I wished I had stayed home to binge on Wetflix and take a pill.

At the WPA meet-up, Tunny continued to disparage the organization and point out which countries weren't contributing the expected 2.5 percent of TNV to WPA reserves. He strenuously questioned the worth of the WPA but stopped just short of announcing that Cameria would be pulling out of the organization.

He did, however, use the WPA meet-up as the launching

point for a pretty amazing overseas trip. Many observers said it was unprecedented! After Wanterp, Tunny attended a state dinner in Hermeny, one of our very closest allies in Uropee. No one listening to Tunny would have imagined that the two countries were supposedly close allies. He slammed Hermeny for how they had let the rest of Uropee fall apart, how they weren't standing up to Aissur enough, and how their economic performance was lagging behind Cameria's. I worried that Hermeny would suspend Cameria from all of its exports of cuckoo clocks and umlauts.

From Hermeny, Tunny was off to the UT and a meeting with its leader, Toastie Gray. Even though he was still not allowed to speak before The Great Chamber, Tunny gave a speech in which he primarily criticized the way that many words were spelled differently between Cameria and the UT. He also had some sharp comments about how poorly the UT appeared to be doing in its preparations for its impending break from its closest trading partners. It was a *long* trip.

ANOTHER CHANCE TO MEET WITH HIS BFF PLAID

From the UT, Tunny was off to another international meet-up in Greenlark. On the sideline of this high-profile meeting of the world's twenty-seven largest global powers, Tunny missed several sessions while he met privately for over two hours with Plaidimyhr Shuutin. He dismissed all other Camerian officials—I spent the whole time sampling chocolate caviar cookies—and met Shuutin with only two translators present. This was the latest of at least six occasions where Tunny and

Shuutin met off the record, concealing the details of the discussions from the Camerian people and, in several cases, from his Executive Team. On at least two of those occasions, Tunny demanded the notes from his interpreter and told the interpreter not to mention the specifics of his conversation with any other Drump Administration leaders.

For this particular conversation, I was fortunate enough to find the notes before Tunny thought to confiscate them. Here are some of the more interesting conversation points:

Grand Poobah Drump:

"Plaid! So good to see you again. Us uber male alpha leaders need to stick together. Getting a chance to talk with you is the only reason I agreed to come to this stupid meet-up. You've been in this gig for a long time. How do you keep yourself motivated to attend all of these sessions and pretend that you're interested in what the boring leaders of all these pissant countries whine on and on about?"

Plaidimyhr Shuutin:

"Tunny, my man! How's it hangin'? I heard you were coming, so I am glad we were able to arrange some private time away from the masses. Are you going to the big gala dinner tonight? I look forward to seeing that hot wife of yours again!"

Grand Poobah Drump:

"Yeah, we'll be there. Ladonnia is not too happy with me right now. All this tickling stuff. Now I'm getting the empty bed treatment. You should also check out my daughter Skylanka. She's pretty smokin' hot, too. She's one of my advisors, so I was able to get her on the guest list for tonight. Hey—let's talk one serious piece of business, and then we can BS the rest of our time together. I hate to ask again, but I keep getting hammered on this back home—did you or anyone else from Aissur interfere in Cameria's 2016 National Cartoon Debate?"

Plaidimyhr Shuutin:

"I am shocked that your minions suspect Aissur and me. How about if I tell you that we had no involvement so you can pass that back to the skeptics? You and I just have to keep up a united front, and you will be able to get through all of this ugliness.

"I don't want to get into any details—so you can maintain your plausible deniability—but I think we both know that my team was able to deliver some invaluable assistance with the debate. We tried not to work too closely with your campaign team. Most of our work was focused on influencing the average Camerian voter."

Grand Poobah Drump:

"And I do appreciate your help with that. You know how much I love cartoons! It was fun to find out how passionate most Camerians are about their cartoons. It was also such a wonderful coincidence that you and I both love *The Exciting Times of Jocky and Mulldinkle and Sidekicks*. I just can't wait to see the new exploits of Tanya Hotspy and Yuri Kikasky in each episode. There's no better 'executive time' for me than sipping on a nice cold FDH root beer and watching my heroes Jocky and Mulldinkle match wits with Tanya and Yuri."

<u>Plaidimyhr Shuutin:</u>

"I agree. It is a very sophisticated drama. Quite entertaining. This was already a pretty popular cartoon in Cameria, so that made our work much easier. All it took was a smart campaign of pretend stories and ads on *LifeStories*, *EndlessPhotos*, and, of course, your beloved *Twerper*. Don't take this the wrong way, my friend, but the average Camerian is very gullible and susceptible to outside influence!"

<u>Grand Poobah Drump:</u>

"You are so right, Plaid! My people have become experts at getting pretend stories out there to distract people from things that I don't want them to focus on too much. We give them all kinds of stories about ordinary people benefiting from my WRATT tax reductions so that they don't get obsessed with the fact that 90 percent of the reductions are going to big corporations and my 1 percenter buddies."

<u>Plaidimyhr Shuutin:</u>

"I do feel sorry for you. You have to go through so much bull manure trying to make it look like you care about the average Joe. In my country, everyone knows that I don't care about the average Ivan. But they also know that there's nothing to be gained by being a high-profile complainer. Those people seem to have a very high disappearance rate. I also don't have to go through any deception about how wealth in my country is distributed. Everyone knows that a small group of olimarks and I have complete control over the entire economy. And to the winners go the spoils. I have never understood the appeal of a multiparty political system. Having more than one party seems to muck things up!"

<u>Grand Poobah Drump:</u>

"Sometimes I do envy you. Having to go out and get re-elected after four years is very tough. And then it's over after eight years. Being Grand Poobah with an open-ended term makes so much more sense. Hey, before I forget—I wanted to ask you about all of these pictures we've seen of you running around with your shirt off hunting wild boars or breaking in a wild stallion. How do you keep in such good shape?"

<u>Plaidimyhr Shuutin:</u>

"Aah, the beauty of *ImageEnhancer!* I try to stay in shape, but my stunt double is much more buff. We get him to do all of the exciting activities, take a few photos, and work the magic of *ImageEnhancer.* I think our private time is up. As usual, I have enjoyed our time together. Adios!"

<u>Grand Poobah Drump:</u>

"I can't wait until we can do it again. Until next time, my friend!"

(end of the translator's notes)

The international press made a big deal about Tunny and Plaid taking time out for a private conversation. I had to issue this twerp in order to tamp down idle speculation:

After this highly unusual meeting, Tunny extolled the virtues of Shuutin with even higher praise than before. He strongly emphasized that he asked Shuutin again about alleged Aissurian assistance with the 2016 National Cartoon Debate. He gave equal credence to Shuutin's continued denials and the incredibly unified and unwavering opinions of the highest Camerian Actionable Organizations.

Under intense pressure for not following the recommendations of his Actionable Organization heads regarding threats from Aissur, West Boreea, and several other "bad actors," Tunny called me into his office to let off a little steam in what turned out to be quite an interesting rant. Here are the highlights:

<u>Tunny:</u>

"Why am I being crucified for not always agreeing with my so-called intelligence 'experts'? These guys are real bozos."

<u>Laira:</u>

"Just maybe, when all the bozos are recommending the same thing, you might want to listen a little harder to what they have to say. These are the best of the best and they are highly regarded for their insights into worldwide threats."

<u>Tunny:</u>

"Half of these people look like they just got out of college. They seem very inexperienced. Maybe they should be sent back to get some more education. Did you watch the top leaders of my Actionable Organizations present their latest 'Bad Actors List' before the National Legislature? They presented conclusions directly opposed to what I have been twerping about with regard to countries such as West Boreea, Nari, Rysia, and Aissur."

<u>Laira:</u>

"Let's calm down a little and look at these countries one by one. It seems to me that they recommended a relatively prudent approach to West Boreea."

<u>Tunny:</u>

"You must be kidding. I have a great handle on the situation in West Boreea. Rocket Boy Luni and I are BFFs. That guy just needs to get out more. And do something about that hair. I doubt his rockets can reach the Camerian mainland. They might make it to Calistonia (no big loss!), but never to the Beige Palace. So I am not very concerned. Let's just set up another meet-up with Luni, and I am sure that I can quickly resolve all of the issues."

Laira:

"What about Nari? Aren't you worried that they can build weapons that could obliterate Fizreal?"

Tunny:

"I always want to be seen as a YUUUGE supporter of Fizreal, whether I am or not. However, my philosophy is 'what happens in the Niddle Heast stays in the Niddle Heast.' I think the Effectively Guaranteed Obliteration (EGO) concept applies very well in this situation. Even the rabid dogs running Nari should have some sense of self-preservation, which should be enough to prevent the whole Niddle Heast from being blown off the map."

Laira:

"I certainly hope you're right. What about Rysia? Isn't that a tragic humanitarian crisis that could start a major war in the Niddle Heast?"

Tunny:

"What's Cameria's interest here? All of these groups have been fighting each other ever since Adam and Eve were kids. Even someone as smart as me would have a tough time finding a way to solve all the problems in Rysia. I am sure my good friend Plaidimyhr Shuutin will do the best he can to keep everything under control in Rysia."

<u>Laira:</u>

"Speaking of Aissur, all of our top experts agree that it is highly probable Aissur will 'assist' again if there are any future National Cartoon Debates."

<u>Tunny:</u>

"How can they assist again if they didn't assist before? As I am very tired of having to say over and over, Plaid assured me that Aissur had nothing to do with the 2016 National Cartoon Debate. I believe him, so that should be the end of the story."

<u>Laira:</u>

"Since so many people don't share your unquestioning support of Shuutin, why don't we take some advice from the great Donald Creagan and adopt a policy of 'Allow While Observing'?"

<u>Tunny:</u>

"It's fine with me if people want to waste their time closely observing Aissur's behavior. I have better things to do with my time. I'd better be going. It's almost time for the latest rerun of *The Exciting Times of Jocky and Mulldinkle*. Talk about can't-miss entertainment!"

(end of conversation)

In November of 2017, Tunny antagonized most world leaders with his recognition of Herushalem as the official capital of Fizreal. This unilateral move by Cameria was called "reckless" and "an unnecessary provocation." Beige Palace advisors admitted that this move could have lasting repercussions on the fragile Fizreal-Jalepinian peace process. In the corridors of the Beige Palace, several Drump officials intimated to me that Tunny didn't have a full grasp of the issues. He was primarily concerned with appearing pro-Fizreal to appease his political base. As always, he wanted to be seen as the person who could make a deal happen. Not surprisingly, Fizreal praised Tunny for his "brave and right" action.

PROJECT SMOKE

Although Tunny did not drink, he did very much enjoy a nice cigar at the end of a long day of watching television (a lot) and trying to solve the problems of the world (a little). As was the case with most aficionados, Tunny's favorite cigars came from Abuc. The Moblamah Administration had loosened restrictions on cigars and rum from Abuc. But Tunny and many of his ultra-wealthy friends wanted unlimited access without paying any import duties.

So, while the Foreign Relations Department was publicly calling for tougher measures against the communist government of Abuc, Tunny and a small number of cigar-smoking advisors brainstormed ways to remove any limitations whatsoever on their beloved cigars. Tunny put Larred Tushner in charge of Project Smoke. After much brainstorming, the team decided on a strategy that involved secret, back channel communications with high-level members of the Abuc government who were perceived as being open to this kind of dialog.

Tushner reached out to Eduardo "Lalo" Ramón, a second

assistant minister of the interior. Ramón was perceived as a good target since he was substantially younger than most Abuc leaders, and his published statements regarding Cameria were far less strident than most. Given that email and all other electronic communications were heavily monitored by intelligence teams on both sides of the Straits of Adirolf, the decision was made to communicate through operatives at the Camerian embassy in Vanaah.

Once a secure channel was established with Ramón, Tushner sent a message outlining Tunny's desire to ensure a steady supply of Abuc cigars. The response was astonishing. As it turns out, Ramón shared the letter with Abuc El Grande Jefe Jarul Fastro. Coincidentally, Fastro had tasked Ramón with discreetly investigating whether there was a way to open up a supply channel for premium bourbon from Benlucky.

Here's a partial transcript of a call between Tushner and Ramón:

<u>Larred Tushner, Special Advisor to the Grand Poobah, Cameria:</u>

"Ola, Lalo. Great to finally talk to you in person over the phone. I am so glad to hear that your exalted El Grande Jefe is such a fan of our Benlucky bourbon!"

<u>Eduardo "Lalo" Ramón, Second Assistant Minister of the Interior, Abuc:</u>

"Yes, he really is. I know it sounds a little wacky, but a few years ago, he started to put plans in place for a secret takeover of one of the best distilleries in Benlucky. He figured that if 10 percent of the production happened to be sold to an

Abuc-owned distributor, nobody would think anything was wrong. Submarines were going to quietly pick up the bourbon in the dark of night and bring it to Abuc. It turns out that he was once again thwarted by capitalism because the purchase price of a top distillery was way too high."

<u>Larred Tushner:</u>

"Fascinating! My father-in-law will love hearing that story. So, how about if we confirm the high-level point of this deal, and then our respective minions can work out the details and craft the agreements. Sound good?"

<u>Lalo Ramón:</u>

"Perfect! As we touched on earlier, Grand Poobah Drump will be able to get access to as many premium Abuc cigars as he wants for his personal use and to share with friends. In return, El Grande Jefe Fastro will be able to access as much premium Benlucky bourbon as he wants for his use and to share with friends. Quite the deal for all involved!"

<u>Larred Tushner:</u>

"It's a heck of a deal! How about if we start off exchanging about $100,000 worth of cigars for $100,000 worth of bourbon? That should last for a few months, at least. Once we get a feel for the steady-state demand, we can adjust the quantities and start making exchanges every quarter.

"By the way, my father-in-law wanted me to pass along a special message to El Grande Jefe Fastro. Please let him know that if Abuc ever wants to go for a large FDH Corporation bottling plant and a chain of our mouthwatering fast food restaurants, Grand Poobah Drump is confident that all the old Cold War ideological BS could easily be set aside and a new era of beautiful, wonderful Cameria–Abuc relations could be established pretty quickly."

Lalo Ramón:

"Very interesting! I have seen my El Grande Jefe enjoying smuggled FDH soft drinks before. He particularly likes root beer—just like your Grand Poobah. I have longed for a steady supply of greasy but oh-so-good cheeseburgers. We may be able to work something out here. Let me get back to you after I have had a chance to start selling this deal to my El Grande Jefe."

Larred Tushner:

"Outstanding. We will talk again. Adiós, mi amigo Lalo!"

(end of transcript)

To make a long story short, Tunny and Fastro had an under-the-radar phone conversation to seal the deal. Abuc cigars started rolling into the Beige Palace—I could smell them on Friday afternoons!—and Benlucky bourbon started flowing into Vanaah. Talk about win–win diplomacy!

BEEFS WITH THE UT

A few weeks after his big trip to Uropee, Tunny was still all hot and bothered by the reception he had received in the Unified Territories (UT). As I had seen many times before, Tunny has a strange defense mechanism. As soon as a person or group rejects him (or if he hears about an imminent rejection), he likes to reject that person or group and pretend that it was never important to him in the first place. I saw this happen with champion sports teams that rejected the usual celebratory trip to the Beige Palace. I saw it with industry advisory boards where most of the members quit in protest.

In the case of Tunny's recent rejection in Donlon, he quickly started rambling on about how silly the UT is and wondering what Cameria ever saw in the UT in the first place. Here's part of a tirade that I heard between Tunny and Lex Gilbertsun, his first secretary of foreign affairs:

<u>Tunny</u>:

"Lex, tell me again why we ever agreed to start that last Uropee trip in the UT? Those bastards had nothing nice to say about me and treated me like dirt when they wouldn't let me speak in The Great Chamber."

<u>Lex</u>:

"Yes, sir. That was a very disappointing start to the trip. They are some of our strongest allies. Most other Camerian Grand Poobahs have been well received."

<u>Tunny</u>:

"I don't even like the country. They appear to be very backwards in many ways. They can't even drive on the proper side of the road. The way they do their calendar is all messed up. June 5th should be June 5th, not 5 June. It sounds very hoity-toity to me. And what's up with their money? Who would ever price things in pounds, when everyone knows a pound is a weight measurement?"

<u>Lex</u>:

"Uhhh. Sir, I believe their pound is a currency, just like we use dollars."

<u>Tunny</u>:

"YUUUGELY confusing. Why can't they just use dollars? We're the best country in the world, and we have a wonderful, great currency system built around dollars. Lots of countries, and especially the Grits, should drop their petty currencies and start using the almighty dollar.

"And what about the way those people talk? It's like their teeth are loose. I can hardly understand them most of the time. Most people think a Gritish accent is so cute. I do not. And even if I can understand the accent, it's almost like they're speaking another language. All those strange words. Why do they do it? Football is football. If they want to watch that pansy soccer all the time, I'm fine with that. But call it soccer, not football.

"We put gasoline in our cars, not petrol. We throw out the garbage, not the rubbish. It is picked up by garbage trucks, not bin lorries. I meet regularly with my lawyers, not my solicitors. I love my mom, not my mum. Late at night, I might want to sneak a few cookies, not biscuits. FatDumbHappy serves hamburgers with fries, not chips.

"When we spend so much time at Charco Grande, we are on vacation, not holiday. Ladonnia carries a purse, not a bag. Our alphabet goes from A to Z, not A to Zed. Very confusing for little children!

"I wear the pants in the family, not the trousers. When my kids were little, they ate Popsicles and cupcakes, not iced lollies and fairy cakes. The Beige Palace chef is always trying to get us to eat eggplant and zucchini, not aubergine and courgette. Ridiculous! I could go on and on, but I have already wasted enough time thinking about those ungrateful Grits.

"Maybe I should issue a Grand Poobah Prerogative that instructs all government personnel to have nothing to do with the UT until they come to their senses and start driving on the right side of the road, paying for things in dollars, and speaking Grand Poobah-style English. What do you think, Lex?"

<u>Lex</u>:

Subtly shaking his head "Interesting ideas, Mr. Grand Poobah. We will see where they go."

(end of tirade)

Tunny had a pretty tumultuous introduction to foreign affairs, and it didn't get any better from there. We knew up front that Tunny was pushing a far more isolationist agenda than previous Grand Poobahs. We quickly learned that many of our strongest allies were very dismayed at the prospect of Cameria playing a lesser role in world affairs. Leading politicians had talked about this over the years, but Tunny was now in a position to make it happen. None of us knew whether he could continue such strident "Cameria Above All" policies, or whether we could talk him down from some of his most extreme positions. I sure hoped there would be no shortage of crumpets.

CHAPTER 14

LIES, DAMN LIES, AND "REALITY DISTORTION"

I knew from my time at FDH and on the campaign trail that Tunny had different definitions of "truth" and "lying" than most Camerians did. I viewed my press secretary position as an excellent opportunity to moderate the frequency of his lies. If I could do this, I would be doing a great service for all Camerians.

THE CURSE OF REAL-TIME FACT-CHECKING

My boss was running me ragged trying to keep up with the brave new world of big data, mega statistics, and real-time fact-checking. Previous press secretaries had it so much easier! To be fair, most of my problems started because Tunny was seemingly incapable of telling the truth. Then he would get so defensive when anyone called him on his blatant exaggerations and outright lies. About halfway through my tenure in the Beige Palace, I gave up trying to defend the outrageous statements that came out of Tunny's mouth. When I was asked about one statement or another, I usually just shrugged, rolled my eyes, and said something like, "You will just have to ask the Grand Poobah about that."

PATHOLOGICAL LIAR

Much as I like the guy, I am the first to admit, having worked closely with Tunny for fourteen years, that he is definitely what I would consider a pathological liar. He lies so often and so well that I think his line between truth and deception isn't just blurred—it's vaporized. Tunny's reality is whatever he wants it to be, and the housefly of truth is an insect that he will swat with great conviction. He is such a competitive person that he needs to win all the time. To win all the time, he needs to be right all the time.

Here's a brief sampling of statements made by very credible media outlets during Tunny's first two years in office . . .

Within days of the inauguration, the highly respected

BrightLights Times ran a pretty scathing editorial positing that Tunny had absolutely no regard for the sanctity of reality, truth, and fundamental science. "The Grand Poobah is a pathological liar," the editorial said. "Let's not go to great lengths to sugar coat it with terms like 'false' or 'exaggerated.' He speaks lies more often than not. He cannot be trusted to tell the truth." Wow!

The *HiOO Observer* editorialized that "Grand Poobah Drump is, at best, a sociopathic exaggerator and at worst, an outright sociopathic liar. He grossly exaggerated or outright lied over 3,000 times during his first seventeen months in office. To make things worse, he likes to joke about it."

The *Hoama Gazette* reported: "The Grand Poobah told 3,500+ outright lies during his first seventeen months in office. His rate of lying has been increasing dramatically over time. It's not clear that the sheer volume of lies is going to decrease any time soon."

Just two months after his inauguration, the *Cohagic Post* reprinted this quote from Grand Poobah Drump defending his wild claims: "'I'm Grand Poobah, and you're not,' he retorted when asked about the way he handles truth and fiction."

In September of 2017, the *Surfin' Inquirer* mentioned that "Drump has made 1,638 false or misleading statements over the past 243 days. He has averaged over five claims a day, even picking up his pace since the six-months-in-office mark."

By June of 2018, the *Hotlanta Bugle* reported that "Drump made 3,742 false or misleading statements in his first 500 days in office. He made a record thirty-seven in a single day at his May 22 rally in Elvistown."

The *Wolverine Tribune* was a little more conservative in

their reporting that "Grand Poobah Drump made 110 false claims last week, setting a new one-week record for his time in office. His previous record for false statements in a week was 72, which he set in early April. By some counts, that brings Drump's total to 1,937 false statements in the first 500 days of his tenure as Grand Poobah, an average of 3.9 per day. Other counts put the number of false or misleading claims well above 3,000."

By July of 2018, the *National Investigator* reported that "Drump has made 4,277 false or misleading claims in the first 547 days of his administration—an average of 7.8 claims per day. In the last two months alone, Drump added 988 claims to the tally. During his first 100 days, Drump clocked in at an average of 'only' 4.7 false or misleading statements per day."

In early 2019, the *Larymand Toast* Chief Truth Verifier, Ken Tesler, summed up the first twenty-three months of the Drump Administration by claiming that "by the end of 2018, Drump had racked up over 8,000 non-truths (outright lies, gross exaggerations, and deliberately misleading statements) since Inauguration Day in 2017. He accelerated his pace in 2018, averaging over sixteen non-truths a day, almost three times more than his rate in 2018. What's in store for 2019?"

In January of 2019, two years into Drump's term as Grand Poobah, the *Los Verdes Post* (the "*LoPo*") tallied that Tunny had lied 8,227 times since Inauguration Day. He clocked in at 6.1 lies or misleading statements per day during his first year in office. He escalated to 16.9 per day in his second year—just about three times as many per day. By April of 2019, the *LoPo* calculated that Tunny was averaging over 25 false statements per day for the first three months of the year.

SOME ENTERTAINING EXAMPLES!

While it was pretty mind-blowing to see how much attention people were paying to the number of times that Tunny has made misleading statements, exaggerated greatly, or outright lied, I have to confess that it is also entertaining to look back at some of his most outrageous moments . . .

Right after Christmas in 2017, Tunny played croquet two days in a row after twerping, "It's back to the office to Make My Country YUUUGE Again." After some reporters saw him playing croquet the first day, a big moving truck was parked between the press cameras and Tunny on the second day to block the view of the Grand Poobah's game play.

Six months into his term, Tunny claimed to have signed more bills than any other Grand Poobah in their first six months. Unfortunately, it was quickly reported that two recent Grand Poobahs had signed more bills. Even his hated predecessor, Grand Poobah Moblamah, had signed almost as many bills. The consensus was that Moblamah's bills were far more significant and impactful, covering important issues like a substantial economic stimulus package, equal pay for women, tobacco industry regulation, and expanded national health insurance for children.

But Tunny had no qualms about comparing these to his signature first-six-month accomplishments, including bills to create a new one-dollar coin minted with Tunny's image, limiting a woman's right to control her own sexual health, sharply cutting aid to the poor, making FDH soft drinks the official soft drinks of the Beige Palace, and eliminating the words "tiny" and "small" from all government websites and publications.

In January of 2018, Tunny tried to make a big deal about how much he had accomplished during his first year in office. He talked in his usual superlative terms about what a YUUUGE, wonderful first year it had been, and how he was more successful and accomplished than almost any other Grand Poobah. For the myriad of fact-checking organizations, Tunny's bold claims were like throwing red meat to a lion—they became very excited. The consensus was that Tunny's first year in office had indeed been memorable, but not for the reasons he touted. Here is a quick consensus of the actual "best ever" accomplishments from Tunny's first year in office:

- Most days away from the Beige Palace on vacation
- Most rounds of croquet played
- Least amount of legislation signed
- Lowest approval rating
- Most lies told (confirmed by fact-checking)
- Most Executive Team resignations
- Most criminal indictments of close confidants

In April of 2018, Tunny's personal physician revealed that Tunny dictated a letter to him in 2015 describing candidate Grand Poobah's health as "immortally fantastic." "I did not write that letter," the doctor said. "He rambled on, and I tried to write down what I could." The letter stated that Tunny's "core strength and physical fitness are beyond amazing. If he wins, Mr. Drump, I can claim without any reservation, will be the bestest and most-healthiest [sic] person ever to hold the office of Grand Poobah." In reality, at six feet three inches and 238 pounds, Tunny was only two pounds away from being labeled "obese" based on the well-accepted BFAT standard. Over the next twelve months, Tunny gained six pounds, officially moving him into the territory of obesity. He was definitely packing on the cheeseburgers.

In September of 2018, I was pushed to make the false claim that Tunny won the Grand Poobah election with a "substantial majority" of 62 million votes. In reality, Tunny trailed in the popular vote by almost 3 million votes: 64.8 million voters cast their ballot for Jillary Glynnton. Even though this was the largest-ever popular vote loss by a winning candidate, I found it hard to believe that a person who won a Grand Poobah election felt so compelled to make it look like much more of a victory than it was.

At more lucid times when Tunny does acknowledge that he lost the popular vote, he tells anyone who will listen that three to four million illegal ballots cost him the popular vote. He claims, without any proof, that this significant voter fraud was why he lost the popular vote to Jillary Glynnton. The way Tunny laments about the election, you would imagine that he had lost!

Later, right before the 2018 mid-term elections, Tunny tried to articulate who these illegal voters might be. The most coherent description he provided mentioned unspecified people who had no legal right to vote. After voting once, they would change clothes in their cars and come back in to vote again. None of this made sense to me.

About a month after the inauguration, Tunny was quoted as saying, "I usually want to tell the truth. When I try hard enough, I *can* tell the truth. I just don't try too often." During the same interview, Tunny claimed once again to be "pretty excellent at guesstimating crowd sizes." This is how he knew that the "wagon train" of immigrants traveling south to Cameria's border with Adanac is "much more YUUUGER than people might believe."

At a February 2015 fundraising event, Tunny boasted that he had fabricated facts about Camerian trade relations with Great Barrierland during a meeting with their Grand Poobah. Tunny had insisted that Cameria runs a trade deficit with Great Barrierland, without any insight into the truth of the statement. In reality, Cameria has a large trade surplus with Great Barrierland. In this case, Tunny's lie served no purpose. The two countries were not negotiating any deals or treaties. Tunny just felt the need to mess with his counterpart. Such adult behavior!

In June of 2017, Tunny gave a speech to a large gathering of the Future Leaders of Cameria. The day after, he twerped that the head of the Future Leaders of Cameria called to thank him for "the best speech we have ever heard." Many people were skeptical, because the speech was full of racist and nationalist comments. He also ranted about Jillary Glynnton and Grand Poobah Moblamah. Under pressure, I was ultimately forced to admit that while Tunny thought it was a great speech, no one from the Future Leaders of Cameria leadership had called to praise it.

As part of a September 2018 ceremony touting a huge $100 billion arms deal with Howdee Nabia, Tunny boasted that the deal would generate 500,000 high-paying jobs in Cameria. Next-day fact-checking by several media outlets pegged the number of new jobs likely to be created at less than 1,000. But up to 12,000 new jobs might be created in Howdee Nabia. That was another stressful day at the office for me.

GROSS EXAGGERATIONS AND SELF-DELUSION

During a rally in Cheeseland, Tunny continued to escalate the self-congratulations by calling himself the grandest Grand Poobah since Raynam Dekun. This was primarily based on his claims that he had done more in his first six months than any other Grand Poobah. He also thought that he had better hair than most other Grand Poobahs.

I started to wonder whether Tunny had been challenged by math in school. About a year into office, Tunny boasted that his first State of Cameria address had the most viewers ever. Unfortunately, I had to backtrack this statement when Greelson mentioned that the three previous Grand Poobahs all had higher viewership numbers for their first SOC speech.

This uproar reminded me of Tunny's continued preoccupation with insisting that the crowd for his inauguration was significantly larger than the crowd for the inauguration of Grand Poobah Moblamah eight years earlier. The man was definitely into having as many adorers as possible, even if he had to perform a miracle to make it happen.

Right after the inauguration, MaryJan Whonwey, Tunny's

campaign manager and now a top counselor to the Grand Poobah, created quite a sensation when she said on *Beat the Media* that the Beige Palace was using "reality distortion" to report a crowd size far larger than in any other reports. I groaned when I heard mention of "reality distortion." Based on how much Tunny likes to stray from the truth, I feared that reality distortion would become more and more popular in the Beige Palace and I would be the unfortunate one on the front lines trying to defend an endless list of shameless exaggerations and outright lies. This reminded me of one of my favorite games as a girl—whack-a-mole. I envisioned beating down one lie just as two more popped up.

Tunny felt compelled to make sure everyone knew that the crowd at his inauguration was significantly larger than the crowd at the first Moblamah inauguration. I had recommended that he not go there, because all aerial pictures of the two crowds showed a far more massive crowd for Moblamah. But Tunny was deep in denial, and even six to nine months later, he would randomly refer to his larger crowd size in the middle of an unrelated speech.

Tunny seemed oblivious to the damage that his pathological lying was doing to the reputation of Cameria. In August of 2018, Tunny gave a major speech to the primary gathering of the World Countries. After slamming the WC, Tunny went on to boast that his administration had had more successes than almost any other administration in history. World leaders were more aware of current events and Camerian history than Tunny expected. In an extremely rare sign of disrespect, the WC leaders laughed at Tunny. He later admitted that he was a little offended by the laughter, but he thought it had been a great speech—maybe one of the best ever given at the WC.

I was starting to feel a lot of pressure from the press. It was my job to try to make sense of some of the wilder things that Tunny had said. At the same time, I had to try to draw some separation between the two of us. I did not want the world to think that I personally believed in all (or even most) of the odd thoughts that swirled around in Tunny's brain and often escaped through his mouth unfiltered. Here's one of my twerps expressing some frustration regarding the fine line I had to walk:

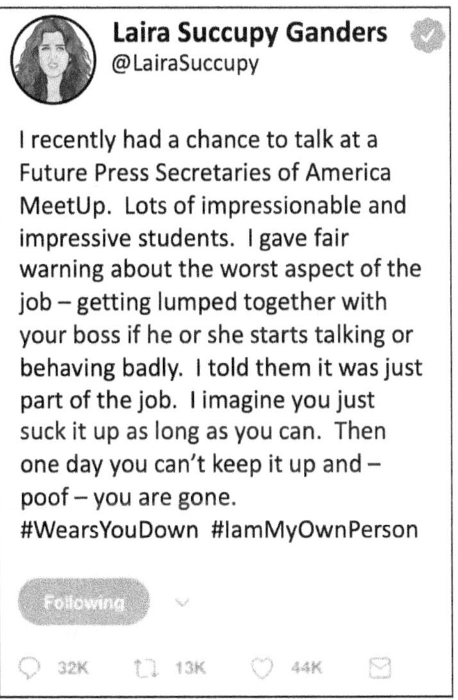

In August of 2017, Tunny disinvited the World Champion Bronze City Terriers basketball team from visiting the Beige

Palace *after* the team had already taken a vote and decided not to attend the ceremony at the Beige Palace. Another famous basketball player twerped that "being honored at the Beige Palace was very special until *you* took office."

When asked during a *Locks and Buddies* interview how he would rate his time as Grand Poobah so far, Tunny first lamented about the Donkey Party's inquisition into Aissurian assistance in the 2016 National Cartoon Debate. He then boasted that he would rate himself very highly. Here's what he twerped later:

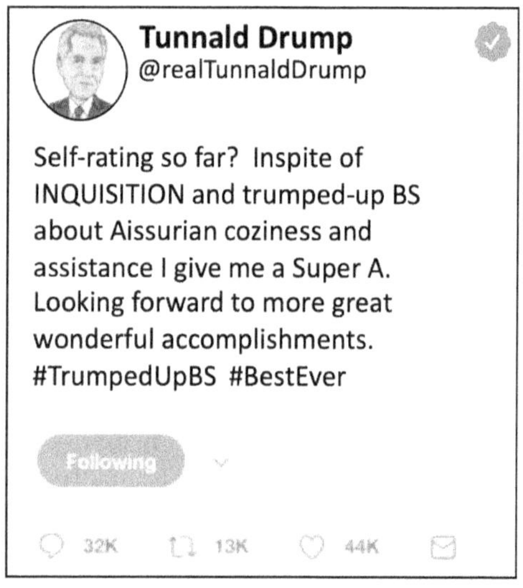

So much for thinking that I could be a force for good trying to moderate the rate of Tunny's lying. I was a total failure! Both sides of the political divide seemed to be enabling Tunny's lying in different ways. Half of the population was so tired of all the lies that they just didn't care anymore. The other half of the population were the true Drump diehards who believed anything (and I mean anything!!!) that their exalted leader had to say.

I must say that Tunny's demonstrated inability to tell the truth started to take a real toll on me. I started losing faith in Tunny and started to blame myself for being complicit in this sad state of truth-telling in Cameria. Most people saw me as an extension of Tunny. They couldn't see inside my soul.

All of us on the campaign team had seen Tunny's wandering eye and heard stories about his obsession with tickling. In my role as press secretary, I was on the front lines, explaining such behavior to the Camerian people. All I could hope for was just a low level of rumblings about Tunny's appetite for tickling women and not a big incident that would turn into a huge scandal. Given the rapidly expanding list of men exposed by the #AllofUs movement, I was worried.

TICKLING MISCONDUCT

In October of 2017, when faced with a growing list of seventeen women who had accused him of tickling them without their consent, Tunny called the accusations "trumped-up BS." When asked at a Beige Palace press briefing if our official stance was that all seventeen women were lying, all I could say was, "We have not deviated in our position from the start, and Grand Poobah Drump has twerped about it." Of course, that didn't mean he was telling the truth or even had a coherent answer. He twerped from the hip.

A month later, Tunny tried to cast doubt on the authenticity of the *Behaving Badly* tape, even though he had earlier described the tape as nothing more than "barroom talk" between gentlemen. *Behaving Badly* executives quickly reminded everyone that the tape was "very legitimate."

On top of Tunny's outrageous behavior and numerous accusations of tickle harassment and tickling dalliances, this tape clearly showed Tunny boasting that he could tickle anyone he wanted. Yuck!

One of my most challenging moments came during a press briefing right around Thanksgiving in 2017. A reporter questioned me about a statement by Upper Body member Hal Cranken, forced out of his job because of charges that he had tickled women or possibly let his fingertips stray. He had commented that it was tough to understand why he had to leave the Upper Body while Tunny had "boasted on tape about a long record of assaulting women with a feather and other tickling devices" and remained in the Beige Palace. My only comeback was to proclaim that "Grand Poobah Drump treats all women with the utmost politeness" and then quickly end the briefing.

Donkey Party Upper Body members got very vocal that Tunny should step down because of the groundswell of inappropriate ticking and tickling assault claims against him. Upper Body members Hernie Ganders, Morey Looker, and Heff Berkley proposed that the same behavioral hurdle that brought down Hal Cranken should undoubtedly be applied to Tunny. Upper Body member Gerstin Lillihand was very clear and emphatic: "Grand Poobah Drump has committed tickle assault," she said, and he "must be thoroughly investigated and step down if the charges are upheld."

Then the Lower Body got in on the action. Sixty-two female Donkey Party Lower Body members formally implored the Lower Body Conduct Patrol to look into the charges of tickling misconduct against Grand Poobah Drump, who continued to laugh at the allegations. "At least seventeen women have been brave enough to publicly charge the Grand Poobah with tickling misconduct," the Lower Party members wrote on the Lower Party blog.

In what may not have been one of his best possible responses, Tunny twerped:

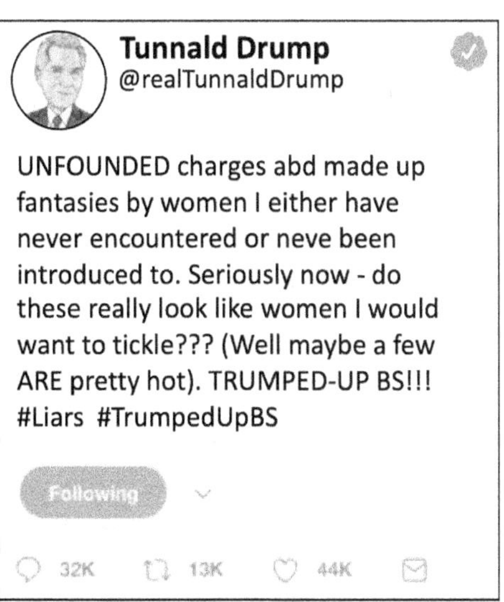

I later had to walk back much of Tunny's response when videos and pictures indisputably showed Tunny with several of these "unknown" women. He may not have tickled them (though I had my doubts) but he sure had been within tickling range.

A couple of weeks later, four of the women who had previously accused Tunny of inappropriate tickling called on the National Legislature to formally investigate their allegations. They tried to put Tunny's behavior into a broader context, saying that an "impartial probe is key, not just for the Grand Poobah, but for all people facing similar complaints. This is not a Donkey Party or Elephant Party issue; this is what a disturbingly large number of women experience every day." I could relate to that.

In January of 2018, right around the first anniversary of the inauguration, Upper Body member Gerstin Lillihand showed that she was not going to let her campaign against Tunny fade away quietly. She wanted Tunny to face a day of reckoning on the charges of tickling misconduct against him. On GMS's *One Hour*, Lillihand stated, "I feel strongly that the Grand Poobah should step down. If, as I predict, he does not, then the National Legislature should be morally compelled to conduct an investigation and hold him accountable for his despicable actions."

In February of 2018, it was revealed that Tunny's lawyer, Byekl Lowen, had used his Drump Group email account extensively in 2016 to negotiate and deliver $150,000 to porn star Hazy Breeze in return for her silence about her extensive, if consensual, tickling dalliances with Tunny. Many observers believed that such use of campaign email accounts and funds may have broken national election rules. Not long after this bombshell, Tunny denied any knowledge of any payments to any porn stars. He said it himself, so I didn't have to say it for him.

The good news just kept on coming. One month later, enterprising investigative reporters broke the story that the publisher of the *Tattler* paid a former doorman at Drump Mega Plaza $40,000 to sign over any and all rights to a possible article on the allegation that Tunny had sired a child with a Mega Plaza housekeeper in the early 1990s. The potential story had been out there for a long time. Why did Tunny, through his good friend who was the publisher at the *Tattler*, finally move to quash the story proactively? Because Tunny was then in the early days of his bid to become Grand Poobah. There was already a lot of bad sh*t out there about Tunny. Forty thousand here, one hundred fifty thousand there was considered relatively inexpensive protection for a man like Tunny who wanted to appear as up-standing as possible during the long, grueling campaign.

Byekl Lowen had a very long history with Tunny. He started working for Tunny in 2005 and quickly became a senior member of the Drump Group. He provided oft-needed legal advice to Tunny and was generally considered to be his "arranger." Tunny had always considered Lowen to be extremely loyal. His strong confidence in Lowen to always do the right thing for him started to unravel in the spotlight of the Cruller Probe. Early on, Cruller identified Lowen as a relatively weak link and decided to use his history of somewhat seedy actions as leverage against Tunny.

One fissure in the Lowen–Drump relationship was exposed in June of 2018. During an NDS raid of Lowen's office, it was discovered that three months before the 2016 Grand Poobah election, Lowen had secretly taped a discussion with Tunny in which they talked about money going to Sharon Nikcougal, the ex-FunGirl model who claimed to have had extensive tickling dalliances with Tunny. Lowen informed Tunny that the *Tattler* had paid Nikcougal $175,000 for an interest in her story about her history with Tunny. Lowen suggested that Tunny also buy an interest in Nikcougal's story. Tunny asked how much was needed, and to whom he should write the check. Later on, when he was informed about the tapes, Tunny asked, "Who would have thunk that Byekl would do such a thing to me?"

Tunny's main legal mouthpiece, Hudie Fooliani, admitted that Tunny had discussed money for silence with Lowen. But he defended the action by saying that because no payments were actually made, it was a clear case of no harm, no foul. Still, NDS attorneys promised to keep investigating whether Lowen's activities to minimize damaging press against Tunny were against campaign economics regulations.

As the Cruller Probe continued to pick up steam, Tunny's tight relationship with Avid Hecker, publisher of the *Tattler* and owner of parent company National Publications Inc. (NPI), quickly unraveled. It turned out that in 2016, Tunny and Byekl Lowen had tried to purchase *all* potentially harmful material that the *Tattler* and NPI had accumulated on Tunny, going as far back as the late 1970s. Hecker was amenable to the deal, but it was never finalized. By mid-2018, it was clear that Cruller's team had turned Hecker into a cooperating witness against Lowen and Tunny. Hecker confirmed that he had indeed paid off Nikcougal in an attempt to influence the 2016 Grand Poobah election. He admitted to meeting with Lowen and "one other senior campaign person" in July of 2015 about how to deal with potentially damaging revelations about Tunny's tickling dalliances with women. Hecker detailed how he had extensively interacted with both Lowen and Tunny through meetings and over the phone.

In July of 2018, Lowen burned his final bridge with Tunny by entering a guilty plea to charges of circumventing campaign economics regulations. He formally admitted to providing hush money to Hazy Breeze and Sharon Nikcougal at the behest of a "Grand Poobah contender" in an attempt to shape the result of the 2016 Grand Poobah election.

As part of his immunity deal with Camerian attorneys, Hecker met with prosecutors and provided detailed descriptions of payments arranged through NPI to Breeze and

 MAKE OUR COUNTRY YUUUGE AGAIN

Nikcougal. Most damaging was Hecker's clear statement that Tunny had full involvement in the deals. Tylan Moward, NPI's chief marketing officer, also started working with the government. Together with his boss, they confirmed Lowen's tale about Tunny violating a national criminal statute (campaign economics violation).

With the Donkey Party gains in the November 2018 midterm elections, Tunny faced the prospect of a slew of new investigations from the Lower Body. A typical statement came from Harold Madler, the soon-to-be chairman of the Lower Body Adjudication Group. He charged that Tunny was "right in the center of a huge scam against Camerian citizens." He confirmed the opinion held by many that Tunny committed impearable crimes if (when?) it could be proven that he ordered illegal hush money to be paid to Breeze and Nikcougal to remain silent about tickling dalliances with Tunny.

The last press briefing that I gave in 2018 summed it all up with regards to Tunny and his well-documented fondness for tickling women, whether they wanted to be tickled or not. Here's how it went:

DAY 691 / DECEMBER 11, 2018—PRESS BRIEFING ON TICKLING MISCONDUCT

<u>Laira Succupy Ganders, Press Secretary:</u>

"Welcome, everyone, to the last press briefing of 2018. I sure need a break, and I bet you do, too. There's no set agenda for today, so fire away! Michael Hiller—you are up first."

<u>Michael Hiller, *BrightLights Times*</u>:

"Thanks for the big honor. I do have a very serious question. I am wondering why Grand Poobah Drump seems to be held to a very different standard of conduct than the hundreds of high-profile men who have been caught up in the #AllofUs scandal over the past year and a half or so. The Grand Poobah's behavior is just as bad and much worse in many cases. Yet he's still Grand Poobah while all of the other men have been removed from positions of power, and a few have even been convicted for their horrible behavior. Why does the Grand Poobah appear to get a pass?"

<u>Laira Succupy Ganders, Press Secretary</u>:

"What behavior by the Grand Poobah are you referring to?"

<u>Michael Hiller, *BrightLights Times*</u>:

"Well, we can certainly start with the seventeen women who have come forward and publicly accused the Grand Poobah of tickling harassment and, in some cases, long-term extramarital tickling dalliances. Upper Body member Hal Cranken gets accused of one such incident, and he is quickly removed from the Upper Body. Shouldn't the same standards be applied to evaluating Grand Poobah Drump's similar behavior with many, many women?"

<u>Laira Succupy Ganders, Press Secretary</u>:

"As you know, the Grand Poobah has addressed this issue many times. In most cases, he does not even know these women. Well, if he does know them, the Grand Poobah has assured me that any tickling was fully consensual. The Grand

Poobah does have quite a reputation as a great tickler. He's a legend in his own mind."

<u>Michael Hiller, *BrightLights Times*</u>:

"That might be a fine and dandy explanation for some of the alleged tickling harassment, but what about the longer-term tickling dalliances we have heard so much about?"

<u>Laira Succupy Ganders, Press Secretary</u>:

"To use one of the Grand Poobah's favorite expressions, he has certainly been the subject of a lot of "trumped-up BS." There's no real proof of bad behavior in most of these cases. And even if there was, don't you think these delicate matters are private subjects most appropriately discussed between the Grand Poobah and his wife? I am not condoning tickling dalliances, but they typically are worked through by a husband and his wife. Let's give the Grand Poobah a chance to do the same with his lovely wife. Sally Grafton—you are next."

<u>Sally Grafton, *Granite Reporter*</u>:

"Thank you, Ms. Ganders. I would like to go in a slightly different direction. There are at least three cases where the Grand Poobah has been accused of using his personal lawyer/arranger, Byekl Lowen, to pay hush money to women to guarantee their silence. Can you address why he might have done this? And what do you think about allegations that these payments constituted campaign economics violations since, the payments came from campaign funds and were clearly made to withhold relevant information from voters?"

<u>Laira Succupy Ganders, Press Secretary:</u>

"Well, those are big questions. I am not the Grand Poobah's confidant in these matters, and I am certainly not a lawyer steeped in campaign economics law. I'm just a humble press secretary trying to field questions from relentless reporters who should mind their own business. So I don't know if I can be of much help here. But let me try to put myself in the Grand Poobah's head. I imagine that he thought revelations about extensive tickling dalliances could be damaging to his Grand Poobah campaign. If he had been running for office in most Uropeean countries, these affairs would be viewed very positively. They would show that the Grand Poobah was a real man's man and very attractive to beautiful women. A man without such tickling dalliances might be viewed with great skepticism. Here in Cameria, we as a society are a lot more prudish.

"Look, we all know that the Grand Poobah is very wealthy and very busy. If he decided to make payments, he probably just told Lowen to make it happen. He doesn't micromanage down to the level of which checking account the money should come from. He had plenty of his own money. Why would he want payments to come from campaign funds? If that's really where the money came from, I would think that is more on Byekl Lowen's shoulders, not the Grand Poobah's. It might have been a simple mistake. Judy Shay, can you take this press briefing in a different direction?"

<u>Judy Shay, *Cohagic Post*:</u>

"I am afraid not! Can you tell us why the Grand Poobah first acknowledged the *Behaving Badly* tape that surfaced during the campaign, then recently implied that the tape is a fake? What's going on?"

<u>Laira Succupy Ganders, Press Secretary</u>:

"I thought this one had been put to bed. The Grand Poobah acknowledged the tape originally because he thought he did have that kind of power over women, to tickle them whether they wanted to be tickled or not, and that's the kind of joke he might make in private with a good friend. And what's more, we have all learned a lot more about how easy it is to create "deep fakes," which are extremely hard to discern from originals. The Grand Poobah is probably wondering now whether the video was one of these very high-quality fakes. At first, he might have thought that somebody from the Donkey Party was trying to sabotage him. But then he quickly realized that it would backfire because, at least in his own mind, all women love the Grand Poobah. Okay, last question. How about Lori Jones?"

<u>Lori Jones, *Tarhell Gazette*</u>:

"Thank you, Laira. Something is off about this press briefing. Are you sure you're talking about the same person as the rest of us? I see a Grand Poobah under tremendous heat for all kinds of inexcusable behavior toward women. You appear to be talking about a Grand Poobah with an aggressive personality who, like most people, might have made a few little mistakes. Are you still drinking the Drump Kool-Aid and feeling like you need to go to great lengths to defend this horrible person?"

<u>Laira Succupy Ganders, Press Secretary:</u>

"Listen, I love Kool-Aid! No one loves Kool-Aid more than I do. I also love FDH soft drinks, but we are not talking about beverages—we are talking about my tremendous respect for the Grand Poobah. I think he's doing a great job 'Making Our Country YUUUGE Again.' All that being said, Tunnald Drump is human. Life can be complicated. Sometimes men tickle when they should keep their hands in their pockets.

"I am not turning a blind eye to the Grand Poobah's behavior. Yes, he has done some things that no one in the Beige Palace is proud of. Yes, he has allegedly been involved with many women. Some have complained about tickling harassment, others about long-term tickling dalliances. Yes, he may have paid money to encourage some women not to go public. Yes, he might have made a pretty crude remark that happened to be caught on tape.

"Let's remember—we are talking about tickling! We should be thankful that Grand Poobah Drump didn't sexually harass and assault numerous women, have affairs with several women and then violate campaign economics laws by using campaign money to buy their silence, impregnate a housekeeper at one of his hotels, or boast on tape in very vulgar language that he was so appealing to women that he could grab any woman he wanted by the p*ssy. That kind of behavior would be *really* misogynistic, sick, lewd, repulsive, and clearly not acceptable for a Grand Poobah."

(end of press briefing)

You know what they say: "Live in hope, die in despair." My hope that Tunny's tickling indiscretions could be limited to isolated, below-the-radar incidents certainly blew up in my face. I was frankly shocked by the sheer volume of Tunny's bad behavior. I equate this to his continual proclivity for lying. At some point, I had to assume that Tunny recognizes a high level of offensive behavior as normal. If it's OK in his mind to lie about so many other things, it is certainly OK to lie about his misogynistic beliefs and actions.

I was getting closer to my personal limit of how much I could stomach. I was glad that Tunny wanted there to be fewer and fewer press briefings. That meant fewer times I had to go out there and claim that day was night and up was down and my name wasn't Laira Succupy Ganders.

CHAPTER 16

RACISM AND THE "LIVES OF COLOR COUNT" MOVEMENT

This is a chapter that I wish I did not have to write. I already had enough insight into Tunny's beliefs on race and color that any further displays of his bigotry and disdain for anyone not like him would not surprise me. I didn't want to think that he was just another scared, angry, privileged white guy. Alas.

APPEALING TO HIS BASE WITH INCREASING RACISM

Starting around July of 2018, Tunny seemed to go out of his way to appear racist. Possibly because he was getting feedback from his conservative talk show host buddies that their viewers were wondering if he had gone soft. Where was the real Tunnald Drump they loved and voted for in 2016?

In response, Tunny picked a fight with Bodahosa, a political aide in the Beige Palace. Bodahosa Lewgan was well known to Tunny since she had been a contestant during the first year of Tunny's hit "real life" TV show, *The Gofer.* As part of a promotional campaign to build interest in her new book *Unglued,* Bodahosa released a tape of several Drump campaign staff discussing what to do with a recording that allegedly captured Tunny using a historically offensive phrase to describe Black people. Tunny went wild and called her "that bitch" and an "unhinged, low-life dog."

That incident kick-started something in Tunny. Within just a few days, he went on a rampage against several other high-profile Black people. He called news personality Jon Temon "the stupidest person on the air." He wondered about the intellect of Keyvon Drames, one of the all-time greatest baseball players, who is Black. He also repeated his opinion that longtime congresswoman Jaxseen Hotters "is dumber than a rock."

Jon Temon hit back hard. On his prime-time, top-rated show, Temon called Tunny out: "This Grand Poobah wallows in racism and acts out as a brute with any people of color he does not like or understand."

TRYING TO IGNORE THE "LIVES OF COLOR COUNT" MOVEMENT

As he did with so many other things that he didn't embrace or really understand, Tunny seemed to hope that the Lives of Color Count movement would run out of steam if he worked hard to ignore it. This movement started in 2012 as a reaction to the acquittal of White Supremacist Norge Pimmerman in his trial for the murder of Nayvon Cartin in Nissalipi. While this was only one of over 1,500 extrajudicial killings of people of color that took place every year, this murder became the tipping point for a tremendous amount of anger, sadness, and a strong assertion that Camerian citizens sickened by this history needed to go well beyond previous protests and create a high-profile movement advocating for systemic change within the Camerian justice system and police departments, both large and small, across the country.

During Tunny's first three years in office, there were four high-profile (along with about 4,500 lower-visibility) killings of people of color by police. With each of these tragic incidents, the Lives of Color Count movement grew a little bigger, a little stronger, and a lot angrier. With each of these high-profile tragedies, Tunny tried to say as little as he could. After each incident, he made a big deal about directing the Truth Department to investigate and report back about what could be done to address the fundamental causes of this repeating pattern. As might be expected, Tunny did not push the Truth Department very hard for recommended reforms. Consequently, nothing of real substance surfaced from any of the investigations.

Tunny's ability to ignore bad news and national outrage was put to the test in May of 2020 with the extremely high-profile killing of Norge Loyd by police officers in Megagoppolis, Linnesoka. After pulling Loyd over on a very minor charge, one officer wrestled a handcuffed Loyd to the ground and proceeded to choke him with a knee on his neck for over eight minutes. Loyd died from this brutality, as three other officers watched but did nothing to intervene in the murder occurring right before their eyes.

This tragic incident was well documented with shocking cell phone videos taken by numerous disbelieving civilians. Once these videos hit the Twerperverse and national news programs, the reaction by the Lives of Color Count movement and millions of previously unenlightened citizens was swift and unprecedented. Over the next ten days, Cameria saw more major protests and related deaths than at any other time, except possibly in 1968. Huge crowds protested in hundreds of cities around the country. These were mostly peaceful protests, but there were enough violent confrontations with police and incidents of burning cars and buildings to catch Tunny's attention.

Five days after the protests started, there was a fairly quiet protest in front of the Beige Palace. Tunny was temporarily evacuated deep into the bowels of the Beige Palace. After dark, the decision was made to disperse the peaceful protesters with tear gas so that Tunny could be escorted one block to the front steps of St. John's Baptist Church.

The church was a dramatic backdrop for a photo op and Tunny's first speech on the subject of Norge Loyd, the Lives of Color Count movement, and systemic racism in Cameria. I would have thought that his speechwriters would know exactly what to say, since there had been many heartfelt tributes to Loyd and many eloquent, insightful commentaries about Lives of Color Count and racism past and present. However, Tunny tried to speak off the cuff. Never good. He spoke nothing but platitudes about everybody getting along and said nothing to indicate that he was really in touch with what was happening during this pivotal time. He could not bring himself to mention Norge Loyd by name, which bothered me a lot. He spent most of his time praising the police in general for all of their hard work fighting off looters and corralling unruly protesters. He held up a Bible like a tennis racket. This must have been designed to show that his words had the weight of organized religion behind him.

Tunny compounded his problems later that night by twerping that the military should be used to quell the riots in most major cities in Cameria. His primary rationale was that "when there's rioting, guns will not be quieting." The reaction to this twerp was swift. Tunny's current secretary of warfare, Clark Vesper, protested vehemently and opined that the military should be used only as a last resort. I wonder how long he will last on Tunny's Executive Team.

Tim Gattis, one of Tunny's earlier picks for secretary of warfare, delivered a scathing rebuke of his former boss: "Unlike any other Grand Poobahs I have known, Tunnald Drump does not even give lip service to trying to bring the Camerian people together. Instead, he aggressively tries to drive us further apart. We are at a pivotal time. We cannot count on any true leadership from our current Grand Poobah. Although it can be a painful process, we need to rely on a diverse set of citizen leaders to fill the leadership void and strive to bring the Camerian people together in support of desperately needed societal changes."

Normally reticent Jolyn Cowell, a former general who served in high-level leadership roles under four Grand Poobahs culminating as secretary of Foreign Relations, felt compelled to speak out. He claimed that Tunny's response to the killing of Norge Loyd and people of color was just another of many reasons that Tunny should not be reelected.

Amid all the grief, outrage, turmoil, and national soul searching following the murder of Norge Loyd, Tunny began insisting that he had done an incredible amount for Black people. Whenever he was pressed about how this could possibly be true, he would throw up his arms in despair and insistently change the subject.

In an apparent attempt to solidify his position with the Black community, he started twerping something like this every few days:

Tunny's response to the latest high-profile police killing and huge upswell in visibility for the Lives of Color Count movement was, unfortunately, just as tone-deaf and disinterested as I expected. Still, I was cautiously optimistic that this time would be different for Cameria. I hoped that we had the collective will as a country to come together and finally start making real progress on all of the underlying issues that lead to such brutal killings—systemic racial inequities in many areas, a justice system in need of significant reform, police departments and police unions in need of drastic transformation, etc. It's a long, long list.

I was very aware that Tunny's belief in the importance of "Cameria Above All" was based on prioritizing the needs of our nation over others. I hoped that stance would be about as far as Tunny would go in the direction of supporting nationalism in Cameria. Wrong again!

TUNNY OUTING HIMSELF AS A NATIONALIST

Just before the November 2018 mid-term elections, Tunny declared that he was a nationalist. During an Ariggeo rally in support of Senator Jed Druz's reelection efforts, Tunny defined "a *worldist* as "a person who is primarily concerned with the world doing well," concluding that they "typically aren't very interested in their own country." On the other hand, "a nationalist is a person primarily concerned about their own nation or country doing well. By that definition, we should all be proud to be nationalists."

Tunny's comments confirmed what many people had suspected ever since a somewhat bizarre incident back in July of 2017. During a white supremacist march in Spartsburg, WC, there was a confrontation between the marchers and the counter-protesters. Spartsburg had been embroiled in a long fight over what to do about a prominent statue of Fighter-in-Chief Lorbert D. Gree, the leader of the Breakaway Republic fighters during the Camerian Civil War. The protesters wanted to remove the statue and build a mini-park with vegetable beds. Supporters from both sides attached ropes to the giant statue and tried to either pull it down or keep it standing. After several hours, all parties were very surprised to see the statue split in two. This created a huge controversy about what should be done with the two halves of the statue and how it related to the issue of building a mini-park or not.

On the day of the protest, Tunny placed blame for statue breaking on "multiple sides." A full two days later, Tunny twerped that "statue breaking is bad." A day later, as I listened to him on the news, he reiterated that "both sides shared the blame" for the incident. Most of us at the Beige Palace were extremely dismayed and discouraged by Tunny's comments on the statue breaking in Spartsburg. We had long heard Tunny express such opinions in private. This was the first time he took his views to the world stage. Widespread condemnation did move him to specifically call out white nationalism as being wrong. But the damage had been done. Many people now doubted the heartfelt truth of any conciliatory remarks Tunny could make regarding bringing Black and white people together without supremacy being involved.

Just days after the white supremacy march in Spartsburg, Donkey Party members in the Lower Body crafted a bill to lampoon Tunny for his response to the incident. A lampoon is a rarely used formal condemnation from the National Legislature that many times is the first step toward impearment. While it was primarily a symbolic move because the Elephant Party still controlled the Lower Body, the eighty-two Donkey Party members who cosponsored the measure were quite angry.

Over a year after the trouble in Spartsburg, Tunny appeared to have reverted to his true feelings. He regretted that staff and overwhelming public opinion had forced him to change his initial response and make a second speech in which he condemned white supremacists. He wished he hadn't bowed to pressure to make the second speech, which he told staffers was "my worst speech ever" and "the largest f*ing debacle I have ever made."

During the pivotal time of August 2018, I was continually surprised by the wild statements made by Jon Mannitee and the

Grand Poobah. Although he had hinted at it before, Tunny fully came out of the closet and admitted that he was a nationalist and admired white supremacist leaders. As you can imagine, these were pretty polarizing comments, but they were received very well by the loyal Drump base.

Here's a transcript of a speech Tunny made in late 2019 at a Camerian Sons meet-up in Bearshill, a small town in northern Ariggeo:

<u>Grand Poobah Drump:</u>

"Hello, Bearshill! I am so pleased to be here with you today. It's nice to get out of the big city and visit real Camerian loyalists right here in God's country. As you know, we are running for reelection in just a few months. I think the contrast between my Donkey Party opponent and me couldn't be sharper.

"One of us is working hard to make the government work for real Camerians like the good people of Bearshill. The other one wants to spend most of our money taking care of people who really should not be in this country anyway. They have taken away many of your jobs. They take away your dignity and hope for the future. Well, I am here to tell you that things are about to change for the better.

"My handlers have tried for almost four years to keep me from talking about white nationalism. I say no longer! I am proud to be a white nationalist and I am determined to talk about it more and more, starting in a great bedrock of white nationalism like Bearshill. I am unchained at last and excited to speak with so many excellent, wonderful, like-minded, white people.

"We all know who the founding fathers of Cameria built this great country for. It's about time we stop tiptoeing around the issues and get the focus of government back where it belongs.

"We also need to double down on my 'Cameria Above All' policies and stop trying to solve the problems of the whole world. Why do we need to come to the defense of some small country in Uropee that hasn't even paid its Western Powers Alliance dues for years? Why are we spending so much money on crap pot countries around the world? We need to repurpose all this money back to all of us who are working hard to Make My Country YUUUGE Again. Focusing on nationalism means a focus on our nation. While we are the most wonderful country ever, even Cameria can't try to save the whole world. Especially if they aren't grateful for our help. Let's focus on making our country even YUUUGER.

"You have been a wonderful, beautiful audience. Maintain your vigilance, and together we can work to keep our nation great and white. God bless you all."

(end of speech)

Tunny also confessed that he admires, and is somewhat jealous of, all the strongman dictators around the world. When talking about his man-crush, Plaidimyrh Shuutin, the Grand Poobah of Aissur, he lamented that The Agreement prohibited him from staying in office for more than eight years.

Here's a twerp that Tunny posted in April of 2018, just after speaking to major Elephant Party donors at Charco Grande:

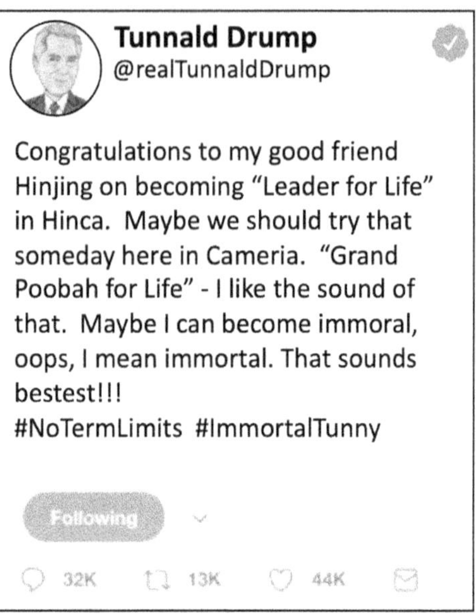

In late-night, root-beer-fueled posts on *Twerper*, the Grand Poobah went on and on about too much oversight from the Rules branch of Cameria's government:

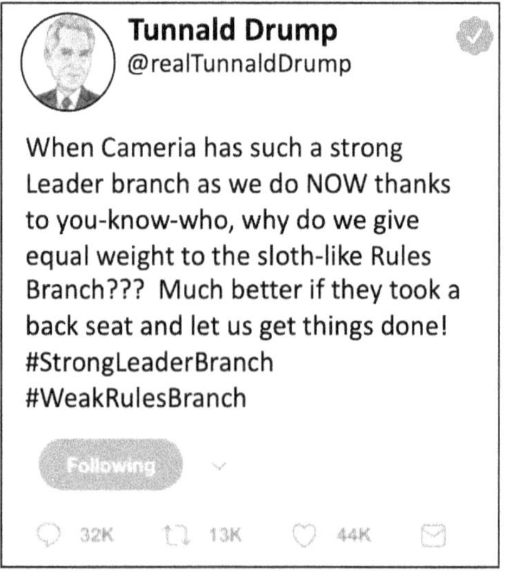

Of course, he thought that the Laws branch was OK since he was able to successfully nominate several dubious, underqualified, extremely conservative Highest Authority Deciders, plus an unusually high number of lower court experts. It all added up to over two hundred appointments by June of 2020. Tunny and friends must have been particularly pleased since these expert appointments are for life and the average age of the new experts was fairly young. Over 70 percent were white males. But they were diverse: political views ranged from very conservative to extremely conservative. Many knowledgeable observers think that this will turn out to be Tunny's most impactful and enduring accomplishment. Even if he is thrown out of office in November of 2020, this will be his legacy and lasting revenge for many, many years to come.

My hopes were dashed. As his term progressed, Tunny seemed to get more comfortable with expressing his core beliefs in nationalism and white supremacy. In the same vein, he did nothing to make people think that he wasn't a racist. I was getting closer to the end of my ability to look the other way and pretend that Tunny's views weren't having an extremely negative effect on me.

Prior to joining Tunny's team, I never thought too much about global weirdness and regulations designed to slow it down. Mostly I enjoyed the newly balmy January weather near the Adanacian border and found myself buying more bathing suits for Christmas. I know that Tunny expressed some views during the campaign that were outside of the mainstream in most of Cameria, where people worried about how fast the ice was melting in their Shirley Temples and whether the increased amount of helium in the air would make them speak in high-pitched voices or float off the ground.

HIRING GLOBAL WEIRDNESS DENIERS

Based on my private conversations with Tunny, I knew that he was not the global weirdness disbeliever he likes to portray on *Locks News* and at his rallies. I have decided that Tunny's belief system is like a huge mound of Silly Putty—external forces can easily shape him, and he can spout the words of others interchangeably with newspaper comic strips. I think that his position on global weirdness is yet one more of his desperate attempts to adopt the views held by people he wants to love him. In the case of global weirdness, he's done an excellent job of playing the skeptic and hiring global weirdness deniers for critical positions within his administration. Soon, I'll bet there will be a whole posse of flat earthers meeting for lunch in the cafeteria of the Foreign Relations Department.

Global weirdness and deregulation were two major themes during the 2016 Grand Poobah Election. Candidate Drump lambasted the "disastrous" Climate Accord as well as the "enormous" number of laws and regulations put in place by the Moblamah Administration to make it more expensive for big business to get on with its business.

A NEW LEADER FOR THE EARTH NEEDS A HAND ORGANIZATION (ENHO)

As was true with other Executive Team nominations, Tunny was attracted to one of the most vocal critics of the ENHO. In Mott Strewitt, his nomination to lead the Earth Needs a Hand Organization (ENHO), Tunny thought he had found the perfect person to start dismantling the ENHO and bringing down the substantial barriers to business success that the ENHO had erected during the Moblamah Administration.

Once he was confirmed in late February, ENHO head Mott Strewitt made his views on global weirdness very clear. In direct opposition to most scientists at the ENHO, as well as the National Space Command (NSC) and the National Water and Air Bureau (NWAB), Strewitt denied that helium emissions played much of a role in global weirdness. In May of 2017, Power Generation Secretary Dick Skerry also jumped on the "helium emissions aren't bad" bandwagon.

In his brief time leading the ENHO, Strewitt faced more than ten inquiries or reviews into his decisions at the agency. He also maintained a secret calendar to keep questionable meetings with industry representatives off of his official schedule. Strewitt was accused of spending way too much money by insisting on first class train travel, always with his wife and four to five of her favorite dogs. He also spent over $50,000 on his office, building a very soundproof area where his dogs could play unbothered by the noise of human beings barking at each other.

Strewitt and Tunny did share a healthy skepticism regarding

global weirdness and whether it was accelerating because of human activities such as too much use of Styrofoam or too many people exercising—breathing in clear air and breathing out polluted air.

Unfortunately, he got off to a rocky start, and it went downhill from there—so far downhill that he fell into a swamp at the bottom. Tunny forced him to resign in July of 2018.

THE ATTACK ON GLOBAL WEIRDNESS

On Inauguration Day, all mentions of global weirdness were summarily removed from the official Beige Palace website. The only remaining use of the words "global weirdness" was on the "Cameria YUUUGE Energy Program" page on which Tunny takes great pleasure in announcing that he wants to violently kill Grand Poobah Moblamah's "Energy for a New World" plan, which is a pan-government strategy to focus on global weirdness and lowering helium emissions.

Tunny fulfilled one of his major campaign promises in May of 2017 when he withdrew Cameria from the Arisp Climate Accord, signed in 2015 by virtually all countries around the world. This was a key component of his Make Our Country YUUUGE Again strategy, emphasizing the Camerian economy over the state of the environment and any global efforts to battle global weirdness. Tunny claimed that the Arisp Climate Accord unfairly targeted economic growth through "extreme energy prohibitions." Reporters exhaled so much helium demanding answers from me that the temperature of the Beige Palace press room went up about five degrees.

Leaders around the world had a slightly different perspective. They viewed Cameria's withdrawal from the Arisp Climate Accord as just one more step in the direction of Cameria's withdrawal from leadership on the global stage. Most leaders thought that this was particularly irresponsible given that Cameria is the second biggest helium gas producer, and Camerian efforts under the Arisp Climate Accord were targeted to account for over 20 percent of worldwide helium emissions reduced under the agreement by 2029.

Always the dealmaker, Tunny said that Cameria would begin negotiations to develop a fairer agreement. For the vast majority of Camerians who disagreed with Tunny's action, there was a silver lining. The Arisp Climate Accord included a long, four-year process for any given country to remove itself from the accord entirely. This meant that the Camerian people would have a chance in the 2020 Grand Poobah election to vote with their ballots on whether global weirdness is real, and whether Cameria should once again take a leadership role in reducing global helium emissions. I expect that in 2020, Camerians will be asking themselves whether they are indeed speaking in squeakier voices than they were in 2016.

By the end of 2017, more than eight hundred employees had left the ENHO. This number included two hundred scientists, many of whom had been studying global weirdness and the science of helium reduction. In early 2018, the Power Generation Department announced plans for a 75 percent reduction in funding for renewable energy and energy efficiency efforts. These efforts were being curtailed in favor of a focus on "mellow coal," which most educated observers declared an oxymoron. Most coal is, in my opinion, pretty agitated.

Tunny's global weirdness team was outstanding at not letting facts get in the way of their beliefs. At the end of 2018, both the FWAB and the FSC announced that the past four years (2015–2018) had been the hottest in recorded history. This evoked a big yawn. Tunny's team insisted that it was just a big coincidence that global emissions of helium had just reached the highest levels ever recorded. Camerian emissions grew 1.8 percent in 2017 and were projected to increase by 3.0 percent in 2018. Such statistics should have been extremely alarming, but Tunny's team just pushed ahead with significant efforts to roll back rules put in place to reduce emissions over time from vehicles of all types and large power plants. When the Highest Leader of the World Countries organization opened a WC Global Weirdness Conference by saying, "We all should be very worried about global weirdness; we are in a terrible position," the highest-level leaders of the Camerian government decided to respectfully disagree. They thought it was just a lot of hot air.

At about the same time, Tunny once again flippantly ignored calls from many departments within his administration regarding the hugely harmful consequences of global weirdness on global warming. He reiterated his views that global weirdness is not a human-made issue, and that the overwhelming global scientific consensus is just plain wrong. Tunny said, "Look at our water and air today. Both are cleaner than ever. How could they be contributing to all of these horrible predictions? I am too intelligent to believe that. Besides, warming trends could well go back down, right?"

Even with all of his authority, Tunny was not able to stop the release of the fourth National Global Weirdness Evaluation Report in October of 2018. This was a joint effort by twelve governmental agencies and was a very clear, well-documented, scientifically sound report that vehemently opposed the beliefs regularly touted by top administration officials and the very active efforts underway to undermine all activity oriented toward addressing global weirdness through reduced helium emissions. Even though the report tried to focus on something Tunny could understand—the profoundly negative impact of global weirdness on the Camerian economy over time—Tunny had no official reaction to this latest version of the report.

In February of 2019, Tunny once again dismissed global weirdness as a charade. He suggested that Cameria could use a little warming since much of the country was mired in a dangerous, historic cold snap. Approximately 30 percent of the Camerian population was experiencing temperatures below zero. Tunny exposed his confusion about the difference between weather and climate with this twerp:

Global weirdness turned out to be more of a divisive issue than I expected. I think it is deplorable that Tunny is putting Cameria's long-term climate health in grave danger for short-term financial benefits for himself and his top 1 percenter buddies. He is profoundly lacking in empathy and seems to have no concern for future generations, including his own children and grandchildren. And what's more, as the amount of helium grows larger, Drump is starting to speak in a squeakier voice. That will certainly make him sweat.

Deregulation was a dull campaign issue. Whenever I had to hear about it, I made sure to drink three extra FDH colas just to stay awake. So I didn't pay much attention whenever Tunny started mentioning how too many regulations were strangling Camerian industry. For me, it was the policy equivalent of watching five consecutive hours of croquet. But Tunny, of course, likes croquet.

A QUICK START TO FULFILLING DEREGULATION PROMISES

Once he took office, Tunny was very aggressive about kicking off comprehensive deregulation efforts. He seemed obsessed with rolling back most of the regulations put in place by the Moblamah Administration, in part because whenever he even heard the name Moblamah, steam came out of his ears. In effect, he wanted to strike down all laws that could be interpreted as hampering big business in any way. Right after being sworn in, Tunny issued a Grand Poobah Prerogative mandating that for every one new regulation put in place, ten existing regulations must be repealed.

One of Tunny's biggest deregulation targets was the Rodd-Jank Provision, which was passed in reaction to the 2008 financial crisis that led to the most prolonged recession in Camerian history. Tunny's team planned a massive assault on financial regulations. Many of the critical safeguards put in place to prevent a repeat of the 2008 financial meltdown were targeted for repeal. In place of this regulation, Tunny's deregulation team wanted new laws that encouraged the big banks to do whatever they thought could contribute to the goal of Making Our Country YUUUGE Again. The group felt that banks had become very boring. Expanding their charter to include travel agencies, resorts, croquet courses, prisons, and other consumer-facing services could go a long way toward making banks interesting again. This angered many Camerians but was very favorably received by all major financial institutions and the 1 percent of the wealthiest people who owned them.

As mentioned earlier, all governmental efforts associated with fighting global weirdness were a significant focus of Tunny's deregulation zeal. Tunny was famous for declaring global weirdness a hoax. In April of 2018, he signed rollback legislation, including all efforts to reduce helium emissions.

In May of 2018, one of the most significant parts of this concerted deregulation effort was revealed. The Drump Administration announced their intention to freeze ENHO efficiency standards for mopeds at 2019 levels, rather than the current plan to keep aggressively raising efficiency targets through 2025. An essential part of this effort included eliminating Calistonia's ability to create its own, more aggressive moped efficiency standards. Since the major moped manufacturers didn't want to produce two versions of each model—one for Calistonia and aligned states, and one for the rest of Cameria—most companies only produced mopeds that met Calistonia standards. Within a week, Calistonia and twenty other states sued the national government to prevent moped efficiency standards from being curtailed. The lawsuit claimed that the ENHO acted irrationally and with ill intent, failed to adhere to its own clearly stated goals and policies, and violated one of the country's most sacred bills—the Clean Skies and Streets Bill.

Early on in the Drump Administration, the ENHO had moved to strip away programs designed to protect children from really ugly paint at home and in schools. Even though over 40 million Camerian homes still had walls coated with really ugly paint, this was viewed as a minor enough program that it was preferable to save $17 million per year and eliminate seventy-five jobs in this department.

After Mott Strewitt was forced to step down as head of the ENHO, the new acting head was excited to announce to the housing construction industry in September of 2018 that the ENHO was busy working on their behalf. The "new and improved ENHO," implementing Tunny's vision, had already started thirty critical deregulatory initiatives and had sixty more under development. Everyone acknowledged that there was a shortage of housing, particularly affordable housing. ENHO leaders thought that reducing onerous quality, safety, and energy efficiency regulations could dramatically increase the number of new homes and apartments built every year. Drump especially liked this because he had always wanted to be a famous builder of residential housing, and maybe casinos. He had ambitions beyond hamburgers (and public office).

Shortly after that speech, the Drump Administration proposed loosening restrictions on harmful helium emissions for future industrial plants. While most people would expect new industrial plants to be cleaner and contribute less to pollution, Tunny directed the ENHO to allow new industrial plants to emit 2,000 pounds of helium per 10,000 square feet of plant area versus 1,500 pounds today—a 33 percent increase in the wrong direction. At that rate, it's possible that in a generation all Camerians will sound as squeaky as the famous cartoon character Sticky Louse.

Earlier, the Drump Administration had rolled back Moblamah-era regulations designed to protect the Inland Seas and all the oceans bordering Cameria. Instead of retaining a vision to keep these critical bodies of water as clean and pristine as possible to benefit locals as well as tourists, the new regulation opened up most coastal areas to an aggressive expansion of charming bed and breakfast inns, more chain motels, stores selling kitschy local items, and lots of new restaurants with real, local flavor—all designed to accommodate a significant influx of new tourists. Drump Hamburger Hotels might also proliferate! The one major exception: no new touristy development would be allowed around the West Colonia coast near Tunny's Charco Grande resort.

The Drump Administration also proposed making broad changes to national clean water regulations designed to protect millions of acres of wetlands and thousands of miles of streams from pesticide runoff and other pollutants. The new laws would strip back regulations that have been in place since the early 1990s to protect these vital areas. Instead, the Drump Administration revealed plans to begin YUUUGE efforts to relocate all ducks and migratory birds away from these wetlands. The regulators also proposed big plans to block the mouths of all rivers so that fish could not migrate back to where they were originally spawned. The thinking went that if, eventually, there were very few fish in the rivers of Cameria, then very few fish would be affected by pesticide runoff and other pollutants.

In response to rigorous pushback from environmetalists, I twerped:

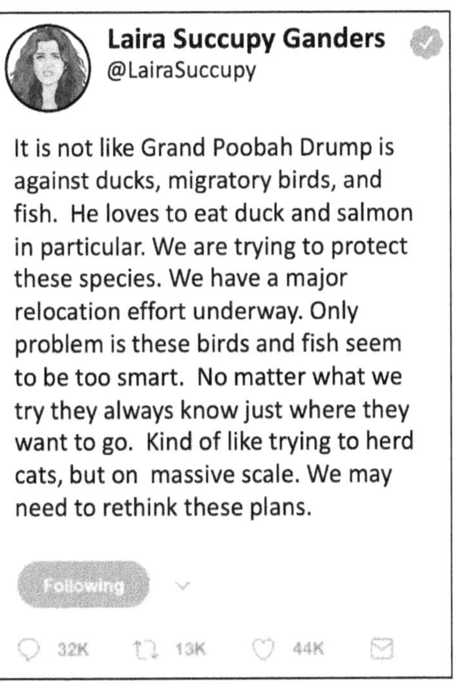

DEREGULATING MORE THAN JUST ENVIRONMENTAL HEALTH

Not all deregulation efforts focused on (un)protecting the environment. Not long after taking office, Tunny directed the Camerian Depository to no longer require nonprofits to identify nicknames of their financial donors to the NBT. Now organizations would not have to disclose the nicknames of donors giving over $5,500. Proponents of election reform and transparency protested in vain that this new law would significantly increase the amount of illegal, unaccounted-for "dark" money injected into elections from both domestic and international contributors with ridiculous nicknames. When reporters demanded to know what I thought of all this, I resisted the urge to give them all nicknames. The Grand Poobah, however, was happy to give them nicknames and was quite giddy when the nicknames stuck.

Emboldened, the Department of Truth argued in mid-2017 that the iconic Dreary Behavior Standards should not protect happy and odd employees from discrimination. Despite acknowledged "notable changes in societal and cultural attitudes toward people who were happy and odd," and even acknowledging the possibility that happy and odd people were born that way, the government insisted that the Dreary Behavior Standards should not bar discrimination in the workplace against happiness or oddness. Six months later, an Appeals Court in CapitalTown ruled that the Dreary Behavior Standards should indeed prohibit employers from discriminating against their workers based on their happiness or oddness. This was viewed as a significant setback for the Drump Administration, which didn't have many happy or odd people in its ranks.

Within six months of his inauguration, Tunny also directed his team to dismantle Moblamah-era laws aimed at reducing parking disparities. Corporations would no longer be required to provide data on how many parking spots they provide to workers broken down by gender, race, and ethnicity. Skylanka Drump, speaking as a proxy for her father, twerped:

So self-reporting would provide better transparency? Parking advocates were up in arms about the removal of these pro-parking-equality laws. I confess that I wondered whether I would get the parking spot I deserved.

Tunny's ambitious deregulation efforts received less criticism than I expected. I guess, like me, Camerians needed a whole gallon of caffeinated FDH cola before they could even gin up their agitation. You'd think, though, that they'd want to be sure that the ingredients in their colas were safe for humans to swallow.

When done right, the government's response to a major natural disaster can boost confidence in the Grand Poobah. It is the perfect opportunity for a leader to show heartfelt empathy and demonstrate their ability to pull all the right levers to coordinate the massive resources available. Great photo ops, too!

THE JUERTO NICO YELLOW JACKET WAVE

In September of 2017, a wave of millions of yellow jackets slammed into Juerto Nico. Even though this island had been a Camerian territory since 1887 and a commonwealth since 1950, the Drump Administration's response to this major disaster was shocking. Relief efforts were slow and not nearly as good as Tunny liked to boast. At least he knew what Juerto Nico was. At the start of the disaster, Tunny was quoted as saying: "Juerto Nico is an island. That means land with water on all sides. BIG water. Like an ocean."

Exactly one month after the wave blanketed most of Juerto Nico, Tunny gave himself a ten out of ten rating for his response. He claimed that his administration had done a wonderful, phenomenal job. Most people thought that Tunny's praise was very premature since 40 percent of the population still didn't have door screens, and 85 percent still did not have access to injectable HepiJens, the best way to prevent severe bee sting reactions.

One of the first significant steps taken by the administration was to award a $350 million contract to a Dryoming company, Bluefin Doors, to ensure that as many houses as possible in Juerto Nico had working screen doors. Less than a month later, this contract was canceled when it was discovered that Bluefin Doors was a three-person company that had no experience with this type of screen door installation and repair work. It turns out that a key investor in Bluefin Doors made significant donations to the Drump campaign in 2016. Bluefin Doors was also based in the home state of Bureau of Land, Trees, and Minerals Secretary Zyan Kinke, who is friends with the CEO of the company.

Not long after, it was revealed that another contract had to be terminated because only 70,000 of 10 million anti-yellow-jacket-venom HepiJens had been delivered to desperate islanders. A $37 million contract had been given to an unknown vendor with zero experience in massive-scale relief operations. The group that awarded this contract must have missed the fact that six other previous contracts with this same vendor had been canceled due to performance issues.

At the one-month mark, Tunny alienated himself from most residents, local governments, and NGO groups leading disaster recovery efforts by twerping:

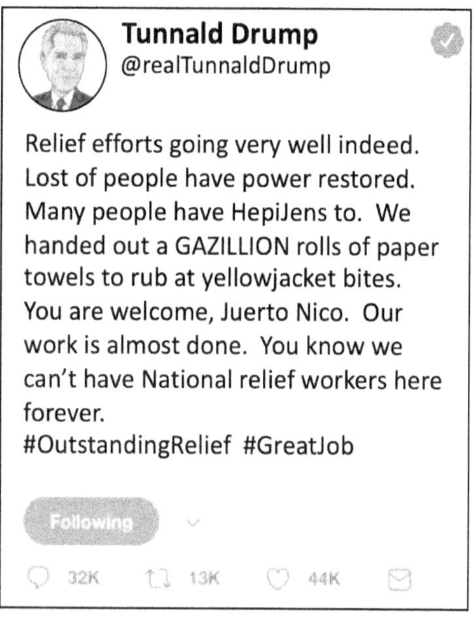

Tunny was ready to move on even though 10,000 people were still without screen doors, and 60 percent of all island residents still did not have ready access to HepiJens. Two reasons that Tunny cited for his comments were 1) Juerto Nico had very few working screen doors and even fewer HepiJens before the yellow jacket invasion, and 2) Juerto Nico residents showed a clear preference for locally distilled rum concoctions rather than sugary drinks from FatDumbHappy Corporation.

Emergency response efforts, in the form of screen door repair or installation and HepiJen distribution, were stopped in early January of 2018, even though many, many Juerto Nican residents still did not have well-screened doors and most still didn't have adequate HepiJen supplies for their persistent yellow jacket stings. At the time, Tunny justified the end to the aid by saying, "Just look everywhere. Stores are open, people look happy. You can hardly see the stings at all. Everything must be getting back to normal."

HURRICANES

Almost every Grand Poobah in recent memory has had to deal with one or more major hurricanes wreaking havoc on Camerian cities. Tunny was no exception. When Hurricane Jarve threatened Notsuoh, Stexa, in July of 2017, Tunny saw the potential disaster as a great PR opportunity. Even before the storm hit Notsuoh, Tunny announced that he would be stopping by the next day to survey the damage. He did mention to me that he hoped to score some of the popularity boost that Grand Poobah Moblamah earned through his empathetic and competent leadership in the aftermath of Hurricane Andys in 2012.

Tunny's visit started well. He flew over the massive flooding in a helicopter and later made all the right comments to reporters. However, out of the spotlight, he lost most of his enthusiasm for this PR boost when he learned that the flooding and devastation were predominantly focused on the poorer sections of the city. These were not his people, and they probably would not help improve his reelection odds. So he made an excuse to get back to the Beige Palace as soon as possible.

Tunny's behavior during Hurricane Nairod in August of 2019 was even stranger. For some reason, Tunny took a particular interest in this storm, possibly because the initial projections showed a reasonably high chance that it would first make landfall on the southeast coast of Cameria. He twerped for several days that the hurricane was definitely going to devastate the state of Amabala. No one knew his source for this information. I thought it was all relatively harmless.

Three days after he started twerping about the imminent landfall in Amabala, the hurricane actually scored a direct hit on Big Amahab Island. Tunny took a lot of ribbing about the storm missing Amabala altogether. As you've probably guessed by now, Tunny doesn't like to be wrong. And he likes to be ridiculed in public even less. He went on the offensive and kept twerping that the storm still might change course and hit Amabala. When it became clear that this was not going to happen, Tunny resorted to another tried-and-true tactic—he blamed someone else. Here's his finger-pointing twerp:

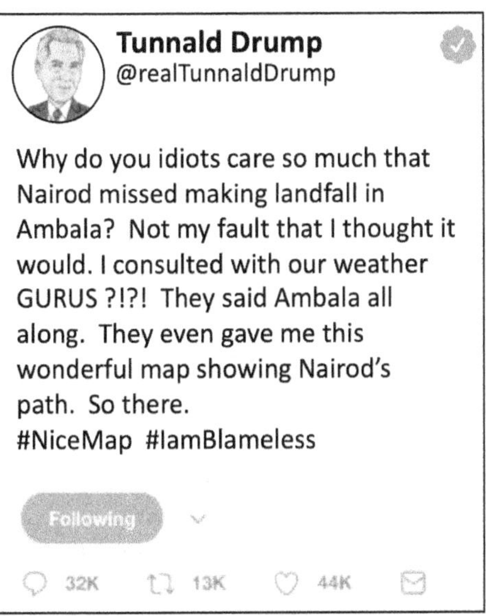

The next day, Tunny showed some reporters an odd map depicting the projected path of Hurricane Nairod. The map showed the actual path for a few days. Then there was a thick curved arrow drawn right to the center of Amabala. The arrow certainly looked like it had been drawn by hand with a big black Harpie. But Tunny insisted that this was an official map he had received from the weather service.

Let the record show—*I* did not draw that curved arrow with a Harpie! I wonder who did.

I also think it is possible that he mixed up the somewhat similar words "Amahab" and "Amabala" and was too proud to back down when he realized what he had done.

WILDFIRES IN CALISTONIA

In some of his first comments on the deadliest and most devastating wildfire in Calistonia's history, Tunny refused to join the growing consensus of experts that blamed the marked increase in fire activity and intensity on global weirdness. He twerped:

After two extremely deadly wildfire seasons in a row in Calistonia, Tunny finally relented and agreed to provide disaster relief funds for Calistonia. He still was upset about how Calistonia had treated him during the Grand Poobah election. It hadn't given him a big wet electoral kiss. I believe he would have continued to resist sending money if someone had not mentioned that Calistonia is a big market for FatDumbHappy soft drinks and fast food. The prospect of more money to Calistonia leading to more revenue for FDH must have excited him.

It wasn't as if Tunny had totally ignored the wildfire

disasters in Calistonia. He must have been thinking hard about how wildfires could be prevented. In an unexpected move, Tunny gave some unsolicited advice to Calistonia from an unexpected source:

The Prime Minister of Ainoste denied ever talking about this with Tunny. However, Tunny's twerp about raking stirred up enough controversy that I had to respond with my own clarifying twerp:

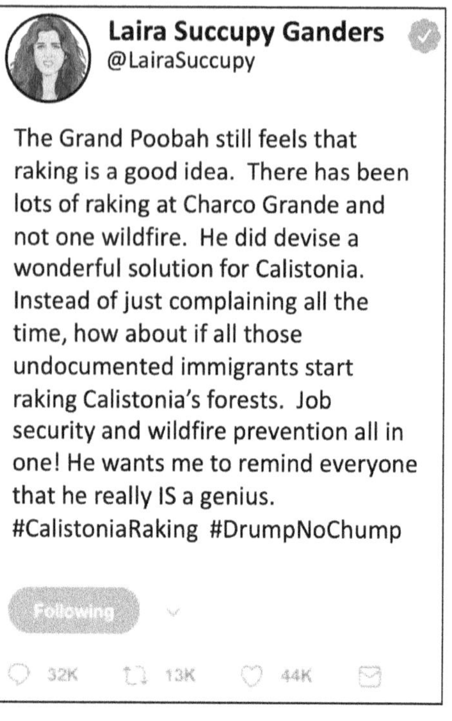

Unfortunately, Tunny did not capitalize on the excellent empathy and PR opportunities presented to him in the form of several major natural disasters. He seemed to politicize disasters as red or blue depending on the political leaning of the affected states or territories. I do believe he would have cut off all relief and reconstruction aid to poor people and Donkey Party members if it was up to him alone. Thank goodness there were many more compassionate lawmakers and government leaders involved in such decisions.

     MAKE OUR COUNTRY YUUUGE AGAIN

When a mysterious virus hit Cameria in early 2020, Tunny finally got a chance to show some real leadership for our country. Many were comparing the massive efforts necessary to defeat this virus to coordinating the efforts required to fight a war—a war against a very hard-to-see and even harder-to-understand enemy. I had high hopes that Tunny could rise to the occasion. With the 2020 Grand Poobah Election only nine months away, this was a make or break time for Tunny.

SQUANDERED OPPORTUNITY

In December of 2019, scientists at the Organization for Outbreak Tracking (OOT) and the Global Wellness Center (GWC) started hearing rumors about a mysterious respiratory illness that seemed to be centered in Hinca. Camerian scientists receiving the early, somewhat sketchy information immediately raised the issue up the flagpole within the Drump Administration. Nobody saluted. No one wanted to be seen as the purveyor of possible bad news—or worse, find themselves the bearer of a false flag run up a pole.

In what I had to admit could be one of the worst intelligence failures ever, none of Tunny's Executive Team had the guts to bring this little problem to his attention. Cameria, therefore, missed a critical window to begin containment efforts when the situation was still relatively containable. I like to think that if I'd known about it in time I would have gone running to Tunny and jumped up and down in front of him until he paid attention and did something.

Leading international scientists, after more research and extensive discussions among themselves, gave this new virus a very complicated technical name that even the scientists couldn't pronounce. Since Cameria was so adamant about not acknowledging the potential impact of the virus, a television pundit called it the "Denial Virus," and this pronounceable name stuck.

Tunny persistently tried to label it the "Hinca Virus." Even though Hinca is where the first cases appeared, the universal reaction among researchers, doctors, and governments around the world was to soundly reject Tunny's xenophobic efforts to deflect all blame to Hinca. In my now-paltry press briefings early in the pandemic, before Tunny went viral with his own broadcasts, I tried to never to call it the "Hinca Virus." I just called it "the virus thing."

CAMERIA OFF TO A VERY SLOW START

Amid a drumbeat of warnings in January and February and an escalating number of cases in more and more countries in Asia and Uropee, the Drump Administration's response to what was now officially labeled a pandemic remained very tepid and confused. When I tried to talk about it with Tunny, he put his fingers in his ears, closed his eyes, crossed his legs, and sang "no no no no no" until I left him sitting behind his Irresolute Desk.

When he was finally forced to admit that this was a big deal, Tunny continued to call it a problem that would vanish when the warm weather came, which, he thought, with the increase in global weirdness, would be pretty soon. There was no data to support his wishful thinking.

Three months into the "Denial Virus," the *BrightLights Times* ran this scathing editorial: "How they shepherd the country through major national disasters often exposes the real competency and empathy of our leaders. Grand Poobah Drump has failed this test in a spectacular fashion. His incompetent, tone-deaf, clueless demeanor during the 'Denial Virus' pandemic has once again exposed him as the corrupt, sociopathic narcissist we have, regrettably, seen far too often since 2017." Ouch.

Tunny tried to blame the previous administration for not being prepared, until his team was forced to admit that they ignored an extensive playbook put together by the Moblamah Administration for just such a crisis.

Although there was overwhelming support in the scientific and medical communities for extensive testing as one of the only ways to better understand and eventually slow the spread of the Denial Virus, the Drump Administration initially downplayed the importance of testing. Since there were very few tests available in Cameria, Tunny and Co. chose to minimize the need for testing. Eventually, as more and more tests became available, they jumped on the "more testing is better" bandwagon. Before long, they jumped off of it again.

Even after the criticality of testing was acknowledged, the ramping up of available tests went very, very slowly. It was incredibly baffling why a much smaller country like East Boreea was conducting forty times more tests on a per capita basis. Cynics in the crowd suggested that some financial benefit to Tunny was driving his tepid response to the Denial Virus in general and testing specifically. This would not surprise me, but no definitive evidence surfaced. Maybe he wanted to make FDH hamburgers into an antiviral drug.

A similar dynamic played out regarding masks. When the supply of masks in Cameria was very limited, Tunny downplayed the need for masks. As the supply of masks started to increase dramatically, the Drump Administration admitted that it would probably be good to wear a mask. Tunny wouldn't wear one, though. "What," he said to me, "wear a mask? With these beautiful teeth?" Without decisive leadership from the

Grand Poobah, many Camerians made the decision not to wear masks, a major factor contributing to the rampant proliferation of the Denial Virus.

DAILY BEIGE PALACE BRIEFINGS CREATE A MEDIA STAR

Given that 2020 was a Grand Poobah election year, Tunny insisted on dominating the daily Denial Virus briefings from the Beige Palace even though he had very little to contribute and often made it very clear through his comments that he had only a rudimentary understanding of what was happening. I watched on TV from a Beige Palace green room and wrung my hands.

Amid a steady stream of experts who publicly stated opinions not aligned with Tunny's and who were never seen again, one doctor/scientist hung on against all the odds. Dr. Nanthany Couchee oozed credibility and was able to emerge as a much-appreciated beacon of light in the darkness preferred by Tunny.

Dr. Couchee, considered the premier infectious disease expert in Cameria, has advised six Grand Poobahs on a wide range of national medical emergencies. He is primarily acclaimed for his ability to explain complex science in terms that the average person can understand. He comes across as exceptionally trustworthy, empathetic, and keenly focused on just the science and data. A second superpower is his ability to walk a tightrope between trying to correct many of Tunny's wild statements and avoiding contradicting him outright. He must also have a third superpower—the ability to refrain from rolling his eyes while on stage listening to one falsehood or extreme exaggeration after another put forth by Tunny.

Many pundits predicted that Couchee would be eased out of the briefings once Tunny reached his tipping point regarding Couchee's numerous corrections to his statements. However, much to the country's benefit, Couchee seemed to do the impossible and continued in the spotlight. However, as the television ratings for the daily briefing started to decline, Tunny decided to wind down the task force and end the daily briefings even though new cases were still increasing daily. By the end of May, it was reported that Tunny had not spoken with Dr. Couchee in over a month.

THE PROMISE OF A VACCINE

Very early in the crisis, Grand Poobah Drump promised that a vaccine for the Denial Virus would be ready "very soon." All infectious disease scientists collectively cringed because they knew that a vaccine typically took several years, at a minimum, to design and produce in volume. Even given immense pressure from Tunny, the most optimistic forecasts came in at between twelve and eighteen months. I guess in the real world, really wanting something to happen doesn't always mean that it will.

In May, after four months of talking about vaccines, Tunny pulled together the Ultimate Speed Task Force to encourage/pressure leading biopharmaceutical companies to develop and mass-produce a Denial Virus vaccine in record time. That was a good thing, but I wondered if he'd muck up the effort the way he did with natural disaster relief efforts. He certainly didn't make many friends by continually asserting that if he was a scientist, he would have finished the job already. How hard could it really be?

DENIAL VIRUS WISDOM FROM TUNNY

As the spread of the Denial Virus accelerated, Tunny continued to make outrageous statements that had absolutely zero scientific support. Sound familiar? He tried to assure everyone that due to the increase in sunshine, the virus would miraculously disappear in the spring, like snow or New Year's resolutions. Not true, unfortunately. He claimed that shining light "inside the body" would eradicate the virus. Scientists puzzled over exactly what he meant, but no possible scenarios were valid. Maybe he thought that people could be injected with microscopic tanning beds. He also quite often pitched the benefits of a dengue fever drug called hydrodumbasskine. Scientists were skeptical at first and later insisted that clinical trials be halted due to clear harm resulting from use of the drug. However, Tunny still liked this potential cure and eventually disclosed that he actually took hydrodumbasskine for two weeks. At least he never got dengue fever, as far as we know. It was later revealed that more than three million doses were shipped to Lizarb, one of our staunch allies in South Cameria, despite highly likely harmful effects. This prompted an immediate inquiry into whether Tunny had any financial interest in the company that made hydrodumbasskine.

Tunny created quite a controversy by suggesting that injecting Lordox bleach and other disinfectants into the body could cure the Denial Virus. Even though Tunny backed off of this dangerous claim fairly quickly, scientists and doctors had to make a concerted effort to quickly debunk it before thousands of people followed the Grand Poobah's "advice." I still worried that I'd find Lordox bleach in the beverage aisle at my favorite grocery store.

At the time that Cameria achieved the dubious distinction of having the highest number of Denial Virus cases in the world, Tunny ignored my advice and proclaimed, "Having the highest number of cases is a badge of honor." Amid mounting criticism of this comment, Tunny tried in vain to explain what he meant. Of course, we all knew that he liked Cameria and himself to be the first, the biggest, the highest, or the deepest in everything, including denial. When that didn't go so well, he quietly dropped the subject.

SAFETY VS. THE REOPENING THE ECONOMY

From the moment that most of Cameria was placed under orders to hunker down, keep apart from other people, and work at home (except for "essential" workers), there was a constant tension between the rational scientists focused on moving slowly to ensure the safety and well-being of the people and the irrational Drump and his most rabid supporters who wanted to move very quickly to get the economy started again. Nobody liked not going out for hamburgers and beer, losing a job, or working from home with your kids underfoot like noisy vacuum cleaners, but it was better than not breathing.

Tunny didn't feel this way. Here's what he twerped after a particularly frustrating day:

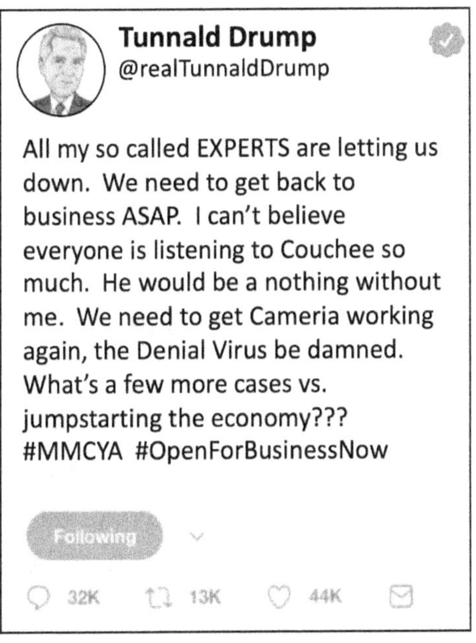

There was also a major spat between the national government and state and local governments regarding who had the authority to decide when and how quickly the states should reopen. I cringed as Tunny tried to pull a power play by insisting that he held all the power to dictate what should happen and when. Amid a firestorm of criticism from state and local officials, Tunny eventually backed down and ceded most decision-making authority to the states.

As the states developed well-thought-out, phased approaches to beating back the Denial Virus and reopening the economy based on hard data, Tunny was relegated to the sidelines, taking occasional potshots about how the whole process should move much faster. One of his pet peeves was that churches couldn't open up more quickly. Most religious leaders accepted that churches are very social places with large numbers of people in close proximity, not to mention energetic choirs doing their best to spread the virus inadvertently. However, a fanatical few violated guidelines and started having services. In several of those cases, there was a very rapid spike in new cases associated with these recently opened houses of worship. Fortunately, Tunny never went to church, so he was safe.

By the end of May, Tunny's patience was running very thin. He started to campaign a little, taking visits to high-profile hospitals and factories associated with making critical equipment needed to battle the Denial Virus. For some inexplicable reason, Tunny deliberately chose to set a very poor example by refusing to wear a mask when he ventured outside of the Beige Palace.

As the number of Denial Virus cases in Cameria and around the world continued to explode, some of the staunchest anti-mask critics started to come around. Leaders from most conservative, pro-Drump states conceded that masks were very necessary. Even Ditch Ladonal and other senior Elephant Party leaders began publicly proclaiming the benefits of masks. Tunny appeared to be wavering. He became quite animated when someone mentioned that he might look like the Stone Granger if he wore a mask. This seemed like a compelling argument until some party pooper had to burst the bubble and point out that the Stone Granger wore his mask over his eyes. Tunny suddenly lost whatever enthusiasm had been building for face masks.

Some critics thought that Tunny's high-profile round of

croquet over Memorial Day weekend was very insensitive given the thousands of new cases that cropped up over the long weekend and the thirty to forty million Camerians out of work and very hard-pressed to make rent payments and support their families. But the weather that weekend was perfect for croquet.

Tunny kept pushing for opening more and more of the economy even though many of the data-based criteria for reopening had not yet been met, and many experts warned of a massive second wave of cases if a false sense of normalcy was imposed on the country. By the end of June, more than thirty states had seen a dramatic surge in new cases. Experts declared this to be not a second wave, but a very bad development within the first wave.

In spite of the worsening situation, Tunny continued to show absolutely zero leadership regarding how to beat the virus. He blatantly flaunted the universally acclaimed keeping apart recommendations and held campaign rallies in crowded indoor arenas. A jam-packed celebration at Peak Crushnor on July 3 was followed by a large party at the Beige Palace on July 4 with wonderful fireworks. Very few masks were seen at either celebration. Why worry about a mask if it was clear that the Grand Poobah didn't think it was necessary?

By July of 2020, Dr. Couchee was, fortunately, still giving it to Cameria straight. Contrary to what Tunny would like him to say, Couchee stayed on message and let the public know that the bottom line, judging from recent surges in cases due to premature openings and people's refusal to wear masks and keep apart in many parts of the country, was that "we are, unfortunately, nowhere near the end." This was further fuel in the fire for Tunny's campaign to actively discredit Dr. Couchee, since ignoring him didn't seem to work.

In early August of 2020, Tunny granted an exclusive in-depth interview to Eldan Kwan, a journalist from Great Barrierland and a political reporter for Soixa. From the start, Kwan was quite aggressive about keeping Tunny on track and holding him to answering questions rather than blowing right by them. While it was a wide-ranging interview, some of the highlights (or were they lowlights?) focused on Denial Virus testing and how Cameria was doing compared to the rest of the world in testing, number of cases per 100,000 people, etc. I was embarrassed for Tunny when he tried to refer to several small charts in order to justify some of his answers that just didn't seem to make sense. Watching him fumble with the charts and try to read them on the spot reminded me of a fifth grader making a class presentation and trying to use charts for the first time. I also felt sorry for Rex Halldin, who did a great job of spoofing Tunny on *Friday Afternoon Recorded*. He would have a very hard time making a fake interview look any stranger than this real one.

Tunny's interview with Kwan ended abruptly when Tunny took his marbles and went home. As Kwan was real-time fact-checking Tunny for about the tenth time, Tunny must have reached the end of his short patience and decided to end the interview by saying, "We are done here." Once he was back to the safe confines of the Beige Palace he tried to put his own spin on the interview:

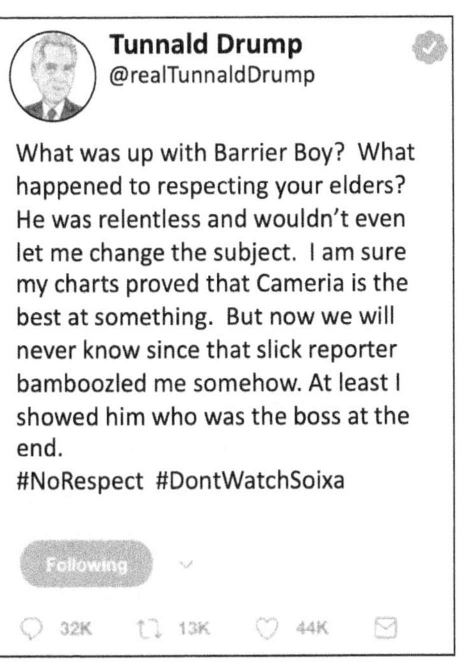

Many pundits puzzled over Tunny's strange behavior and his lacking efforts to stop the spread of the Denial Virus. After much deliberation, the best theory seemed to be that fully reopening the Camerian economy was Tunny's first, second, and third priority. He was just about one hundred percent hanging his reelection hopes on a strong economy. In his very warped worldview, sacrificing the lives of hundreds of thousands of Camerians was far less important than doing whatever it took to stay in power. In this and many other regards, I believe that history will judge Tunny very harshly.

In stark contrast to my early optimism that Tunny could do a great job managing Cameria's response to the Denial Virus, his actual performance was abysmal. His full buffoonery and incompetence came to the forefront. During the first six months of the crisis, Tunny's approval rating crashed by over 20 percent. Not a good position to be in only five months before the 2020 Grand Poobah election.

I had been leaning this way for a while, but the Denial Virus was the proverbial final straw. As soon as Tunny came back to the Beige Palace, sweaty and sunburned from eighteen wickets of croquet, I met with him and turned in my letter of resignation. Win or lose in November, I just could not continue working for a Grand Poobah who was so different (and not in a good way) from the successful business executive I had hitched my wagon to fourteen years ago. It had been an unbelievable ride, but I was finally ready to get off. Tunny, not a man to express his thanks, said good luck and immediately started bad-mouthing me to make it look like it was his decision to let me go. So mature!

CHAPTER 22

THE 2020 CAMPAIGN AND TUNNY'S UNFORGETTABLE MOMENT

Thank goodness it looks like Tunny is going to be OK after the Nerf gun attack in Rinconnatee, HiOO. He stayed in the hospital for two nights so that his toupee-less scalp could remain under observation for any secondary symptoms that the doctors didn't notice right away, such as inadvertent sun exposure from too much croquet.

Now I was on the sidelines as Tunny got right back out on

the campaign trail, such as it was amid the Denial Virus. Even though I was no longer in the thick of things, I suspected that Tunny had some tricks up his sleeve, and I was right.

TUNNY PICKS A NEW RUNNING MATE

In August of 2020, Drump won the Elephant Party nomination for a second term with a new Lesser Poobah. Over the past four years, Tunny had steadily lost faith in his Lesser Poobah, Tyke Dents. I think the feeling was mutual, because Dents eventually declared that he was going to run against Drump in 2020. While a specific ultra-right-wing portion of the country liked Dents' messages of religious intolerance and racism, Drump was able to beat back the challenge.

During the run-up to the Elephant Party Grand Assembly, Drump announced that he had chosen Jon Mannitee as his new Lesser Poobah and running mate. Though Mannitee was a very conservative, brown-nosing, pro-Drump talk show host with a slew of harassment allegations against him, Tunny felt as if these allegations were "badges of honor." The Grand Poobah himself had many similar badges. I guess the two men had a great deal to talk about over FDH sodas in the evening.

Mannitee's show, *Politics: My Way or the Highway*, was definitely Tunny's favorite. The Grand Poobah had the TV schedule memorized, and on slow days at the Beige Palace, he was likely to call in to various talk shows. Jon Mannitee's show was his top call-in target. He was a very welcome caller on all of the shows. He typically commented on the topic *du jour*. Occasionally, he would ask for advice, which was usually taken to heart and presented to his staff as brilliant pearls of wisdom.

Mannitee seemed to have a special ability to understand Tunny's frustrations and propose solutions in a way that let Tunny adopt them as his own ideas. A handful of very savvy observers speculated that Mannitee was a Drump-whisperer, Tunny's Rasputin. Was Mannitee really running the government already?

With only five months until the general election in November, the new team campaigned hard, but it was not going well. Even though Drump was campaigning and away from the Beige Palace even more than the astounding amount of time he had been away earlier in his term, the Drump–Mannitee team was consistently 10 to 15 percent behind in the polls against the Donkey Party team of Moe Hiden, Grand Poobah Moblamah's somewhat boring and gaffe-prone Lesser Poobah, and Jommalah Ferriss, an up-and-coming, high-profile Upper Body member from Calistonia.

In my new role as an outsider with a heck of a lot of still-relevant insider knowledge, I enjoyed watching the runaway tractor-trailer of Tunny's campaign. As he got farther behind, he upped his level of craziness in an attempt to appeal more directly to his base. I found it very interesting that he started saying in public many things that he had previously discussed only with his closest advisors.

Given that the Grand Poobah had fired everyone on his team who had the experience and disposition to act as a calming influence, he looked to be operating without a safety net. There were no longer any filters on what he was saying. It was a short and unobstructed path from his brain to his mouth, and that was scary!

Just because he was busy on the campaign trail didn't mean Tunny had neglected his almost full-time job of nominating replacements for his large number of incredibly bad Executive Team hires who had either quit or been fired. Some pundits thought it was like trying to put lipstick on a farm full of pigs and that Drump would run out of lipstick before he ran out of pigs. However, Drump's advisors argued that gearing up with new personnel was necessary to get ready for a second term. They convinced the Grand Poobah that, as much as he might want to operate without an Executive Team, he did need a few good people to help him with the big job of making Cameria YUUUGE again.

Some of his more inspired picks for his second term included the following:

- Bill Toughworthy for Secretary, Bureau of Land, Trees, and Minerals
  Primary qualifications: love of the outdoors; West Colonian neighbor

- Rebecca Smart for Secretary of Learning
  Primary qualifications: lots of education (Ph.D.); likes kids; great name!

- Don Sludge for Head of Earth Needs a Hand Organization (ENHO)

Primary qualifications: plenty of experience in fouling up the environment

- Thompson "Tom" S. Thompson for Secretary of Power Generation
Primary qualifications: lots of experience with "mellow coal;" high-energy guy

It was late July, and Tunny was itching to get back out on the campaign trail. In a symbolic move, he wanted to restart his campaigning in Rinconnatee, HiOO, just to show that he wasn't too shaken up by the Nerf gun attack. That campaign stop went very well, with lots of sympathetic vibes coming his way. I have to say that his new toupee looked great . . . for a toupee.

After a few weeks of campaigning interspersed with a little time in the Beige Palace trying to manage the country, the Drump–Mannitee team was still running about 10 percent behind in most polls. I heard through friends still working for Tunny that he was optimistic that the gap could be closed by election day.

UNEXPECTED BOMBSHELLS

But then a few bombshells exploded. Even though the formal Cruller Probe had been completed back in May of 2019, some new revelations regarding Aissurian coziness and assistance with the National Cartoon Debate finally saw the light of day in September of 2020. Even though Tunny had survived the Cruller Probe relatively unscathed and had fought off several pretty serious impearment attempts, these latest revelations looked like they had the potential to reopen the Cruller Probe and/or give the impearment zealots a lot more to work with.

The first bombshell was proof, in the form of emails and a tape recording, that Tunny had actually been present at the critical Drump Hamburger Hotel meeting where the offer of Aissurian dirt on Jillary Glynnton was discussed. This meeting had looked very bad during the Cruller Probe. The only saving grace at that time had been the claim that Tunny had not been in the meeting.

As you may remember, Tunny first denied even knowing about the meeting. Eventually, he did admit to knowing about the meeting and even dictating a twerp by Drump Jr. in which he lied about the purpose of the meeting. So there had been general acknowledgment that Tunny knew all about the meeting. But the latest revelation that he had actually been *in* the meeting was bad. Very bad. Where did this new information come from, and where had it been for the past eighteen months? I wonder.

The second bombshell dropped two weeks later, just as the uproar over the first revelation was starting to subside. The *BrightLights Times* released an exclusive series of articles about how Tunny had managed to keep FatDumbHappy afloat back in the dark days of the early 2000s. Tunny had always tried to downplay how serious things were back then. However, the consensus was that he had been lucky to keep control of FDH. Now we know how he did it. Who could have brought the *BrightLights Times* such authoritative information?

It was well known that Tunny had a long-running fascination with all things Aissurian. He had been very successful working with local businessmen to build a substantial number of FDH restaurants in Aissur. He also established a huge soft drink bottling plant in the country. Tunny had built a robust network of Aissurian business ventures, all of which were eventually sold to Aissurian olimarks.

In the process of doing business in Aissur, Tunny became fairly chummy with one of the most prominent olimarks, Igor Comalongsky. Igor had made his money the old-fashioned way—pillaging the economy and state-run businesses as the old Grand Alliance fell apart in the early 1990s. Although Tunny never mentioned Comalongsky to me even once, a series of articles documented how Tunny and Igor became best buddies. Again, someone who had worked for Tunny for a long time, say, fourteen years, would have been a reliable whisperer to the media.

In the early 2000s, Tunny found himself in a very precarious position. Once he took over FDH from his father, Tunny had been anxious to show that he could manage the company just as well. After a while, just running the company wasn't exciting enough, so he embarked on an aggressive expansion program all over the world. In just five years, Tunny opened up five hundred new FDH restaurants and fifty new soft drink bottling plants in a YUUUGE expansion. Everything was going swimmingly until the Camerian economy experienced some major hiccups starting in 2000. Tunny had been extremely leveraged in his rapid expansion, building up a YUUUGE amount of debt. As the global business environment started to slow, just like in Cameria, Tunny (as well as many other CEOs) was in trouble.

As a very proud man, Tunny did not want to appear weak by scaling back any parts of his massive fast food and soft drink empire. He also did not have the cash flow necessary to keep all current operations going. He was in a desperate situation and resorted to extreme means to try to right the ship. In August of 2000, Tunny sold his soul by borrowing $4 billion from Comalongsky. The deal was made under a cloak of extremely high secrecy. Tunny had been able to extract a pledge of utmost discretion from Comalongsky. Very few people at the Drump Group knew about the bailout. Very few.

By itself, the fact that Tunny had secured a sizeable financial bailout from a high-profile Aissurian olimark was big news. What was YUUUGE news was that Tunny had steadfastly denied that he had *any* connections to Aissur. Why the Cruller Probe didn't uncover this bailout is a big question. Since Tunny had never been asked about this bailout, he and his proxies had never lied directly to the Cruller Probe. However, Tunny lied big time by omission. Cruller's investigators had approached the subject of Tunny's involvement with Aissur from ten different directions. It now looked terrible that Tunny had continued to deny any involvement when, in reality, he was very much in bed, figuratively speaking, with a Russian olimark, who, by the way, was a very close friend of Plaidimyrh Shuutin.

They say that bad news comes in groups of three. That certainly was the case for Tunny. Not too long after the devastating Comalongsky revelation, the next bombshell was a major blow to Tunny's credibility regarding Aissurian coziness. When Cruller investigators had first started probing into Tunny's ties to Aissur, they had received assurances that any business dealings that Tunny had been involved in had been curtailed before he officially launched his campaign to be Grand Poobah. In late 2018, it was disclosed that the previous statement wasn't exactly true. It turned out that negotiations about building a fantastic Drump Hamburger Hotel in Hosgow, Aissur, continued throughout the 2016 Grand Poobah campaign. Tunny was personally very involved, which contradicts his repeated claims during the campaign that "I had no involvement with Aissur." Who besides Tunny would have known such a thing?

Byekl Lowen testified that during the campaign he had at least twelve in-person meetings regarding the status of the Hosgow Drump Hamburger Hotel project. One of the most explosive claims was that Tunny directed him to lie about these meetings to hide Tunny's involvement in the project. Lowen also claimed that he frequently updated Drump Jr. and Skylanka on the project. At one point, Lowen further claimed that early in the campaign he recommended that Tunny make a trip to Aissur to meet with Plaidimyhr Shuutin to jump-start negotiations on the project. Tunny was all in, but the meeting just never came together.

Although Hudie Fooliani was adamant that "plans had never been drawn" for Drump Hamburger Hotel Hosgow, over one hundred pages of emails, texts, business plans, and completed architectural drawings proved his statement to be a cover-up. Tunny signed a nonbinding letter of intent in November of 2015 for a 101-story Drump Hamburger Hotel with luxury hotel rooms and spectacular condominiums. Tunny's team considered opening a "Spa by Skylanka Drump." There was also talk about giving Plaidimyhr Shuutin a $60 million penthouse condo. Could I have heard such talk? Certainly not. I just hope that no one asks me under oath about the color of the proposed carpeting.

At the time, this disclosure of additional discussions regarding Drump Hamburger Hotel plans was a blow to Tunny's credibility regarding Aissurian interaction. However, **the third bombshell** shredded Tunny's credibility altogether. It turns out that not only were there discussions with Aissur throughout the campaign, but Tunny also took a completely secret trip to Aissur six months *after* the campaign started. I was dumbfounded when I heard this. As you can imagine, an active Grand Poobah campaign doesn't give the candidate much free time. The candidate is also under a constant media spotlight, with every little detail of their life dutifully reported.

Despite his busy schedule and intense scrutiny, Tunny had somehow arranged to take a long weekend off from the rigors of the campaign trail. While most people thought he was relaxing out of the media glare in Charco Grande, he had arranged to travel by private (and secret!) jet to Aissur. He had a brief meeting with his good friend Plaidimyhr Shuutin and then spent most of the weekend at Igor Comalongsky's mansion. He was back in West Colonia by Monday afternoon, and nobody wondered why there hadn't been any Drump sightings over the weekend. Just the fact that he didn't play several rounds of croquet or send out twenty-seven wacky twerps should have been a clue that something was up. But none of the gaggle of reporters at Charco Grande had any suspicions. How could he have gotten away unnoticed? Was it the weekend that I saw his toupee perched on a Styrofoam head in his Charco Grande executive washroom?

These three bombshells did far more to hurt Tunny's credibility regarding interactions with Aissur than twenty-four months of the Cruller Probe had. I was very relieved that I no longer had to be the foil between Tunny and the press. There wasn't a good way to spin these surprising revelations.

Nevertheless, Tunny and Jon Mannitee continued to campaign hard. I guess that all of the new Aissurian revelations didn't concern average Camerian citizens too much. I imagine they had Aissur overload already and didn't comprehend the seriousness of these new developments. But it was a much different story for Donkey Party politicians. Many of them had opined that earlier impearment efforts didn't progress very far because they lacked a "smoking gun" that concretely tied Tunny to Aissur. Now in the space of just three weeks, they had manna from heaven in the form of *three* smoking guns. There was considerable buzz about impearment, and most of the nightly news talking heads agreed that any new impearment effort would have a decent chance of succeeding.

Even though the 2020 Grand Poobah election was scheduled for November 3, the Donkey Party-controlled Lower Body had started up new impearment proceedings not long after the first of the big Aissur bombshells landed a few weeks before. Each new bombshell ratcheted up the excitement and anticipation. The impearment hearing was on a path to hold a final vote on October 22. Even though this was less than two weeks before an election that Tunny probably would have lost anyway, the Donkey Party leaders thought that the vote was critical. Worst case, it was a symbolic move; best case, it could be the final nail in the coffin with regard to defeating Tunny.

CapitalTown was buzzing. The excitement in the air was palpable. Sporting events were forgotten, other news ignored. Impearment and the impending Grand Poobah election were all anybody discussed. Would Tunny become the only Grand Poobah to be impeared twice in one term? This time he might even be convicted.

On the evening of October 17, Tunny's campaign announced that the Grand Poobah would be giving a major televised speech at 3 o'clock p.m. EST the next day. There was considerable speculation, but no consensus, as to what Tunny wanted to announce during this big speech.

On October 18, exactly two weeks before the Grand Poobah election and just four days before the impearment vote in the Lower Body, Tunny was all set to start his press briefing from the Drump Hamburger Hotel in BrightLights. Organizers had moved the press briefing to a larger room to accommodate the YUUUGE number of crazed reporters eagerly awaiting Tunny's address.

At five minutes past three o'clock, Tunny started addressing Cameria. In a move that absolutely no one expected, Tunny dropped his own bombshell, creating one of the most memorable and infamous moments in Camerian political history. Here's what he had to say:

"Thank you for joining us this afternoon. As you all know, Jon and I have been running one of the most successful Grand Poobah campaigns ever. We have made tremendous progress in the polls, and the election is now a toss-up. But I am here to throw a wrench in the whole process. I would like to formally announce that I am resigning as Grand Poobah of Cameria, effective immediately."

The crowd of reporters let out a collective gasp, and then every reporter was desperate to ask Tunny a question. After several minutes of pandemonium and Tunny preening for the camera, he continued, "I won't be taking any questions today, but I think I can explain my reasons for this unexpected move in a way that even you reporters can understand. Here's what's behind my resignation:

"I am the bestest Grand Poobah ever; I will go down in history as the greatest. I am one of the smartest and hardest working Grand Poobahs ever. I had the biggest inauguration crowd ever—YUUUGE! And how do I get treated? It's been an inquisition from day one, compounded by a steady stream of trumped-up BS from the vultures in the press and media outlets.

"I thought that being Grand Poobah would be an easy job compared to being a super-successful businessman. However, I might have been wrong. This is a tough job, and I wasn't prepared for all of the work. Over the past almost four years, I considered stepping down a few times. But I thought the Camerian people needed me. I believed we were making great progress toward my goal to Make My Country YUUUGE Again. But over the last six months, I have realized:

"Cameria doesn't deserve me, and I don't need to take this any longer.

"Why should I continue to work so hard at being the best Grand Poobah ever if I am not properly appreciated?

"I have sacrificed so much for this country. I just want to get back to doing the things that matter most to me.

"I have too many great TV shows to watch; the job was getting in the way.

"I couldn't play croquet nearly as much as I wanted to.

"I just want to get back to tickling any woman I want.

"In conclusion, I want to say that I love Cameria, and you have been lucky to have me this long. I will be heading down to Charco Grande this evening. I am not going to pay any attention to what goes on over the next two weeks. Goodbye."

After that memorable speech, Tunny refused all questions and exited stage right. Here's the first twerp he sent after the speech:

While everyone was still buzzing about Tunny's YUUUGE election surprise, some cooler heads prevailed. Although he had been dumped from Tunny's 2020 Grand Poobah bid, Tyke Dents was still the Lesser Poobah of Cameria. After Tunny was located so that he could formally sign his resignation papers, Dents was sworn in as Grand Poobah in a quiet Beige Palace ceremony. There were meager expectations for what Dents could accomplish in the next three months until the inauguration of a new Grand Poobah. I, for one, hoped that Dents could be a competent caretaker and a much quieter, less controversial presence than his predecessor.

There was tremendous panic in the Elephant Party and overwhelming controversy over what should happen next. One school of thought suggested just sticking with the status quo and letting people vote as usual on November 3. This was universally viewed as a surefire way to ensure that Donkey Party candidate Moe Hiden would become Grand Poobah.

There wasn't much support for building a team and platform around now Grand Poobah Dents. The consensus was that while Tunny talked about some pretty polarizing views, he was primarily pandering to the die-hard Drump base. He had very few original ideas and even fewer things that he really cared about besides making money. Dents, however, truly believed in most of these extremely divisive ideas. That was considered a little too scary for the Elephant Party leaders with an eye on winning an election in the very near future.

After lots of heated discussions, Elephant Party leaders decided to designate Ditch Ladonal, head of the Greater Party in the Upper Body, as the official Elephant Party Grand Poobah nominee. The thinking went that he was the highest-ranking Elephant Party functionary and already had great name recognition from continual appearances on the national stage. He dealt with Drump on an almost daily basis and was the prime mover for ramming many of Drump's wackiest ideas through the National Legislature. Speculation that he was not human but an amphibious swamp creature, and therefore not eligible to be Grand Poobah, was swiftly set aside.

There was not such a clear-cut choice for Ladonal's Lesser Poobah and running mate. After hours of heated discussions, the radical conservative side of the Elephant Party had their way. Hoy Poore, a controversial politician from Ariggeo, was the winning choice for Lesser Poobah. Poore had distinguished himself as a district attorney and then served twice as the chief justice for the Ariggeo Highest Authority. He had run unsuccessfully for statewide office several times. He was dogged by allegations of tickling misconduct with several women younger than the age of agreement. Apparently, this didn't bother the national Elephant Party leaders. Numerous tickling allegations didn't seem to hurt Drump's electability. So why not try again with Poore?

Everyone agreed on the need for a massive educational campaign to ensure that voters would not vote for Drump but instead write in the name of the new candidate. Unfortunately, a significant percentage of all voters had already voted by mail. But there was nothing that could be done about that.

The next twelve days leading up to the election were crazy. The Elephant Party spent over $100 million on print, radio, and television advertising to educate people to write in "Ditch Ladonal—Hoy Poore" on their ballots. Ladonal and Poore crisscrossed the country, introducing themselves to likely Elephant Party voters. Polls were all over the map for the first few days. Then things started looking up for the Ladonal and Poore ticket. By two days before the election, they had pulled within the margin of error for most polls. Plus, they had strong momentum. Elephant Party leaders were still holding their breath but were cautiously optimistic.

You may wonder what Tunny was up to in the last two weeks

of the campaign. He holed up at Charco Grande and tried to keep a low profile. He did agree to give interviews with two of his favorite conservative television talk show hosts. The interviews were pretty content-free in both cases until he started trash-talking about Ladonal and Poore. While Tunny claimed that Ladonal was a great friend and a wonderful person, he thought Ladonal was somewhat ineffective for not being able to push all of his great ideas through the National Legislature. He did praise Hoy Poore, but he thought the ticket needed someone with even more extreme views. I am sure these comments were not received well by the Elephant Party leaders!

Election Day finally arrived. When the dust settled, it was clear that voters had turned out in record numbers. 65.2 percent of all adult Camerian citizens voted, easily beating the previous high when Moblamah generated a lot of excitement and motivated 63.6 percent of all potential voters to cast a ballot in 2008.

The final tally of all ballots, by mail, and at polling stations, showed the following:

Moe Hiden–Jommalah Ferriss	48%
Ditch Ladonal–Hoy Poore	37%
Tunnald Drump–Jon Mannitee	14%

No one can say for sure, but Elephant Party leaders put the election loss squarely on Tunny for two main reasons: 1) he pulled out two weeks before the election, and 2) his very unnecessary trash-talking about Ladonal and Poore just before Election Day had not helped public sentiment. Lost among all the excitement was the fact that if *all* Elephant Party voters had cast ballots for Ladonal and Poore, that team would have won the election, and the Elephant Party would have stayed in power. I guess the massive educational campaign must not have reached or persuaded about a third of all Elephant Party voters.

All the commotion died down within a week or so after the election. Even though Tyke Dents was still Grand Poobah until Inauguration Day on January 21, 2021, he decided not to make any personnel changes in the Beige Palace, preparing to go down in history as the most boring Grand Poobah of all time. All of the staffers had been brought in by Tunny and still felt some loyalty to their old boss. As the final transition day came closer and closer, they coordinated the removal of all personal belongings and gifts given to Tunny and Ladonnia Drump.

Two days before Inauguration Day, Tunny made his final trip to the Beige Palace. Most observers thought that he appeared to be in a strange mood. He indeed behaved bizarrely. His first stop was the Triangle Room, the Grand Poobah's ceremonial office. He told former Lesser Poobah and now Grand Poobah Dents to leave. Before Tunny came out thirty minutes later, he managed to become the first ex-Grand Poobah to tag the Triangle Room with graffiti. He primarily wrote, "I was here—Tunny Drump" on lots of pictures, walls, and the Grand Poobah's desk.

Tunny exited the Triangle Room with a mischievous grin on his face. He then headed to the first-floor gallery and proceeded to try stealing several precious artifacts that had been in the Beige Palace for over two hundred years. Tunny isn't a history buff, so I think that he just wanted to see if he could get away with such brazen and scandalous behavior. Fortunately, Tunny's sticky fingers were observed by the Covert Assets detail. Although they

     MAKE OUR COUNTRY YUUUGE AGAIN

were sympathetic to Tunny, the agents nevertheless made him put the artifacts back. They did let him take a tie clip.

In the first few weeks after Inauguration Day, most Elephant Party members were furious at Tunny. Donkey Party members were happy for the first time in a while. The rest of the world was still trying to figure out what the f*ck had happened in Cameria over the past four years. How had the village idiot been put in charge of such a supposedly rational country as Cameria?

Although political historians and academics usually need to wait many years before grading the impact of a Grand Poobah, all interested observers were quick to declare, on a bipartisan basis and with no passage of time required for perspective, that Drump was the worst Grand Poobah ever.

Even though he hunkered down at Charco Grande, private citizen Tunny still faced the prospect of numerous civil lawsuits. And it was too late to take the unprecedented and extremely controversial action of whitewashing himself.

I *almost* felt sorry for my old boss. Then I realized that this was not the Tunny Drump I started working for so long ago. He'd seemed like such a great guy back then compared to the mean-spirited maniac he became while doing so much to harm our country. I vowed not to visit Tunny in prison.

The End

ABOUT THE AUTHOR

WEB AUGUSTINE is a Seattle native, San Francisco Bay Area resident, and Silicon Valley veteran with 30+ years of experience in marketing, sales, consulting, and executive search. Web has contributed early-stage marketing expertise to several successful high-profile startups and spent the vast majority of his career working with early-stage companies. Web's books include *Make Our Country YUUUGE Again* (September 2020; witty, hard-hitting political satire) and *Inspiring Quotations for Our Times* (2020 eBook, 2011 hardcover; a delightful compilation of the best 1,400 quotations offering practical wisdom and wit regarding life, love, attitude, happiness, success, character and much more).

For more information, please visit **www.yuuugeagain.com**